CUBA
ON MY
MIND

KATIE
WAINWRIGHT

LIVINGSTON PRESS
THE UNIVERSITY OF WEST ALABAMA

Copyright © 2010 Katie Wainwright
All rights reserved, including electronic text
isbn 13: 978-1-60489-062-4 library binding
isbn 13: 978-1-60489-063-1 trade paper
Library of Congress Control Number 2010930361
Printed on acid-free paper.
Printed in the United States of America,
United Graphics
Hardcover binding by: Heckman Bindery

Typesetting and page layout: Joe Taylor
Cover design and layout: Jennifer Brown
Cover photo: Katie Wainwright
Proofreading: Connie James, Joe Taylor, Patricia Steib, Emily Mills

Parts of this work appeared in
Pangolin Papers
Microcosm

This is a work of fiction.
Any resemblance
to persons living or dead is coincidental.

Livingston Press is part of The University of West Alabama,
and thereby has non-profit status.
Donations are tax-deductible:
brothers and sisters, we need 'em.

first edition
6 5 4 3 2 1

CUBA

ON MY

MIND

In memory of
Angela Martinez de Cameron

Chapter 1

The big hand clutching mine had warm fingers. Why black grime under the nails? Mud from the cane fields stained red. And the gasoline smell — diesel, maybe? I raised my eyes and looked into a distant yet familiar face, wrinkles and creases erased, the skin smooth; the deep cleft in the chin still there. Who was this man with a red halo bending over my bed? Not my Olaf. My Olaf smelled of field sweat, dark circles under the armpits. He came inside seeking shelter from the tropical heat and stifling humidity. This place was cold.

"Who are you?"

The man released my hand and carefully straightened my arm as though his grasp could break my fragile bones. "I'm your grandson. I'm here for your birthday party Sunday."

The deep, rumbling voice halted my sliding mind and drew me back to now, to here, to the bed where I lay dying. "You're little Olaf?" He'd sprouted a red beard and a mustache. He looked so much like his grandfather!

"Everybody calls me Wayne, Gramma. You're the only one calls me Olaf, but that's okay."

"You're here for my birthday? Is it August?"

"You do remember things! Mom said you forgot a lot. You were going to tell me about Cuba before I went back to school, remember that?"

Oh, yes — he wanted my story before he returned to Tulane next week, or was it next month? Time slipped like water through the fingers.

I was propped on a white cloud, pillow cases monogrammed with my daughter's initials, kKv. The sheets on the antique four-poster bed were tangled like frothy white waves. I was surrounded by life savers — oxygen tank, IV, needles, bottles, vials, and an aggravating home care specialist named Surviva.

My grandson had wanted me to take him to Oriente Province, to Banes, the mountain village where I was born, but we never got there. The United States didn't allow travel to Cuba. A visitor had to slip in illegally through Mexico, Canada, Haiti or any nearby island. I was afraid to do that. Too many of my relatives and friends ended their lives in dungeons, the lucky ones in exile. Presently, there was no way I could travel to Cuba or anywhere else for that matter.

Since I was never going back, Olaf thought I should record my history, connect my past to his present and give my life permanence. Future generations hearing my voice on tape would become excited as though they'd discovered hieroglyphs carved on an ancient cave wall.

I didn't want to disappoint my grandson. He'd spent time with me these past days. We'd gotten to know each other better — *bonding* — as they said now. To be frank, I'd lost track of Olaf. We lived a thousand miles apart, visited sporadically — vacations, Christmas, sometimes Thanksgiving. He was no longer the little boy I remembered.

"C'mon," he prodded. "You know you can do this. Do it for me. We're going to Cuba — " he gently rubbed my arm — "one day soon."

Remembering was a chore. When I boarded the ship my childhood years sank into the sea. Could I revive drowned memories? In thought, resuscitate the dead? Breathe life into the watery graves of those who were no more? I'd never been one to look over my shoulder. Even now, I looked ahead, anxious to be on my way and reunited with my love.

"If you really want to know — Castro is dying and I'm not far behind and I have lingering thoughts of the island floating like a crusty green crocodile on a blue sea. Why do I call it a crocodile? Go bring me the map, I'll show you, but it's more than the shape, you know. It's all that scaly green — green hills and forests and palm trees waving in the wind — deceptive tropical paradise, slumbering, so docile one never suspected it could grumble, open up big jaws and swallow a way of life."

Olaf left the room and returned with a world globe and a tape recorder. "I'm back, Gramma. Can you hear me?"

"Don't exhaust her," my daughter said.

Good daughter ... good mother ... how did I end up here — in this house? — in this room?

"Rehab hospital," James had said. "That's where your mother needs to be."

"No," replied Katherine. "She doesn't belong there. She's too far gone."

"Extended care, then — "

"James, please. She's my mother."

"Assisted living? We can pay for that."

"I want her here, with me."

Riding in the car's back seat from the airport to the house, eyes closed, my daughter and son-in-law assumed I was either asleep or deaf. But I heard them, heard the arguing and understood my intrusion into their orderly life. James wasn't keen on having his dying mother-in-law taking up space, not to mention Katherine's valuable time. He didn't tolerate disruptions well. That's why my previous visits had always been short ones.

A dying person changed the tenor of the house, demanded full attention. Death hung like pallor over every room, silent spaces, contrived quiet. Death bleached the color from life, turned the world a dismal gray. Laughing would've been a relief, but finding anything funny in death would've mortified Katherine. Her intensity left no room for humor, not to mention that absurd hilarity would give James a ready excuse to ship me to a loony bin.

Living in my daughter's house, in her care, at her mercy, I had to be careful, watchful — no telling what little nothing would trigger her hormones or James's wrath. A shiver went through my rusty old bones.

"Are you cold, Mama?" Katherine asked.

The August heat in New Orleans was stifling, yet I was always cold. Katherine's handyman had climbed a ladder and closed the bedroom ceiling vents. The central cooling unit ran constantly. In the night's dark and heavy stillness, unable to sleep, instead of sheep I counted the shudders that sent cold blasts through the house followed by the quick vibrations as the unit reached its peak and cut off.

I motioned Olaf to come closer. My memory was faulty. Life was a confusing voyage. Some events stood out and others blurred. I would tell Olaf things I remembered. They might be true or maybe I dreamed them.

***

Olaf looked about the room searching for a place to start, a beginning. Katherine had personalized my space with items she thought important to me: pictures of my parents; one with Olaf and me, toddler Katherine astraddle her daddy's shoulders; mahogany boxes with intricately designed woodwork; the brown wicker rocker that sat on our tropical veranda for years like a bruise amidst milky white chairs.

"Tell me about this." He pointed to a framed diploma. I didn't know where Katherine found the oversized scroll. She had it matted blue and framed in gold. She gave it to me one Mother's Day.

"That's my mother's *Corte y Costura* diploma, isn't that right, Katsy?"

My daughter nodded yes while she fiddled nervously with the vials on the night table. She arranged the little bottles in an even row like soldiers lined up for battle. I had no idea how she came by this impulse for perfection — certainly not from me or her daddy. "I'm meeting James downtown at five. I can't be late." She wiped an imaginary spot from the dresser top. "Surviva, be sure Mama gets her meds on time."

As soon as Katherine left I made a face at Surviva. Her ever present bulk was oppressing. She filled the room with bad karma. "Get out."

"I ain't goin' nowhere. I's paid to be sittin' here, and here I stays." She had already plunked her big bottom on the wicker rocker's bright flowered cushions and was busy filing her nails. She gave more attention to her long claws than she did to me.

Olaf took up for me. "Do you mind taking a break — go get some coffee — and giving my Gramma and me a little space?"

"Yessir, I does mind — " impudent as usual.

Olaf took a sudden step in Surviva's direction, a twist and a turn and both his big hands rested on the rocker arms. He leaned into her face and hissed through his teeth, "Please."

She leapt from the chair, almost knocking him over. "It's your house, but I'll be right outside there." She put her fat fists on her hips. "Leave this door open, y'hear me?"

Olaf slammed the door in her face. I liked that boy. He had his grampa's grit.

"Now tell me," he said, pointing at the framed diploma, "about that."

Faded memories rushed back and suddenly I felt an overwhelming need to relieve my soul, leave the past behind and go to the next plateau like an empty vessel ready to be filled anew. "My mother was an accomplished seamstress. She studied in Paris and Barcelona with the great couturiers. She made all my clothes."

I distinctly remember the blue and white striped culotte. I was a headstrong child and refused to wear it.

My nanny, Carmen, an ornery creature, a peasant from the hills, a square woman strong as any man, said, 'You're wearing it. Your mother made this for you with her own two hands and abundant love. Put it on right now.' You couldn't argue with that woman. She was mid-thirties, unmarried. Not having found a husband gave her a hard edge. She was forever searching, unable to relax, working to preserve her looks, fighting wrinkles with facial lotions and creams, vain attempts to preserve a youth fast slipping away. No matter how you looked at her, she wasn't pretty from any angle, her big, round face a cross between the Taino Indian's high cheekbones and a peasant's coarseness — thick lips and a flaring nose; black hair like a horse's mane, thick and wiry. Her skin was pale unlike the others whose coloring was mahogany. She jealously protected her face and arms from the scorching sun.

Getting in and out of the culotte was tedious and complicated. The silly outfit looked like a skirt but was actually pants, top and bottom starched stiff like sun-dried seaweed. I stood defiant and uncooperative while Carmen fastened the buttons. The culotte had eight or ten buttons made from whale bone, four holes in each center, secured in place with dark blue thread. The ruffles crisscrossed in front, went over the shoulders, hooked in the back.

The other girls at the U. S. Sugar Company School, the American School, the Cubans called it, were envious. The culotte was the latest Paris style. Mama kept up with the trends. She was more than a seamstress — she was an artiste with a needle and thread. I've never met anyone who could sew like she did, though I didn't appreciate her talent when I was young. Who wanted to stand for hours to have a hem pinned up when there were many more exciting things to do outside?

In school we had no organized activities. We instinctively knew when it was time to stash the golf clubs and find the baseball mitts. Our favorite game was plain old hide-and-seek.

We didn't simply duck around a corner. We hid in caves; high in the tall tree limbs; behind the roof gables — big time hiding places. When school let out on this particular day, we bolted from the building, ran around No. 3 green and raced uphill to my house. I can't remember a single kid ever walking. We ran everywhere.

This particular afternoon, Olaf was "it." He covered his eyes; counted to ten. We scattered. I left the yard and vanished behind the house into the wooded area that sloped to a little stream. When I walked under the guava tree, the vultures made whirring, disturbed noises — ugly birds. They slit the juicy guavas with their curved beaks, devoured the soft pulp and let the rinds fall and hit the ground. I started to crouch behind ironweeds, the big, flat leaves a perfect screen. But then, I remembered that a few days before in the ironweeds surrounding the *ceiba* in our front yard, Carmen had killed a huge snake. The snake uncoiled, raised up, big and round as a grown man's thigh. Eduardo, the gardener, jumped back six feet. Carmen yelled, 'Give me that!' snatched the machete from his paralyzed hand, raised it above her head and brought it down. With one clean whack she cut off the chicken snake's head. The way she wielded the razor-sharp blade made Eduardo look bad and insulted his machismo. He sulked for days.

Carmen wasn't afraid of snakes. She wasn't afraid of anything.

I found a tall clump of *mariposas* – delicate white ginger lilies with fluttering petals shaped like butterflies. They formed a screen, a safer place to hide. *Mariposas*, Cuba's national flower, had a scent like no other. The drought-burned leaves rustled and crackled. The shallow stream with no name ran near by, the clear water gurgling over rocks and fallen tree trunks. It was the dry season — we only had two seasons, dry and wet, always hot. Brown dust covered my sandals.

The heat! The heat! The shimmering waves rose, sapping life from every moving creature. Birds sought shade in the leafy overhead canopy, not twittering. Frogs sank into cool ditches, saving their energy for nighttime croaking. Lizards hiding in the ferns changed their skins from brown to cooler green.

Voices drifted through the mahogany, ceiba, and banyan trees, huge trees so big they made the live oaks here look dwarfed. 'I caught you!' Olaf called. Trills and laughter followed as the discovered one stepped from the hiding place. After a while, Olaf had found everyone but me. I heard him calling, 'Catica! Cata! Lina! Lina!' — then my full name — 'Catalina!' With each call, I burrowed deeper into my hiding place.

Olaf's calls became fainter, ceased. I knew the ploy. Make me think he'd gone away, so I'd pop up and he'd find me. I held my breath and didn't move listening for a falling step, a snapping twig, the whirring vulture wings, signs someone was approaching. After quite a while when nothing happened, I rose slowly and peered over the ginger lilies. A deep quiet enveloped the late afternoon. The humid air hung heavy. I was looking straight ahead, staring at every bush and tree trunk when from behind, a heavy arm encircled my waist, a muscular arm covered with hairy swirls like black widow spiders.

Not the arm of a classmate –

The arm jerked me with great force, lifted me a foot off the ground, my legs dangling and kicking air. I shrieked. The vultures flapped their wings, shook the guava limbs and took flight. The man smelled awful. I struggled to wriggle out of his grip and take a look at his face so I could tell Daddy. He'd have the *Guardia Civil* stand the man blindfolded against the brown-stained concrete wall.

I raised an arm and with stiff fingers jabbed at his eyes. Even if I didn't blind the awful man, making him blink would give me a second or two. I missed his eyes and my hand slid down his beard, not a soft, silky beard like Daddy's, but a rough, stubby growth, uneven and unkempt. I wrestled with this sweaty creature, fighting for my life. He snorted and panted, foul breath hot against my cheek. With a forward thrust, he threw me down. I rolled to one side, ate a mouthful of dirt and rolled back. He pinned one knee on my chest, and planted one mud-encrusted boot next to my head. He bungled the attempt to rip off my clothes.

Thank goodness Mama was an excellent seamstress who double-stitched all garments. She bought only good strong cloth, indestructible material that wore well and lasted forever. He couldn't undo the straps, all those buttons and crisscrossing ruffles; couldn't pull up the skirt because it was sewn onto the shorts; couldn't yank down the shorts because they were anchored to the buttons. He finally jerked a button through a buttonhole, then another one. A scream stuck in my throat, the arrested breath a painful, choking lump. His knee pushed me into the ground. Dirt matted my hair. My fingers groped the dry, dusty ground, reaching for a rock, a limb — anything. He flung the culotte's straps aside. My heart beat against my ribs like a bird trying to escape its cage. A panicked cry tore from my throat.

The scream scattered the vultures. Their wide-spread wings covered the sun like a black shroud. *Camouflaged trousers — mud-covered, torn — wet — he came from the river. Important to remember that, and the beard and the —*

His full weight struck me like a landslide and he toppled, unbalanced to one side. His leg twisted away from his body, his army boot toes up. A warm gush soaked the blue and white striped culotte.

I looked up and in dizzying circles saw green leaves, blue skies and the silver glint of a machete dripping red.

***

"Gramma — "

The heat smothered, made breathing difficult. My chest heaved. I thrashed about, struggling, suffocating.

From far away someone said, "See how restless she is? You gotta let me give her this shot. I ain't waitin' forever."

Surviva! Who let her back in?

"In a minute," Olaf replied.

"See here! She can't go much longer — " quarrelsome tone, impatient — "Look at her wriggling and squirming! Sinking into that mattress! I ain't takin' part in this. First thing y'know, she dies and Miz Kennedy'll be blaming me." Surviva loomed at my bedside. "It's time for your shot."

"Somebody grabbed me!" I fought to get away.

"Quit that thrashin'! I's pullin' you up on the bed, tryin' to make you more comfortable." She gripped my middle.

"Gramma — can you hear me?"

"You ain't killing her on my shift." Surviva pushed against my hip. "Don't give me a hard time. Turn over."

Olaf said, "Be gentle with her. I'll give her the shot."

"It's my job."

"I'll take the responsibility."

"Miz Kennedy ain't gonna like this."

"I'll talk to Mama."

"You can talk to anybody you want to. It's my quittin' time and I'm leaving. She needs her shot. You get that trash heap from behind my SUV or I'll run right over it."

"My Studebaker — the car I'm restoring? You wouldn't dare."

"Stude-whatever — I'd dare alright. I heard Mr. Kennedy say he wanted it gone. He told Miz Kennedy send it to the city dump, if they'll take it. He said that rattletrap been runnin' down this neighborhood long enough."

She touched a nerve. "My father doesn't know a thing about cars. That auto is *vintage* — one of a kind! Valuable."

"Mr. Kennedy knows a heap o' trash when he sees one — Gramma, turn over or I'll flip you myself."

Olaf grabbed the needle from Surviva. "Don't touch her. Get out of here."

"Miz Kennedy goin' to hear about this — " Surviva's lower lip touched her chin.

"From you?" asked Olaf, "or from me?"

I loved my grandson more every minute.

Cuba on My Mind

Chapter 2

Olaf was back. He was here last week or maybe yesterday, or was it this morning? I didn't know anymore. The weeks, days, minutes ran into each other and dispersed like sand flung into the wind. *What is man that Thou art mindful of him?*

My thoughts bobbed back and forth like driftwood floating on ocean waves. I wouldn't leave this shore until the last breaker spilled upon the beach.

"Gramma? — "

"I hear you."

"Did they put the man in jail?"

"What man?

"The one that tried to rape you — "

"Rape me? Nobody tried to rape me."

"Remember, you said you hid in a flower clump — " he gave up. "I brought you something."

As clearly as if he'd opened a vial, Olaf brought the scent of the tropics into the room.

My fading eyes struggled to focus. I saw flowers on the wall: fire red bougainvillea, spiky hibiscus, purple orchids dripping from tree limbs, crepe myrtles raining pink confetti, Poinsettia trees aflame, impatiens spilling from every crack, pink blotches everywhere, impossible to kill those pesky little flowers. The ginger lilies started close to the floor and grew and grew until they covered the walls, the ceiling, the floor, the dresser and spread onto my bed. Inhaling deeply, I smelled my island home. *"Mariposas."*

Olaf placed a flower in my feeble hand. I cupped the white blossom. The heady aroma that once stirred passions lay like a gravestone on my bosom. "You're a good boy. Where did you find them?"

"At a friend's house — "

When Mama and Daddy moved to the States, Mama searched the garden nurseries until she found *mariposas*. She planted them by the back steps. She loved their smell as she entered or left the house. She was devastated when winter killed them, thrilled in spring when they resurrected. She asked for them on her deathbed, rubbed the petals fragile as tissue paper between her fingers until her hands stilled.

Katherine swirled into the room and took the long-stemmed flowers from Olaf and handed them to Surviva. "Put them in a vase, please."

Surviva lifted her big carcass from the wicker rocker. Her sitting in Olaf's rocker so offended me! As if it belonged to her!

Katherine leaned over and pecked my cheek. "You're looking much more chipper today."

"Pee-yew! — " Surviva said. "These things stink."

"They kinda smell like gardenias," Olaf said.

I set him straight. "Gardenias have a strong, repugnant odor, indelicate. The grace of *mariposas* is their subtlety. They make their presence known without overpowering. Can you prop me up a little, please?"

Katherine plumped the pillows, pulled my skeletal body up higher, and asked, "Are you in pain?"

We were born in pain, struggled against pain from start to finish. Pain was a friendly ache, a familiar torture, existence verified and made bearable by knowing there was an end. "I'm really not in pain. It's more like an out-of-body experience, floating all over this room. Right now, I'm a feather up there in that corner next to the ceiling and I am looking down on you." My laugh had turned into a dry cackle.

Katherine sighed, "I've so much to do today," already put upon, behind schedule, no time to listen to my ramblings. "The caterers are coming and the florist and the music people."

"Another party? — " Olaf asked. His mother was always hosting parties. "I told Irene to take me off your list."

"That's choice," replied Katherine.

My daughter had a social secretary. Computer files held guest lists, party menus, music, theme, calendar, dates, apparel and jewelry.

Katherine had to take care not to repeat herself since mostly the same people came to every party.

She looked anxiously at me as if assessing my remaining time span, "Your birthday party."

"I don't want a birthday party." All that commotion! Who needed it? Just let me go in peace.

"Sure you do," my daughter replied with that firm but sweet voice adults used when disciplining a child.

Then she was gone, whirling through the door like a little tornado, taking with her all the hustle and bustle that crowded the room. Olaf and I absorbed the serenity. After a time peace settled in and I asked, "Who would she invite to a party for me? I don't know anybody here."

"She and Dad will ask their old cronies. They'll drink themselves into a stupor, then have an argument and go to bed. They do it all the time."

Katherine tore back in again. "Did I leave my car keys? Didn't I have them in my hand? Don't tire her out, Wayne Olaf. We have to keep her in mint condition for Sunday."

"Who's coming to this party?"

"For heaven's sake — I don't have time right now, but you will truly be surprised! You are going to love it."

"Well, forget this foolishness, because I'm not going to any party."

"Let's not argue, Mama. Believe me, there's nothing James would rather do than cancel." Realizing what she'd said, she tempered the truth. "He's so busy."

"Make him happy. Make me happy — cancel."

"Now, Mama — "

"I'm skipping it, too," Olaf said.

I loved that boy.

Katherine looked injured. "I'm always the one between the rock and the hard spot." She'd left the car keys on the dresser, right next to the perfectly aligned medicine bottles.

Olaf pointed at me. "You're the rock." He tapped his chest. "I'm the hard spot."

We both laughed.

"Oh, please!" said Katherine.

"Katsy, do you remember José?"

"José who? — I wasn't there, Mama. I've never been to Cuba."

"You were born in Cuba."

"Not me, Mama. I was born in Hawaii. You were born in Cuba."

That was rather confusing. I would've sworn she was born in the company hospital overlooking the 18th green. I closed my eyes to concentrate. Frequently it was impossible to connect the bits and pieces drifting by.

"You never knew José, our chauffeur? Are you sure?"

"I'm sure," she replied from the doorway, her busy morning already melting, the hours disappearing into noon.

"I'll tell you about José, then, Olaf." The recording machine clicked on, spurring my thoughts and loosening my tongue. "He was the *chofer*, but he wasn't always in that employment. Once, he was a greens keeper. What happened to him was my fault. Sometimes young people do things on impulse, not taking the consequences into account."

***

The *guajiros* worked the fields, but José was too rheumatic to swing a machete and cut cane, so he tended the company's golf greens.

Our company golf course was the best in all Latin America. Dignitaries came from all over to play. Daddy said the golf course was a *retaining* expense. The company would do whatever necessary to get the personnel to stay. Most did for a year, maybe two.

Men came to the tropics, fancying the experience a great adventure. After they'd been there a few months, living without a controlled, mindless routine, estranged from their former life's futile bustle, Daddy said they became like lost sheep. Adjusting to *mañana* time, accepting the tropic's slower rhythm, the snail pace, allowed time to think and reflect. That was more than most could endure. Rather than search their souls and find their true selves, down time made them nervous and irritable. Before their contract was up, they were looking for excuses.

The wives disliked the isolation, the limited social life, the lack of shopping. We had no mall, only the commissary and a freighter that docked every other Thursday. It brought supplies and took away sugar. The women soon became bored, listless and began nagging to go home.

All day José squatted on his haunches and went over the greens' velvety surfaces inch by inch, pulling stray weeds with the sure, swift movement of a woman plucking an eyebrow. As he yanked, he sang *Cielito Lindo* or *Siboney* in a rich, tenor voice. The melodies soothed the sore and thankless labor.

When the *gringos* came, José stopped singing and scooted out of their way on all fours like a frightened animal. The players bent over their putters and concentrated on tapping the little white ball into the cup, never noticing the one who kept errant weeds from taking permanent root.

Nights, José, bent like a shepherd's crook, arrived at his thatched hut. His wife was Nanny Carmen's cousin. Nanny never kept anything to herself. She broadcast whatever news she gathered. After a visit, she was the one who told Mama about José, how over his plate of black beans and rice, he said to his woman, 'How much longer can I do this?'

The practical one answered, 'Until death. There is nothing else.'

'Perhaps I can ask for the cane fields.'

When sweat streaked down a man's forehead and sun blurred his vision, the green cane stalks dipped, swayed and slipped through the cutter's fingers like a wave from the sea.

'One day in the fields will kill you.' José's wife said.

More afraid, less sure of himself, he suggested, 'Maybe the mill.'

The powerful grinding machines chewed up hands and spit out bone. Steam rising from cauldrons of boiling molasses burnt arms and scalded faces.

'You might as well be dead as work in the mill,' his wife said.

She was right and getting a transfer wasn't easy. The company determined a man's job, paycheck, living quarters, credit at the company store.

Every day José bent over the greens, the sun like a heat lamp in the sky. His bones ached and his parched lips tasted salty.

Late one afternoon, not long after Nanny related the conversation between José and his woman, after Daddy sank his last putt, he said to José 'Get up. You see that school?'

José looked at the yellow building surrounded by Royal Palms. It was 150 yards from No. 3 green, built on pilings, a play area beneath, a long flight of stairs to the two classrooms above. José often stared at us when we ran up and down the stairs. Sometimes when his song reached our ears, we stopped long enough to jeer and mock him.

'I see the school,' José said. 'It is a very fine school.'

Daddy was a Scotsman with a stern, taciturn demeanor that hid a kind, generous heart. A lone figure detached from his surroundings he kept his ear to the ground, said little and observed much. Without ado or fanfare, without uttering a word, without signing a memo or giving an order in triplicate, he rescued José. 'Tomorrow you will be the janitor there.'

Margo Kelly, the English teacher in charge, outlined José's duties: dust, mop, wash the company cistern and fill the white ceramic filter placed right inside the doorway, wipe the blackboards, beat the erasers, clean the toilets, dump the trash and fill the water filter twice each day.

José was convinced his new assignment was a miracle from God. Every day he arrived singing straight from his heart, so happy was he no longer to be crouching over the greens. He made several attempts to thank Daddy, but Daddy ignored him, wouldn't even acknowledge the man's existence. So José talked to Mama. She passed on to Daddy the peasant's grateful thanks. That's the way Mama and Daddy did things. He was distant. She was near. She was his connection to Cuba.

Mornings, carrying two water buckets balanced on a pole across his shoulders, José neared the school, a song on his lips. We laughed at him and imitated his crab-like walk. Ignoring us, he climbed the 22 steps and didn't stop singing until he set foot inside the school foyer. Miss Kelly was always shushing him, but knowing how happy he was to be off the greens, she was good-natured about her request.

He removed the heavy lid and poured water into the ceramic

filter. The sand in the middle section sifted the impurities. The six tablets he added killed bacteria and germs. By the time we turned the spigot to fill our paper cups the water was safe to drink.

Afternoons, José refilled the water filter. In between duties, he sat in the shady spot under the yellow building, watching us play at recess, noticing our bright colored clothes, our good shoes. We yelled at him in Spanish and English. We opened our cellophane-wrapped sandwiches, took two bites, and threw the rest aside. When the bell rang and we raced up the stairway, José picked up the discards.

One day, I asked him where he learned to sing.

'It is a gift from God,' he replied.

'How long have you had this gift?'

'My mama says I arrived from the womb in glorious song.'

Next morning, he walked up the steps, buckets balanced on the pole across his shoulders. He reached for the door, turned the knob. Water splashed on his head, drenched his face and doused his melody. The pole tilted. He lost his balance, fell backward, head over heels, head over heels, 22 flips. He hit the bottom step, a crumpled heap.

Before school dismissed, Daddy was in the classroom, his face splotched red, not a good sign. 'All right, chaps. Who did it?'

The eight students looked intentionally blank as Daddy's gaze swept from one side of the room to the other, stopping briefly on each one of us: the Cormans — Elise, Dwayne and Dorothy — Olaf, me in the upper grades, on the east side of the room overlooking the golf course; the Broussard twins, André and René, and Olaf's little sister, Gretchie in the lower grades across the room.

Finally Olaf, staring straight ahead said, 'We don't know, Sir.'

'Bullocks! — ' Daddy's piercing blue eyes could drill through rock. 'One end of the rope is tied to the doorknob, the other to an overhead pail filled with water — don't tell me you don't bloody know — ' the madder he got, the more he lowered his voice and he was close to whispering — 'that rig didn't get up there on its own.' Daddy disliked discipline sessions. He always left that to Mama. He had a company to run and no time to waste. The teachers should be able to handle these situations. He came straight to the point. 'Either one of you did it, or all of you did it.'

I raised a shaky hand. 'I — '

Olaf was on his feet. 'I did it. I put that bucket up there.'

He did raise the bucket, because he was taller than I was and could reach easier, but the prank had been my idea. I couldn't let him take the blame. I slid from my desk and stood next to Olaf. 'I thought it up — a joke to dampen his enthusiasm for singing. We meant no harm. Is he dead?'

'No, but he's no use to us anymore. He lost an arm. The company will have to lay him off. His family will starve. He will hate us forever.'

What remorse I felt! What anguish! My voice caught. 'Can he work at our house when he recovers?'

'I doubt it.' Daddy turned to Miss Kelly. 'And what am I to do with children who so thoughtlessly inflict damage? What is your suggestion?'

She pondered a minute, maybe less. 'Shall I deny them recess and keep them all in after school for a week?'

A protesting storm rose from the innocent ones. 'We didn't do it!' 'It wasn't our fault!'

Daddy pointed to me, to Olaf — 'Those two.'

We groaned. No worse punishment existed than to be cooped up in a school building when the lush, brilliant outside world beckoned.

Daddy placed his pith helmet on his head. 'That's settled then. Carry on.'

I remember him so clearly — the florid, sunburned face, the trim white beard and handlebar mustache. The cold beam in his eyes fell on us and froze our movement. Olaf and I sat like statues, afraid to blink, afraid to breathe.

For one whole week while the others played golf, went swimming or fishing or hung out doing nothing, Olaf and I were caged inside the school room. For added torture Miss Kelly made us memorize American poems by Edgar Allan Poe about ravens and a dead Annabel Lee. She forced us to read Wadsworth's Hiawatha from beginning to end, totally incomprehensible to us, and gave us a test on it. When she flopped down Shakespeare, I got sick to my stomach and Olaf opened the window and jumped from the second story to the soft ground below. I bolted right behind him. Daddy had us punished in principle, as an example. It truly didn't matter to him if we completed our sentence or not.

In three months José healed and shuffled into Mr. Corman's office his eyes begging from sunken sockets, hunger pleading through a thin smile, wanting his old job back. 'Please. I can pluck grass with one hand,' he assured the Recreation and Entertainment head. The American played 18 holes seven days a week, walked on the greens José had meticulously kept. Certainly, that had its worth.

'No,' replied Mr. Corman. 'That's been filled.'

José's heart hit his empty stomach. 'Is there nothing I can do?' he asked Mr. Corman.

'Go see Broussard over in Transportation.'

Hat in hand a pale one-armed José crossed the office hallway.

The Frenchman glanced up from his paperwork. 'You survived, eh? — tough little bastard. We have a job for you. The administrator has requested you be his new *chauffeur*.'

'Me? With one arm? — '

'Who asks my opinion?" Mr. Broussard halfway turned in his chair. "Julio! Julio! Bring me that box!" Mr. Broussard had a second thought and swung back and faced José. 'Can you drive?'

José mutely shook his head.

A young clerk entered carrying a box he placed on the desk. Mr. Broussard pawed through it. 'Here — take this.' The navy blue uniform had a jacket with gold buttons and military epaulets; same color trousers with a yellow stripe down the side, and a visor cap trimmed in fancy braid. 'And Julio, borrow a car from the pool and take this man to that field behind the warehouse and teach him how to drive before Mr. McAuley finds out his new, one-armed *chofer* has no notion how to do it.'

Mr. Broussard knew Daddy could slay dragons, but the little foxes that spoiled the vines drove him crazy.

José proudly wore his uniform when he sat behind the wheel of Daddy's four-door Buick. The distinctive clothing, far superior to his workman's garb, gave him stature. He twirled his mustache upward, tilted his chauffeur's cap at a raffish angle and sat up straighter, tromped the gas and aimed the Buick as he'd been taught. Before long, he had the hang of it.

The chauffeur's days were filled with short trips to the office, the market, the American Club, across the Banes River Bridge into the Cuban sector to take Mama and me to visit grandmother. As he drove through the streets, people took notice, some with envy in their eyes, others with awe, with pride. José could drive! With one arm! Because he no longer squatted for hours in one position, his rheumatism improved.

One afternoon I rode in the back seat and quizzed him. 'Manco,' — for "One-armed" everybody called him now, as if José, his proper name, had vanished along with his missing limb — 'you never sing anymore.'

'I do. I do, but not around the gringos.'

'Daddy said you would hate us forever, but you never got mad.'

'Why should I?'

I pointed to his left sleeve, folded and pinned above the elbow, a practical joke turned tragic — my fault. Sometimes things happened that couldn't be fixed no matter what, a cross carried forever — 'Because of that.'

'The arm,' he replied, 'was a gift from God the same as my voice. I am grateful I had two arms and God took only one as a small sacrifice for this job. He left me the other to embrace my woman and my children.' He looked into the rear view mirror. His gaze caught my eye. He had a clear, honest look, a peasant's look, void of greed or treachery or revenge. 'I am a lucky man,' he said. 'And I have never thanked you in a proper manner.'

His remark astounded me on both the luck and gratitude levels. It seemed to me he didn't have much of the first and little need for the second. 'Thank me — whatever for?'

'I thank you, Catica,' he said, 'for everything you must forget.'

***

The bedside lamp was on, so it must be dark outside. The yellow glow lit the side of Olaf's face, sent a copper gleam through his hair and touched upon the red mustache. His profile reminded me of Van Gogh — with both ears, of course. I yearned to capture Olaf's face on canvas, bold strong strokes in primary colors. Where were my paints? Had Katherine put my artist kit away or had Surviva stolen it?

Olaf had asked me a question. What? I closed my eyes and concentrated, chasing wisps across my mind. "What? What?"

"I said how did your father end up in Cuba?"

"My daddy like every man in the colony was an adventurer. They were restless men, staying a few years, moving on. They told the most exotic tales. Boredom was their enemy; routine their constant foe. They needed the extra fillip of living on the edge. Daddy came to build a railroad for U. S. Sugar in Honduras, worked his way up Central America, crossed the sea to Cuba and began building sugar mills and houses for the company. Before long, he headed the construction division. Then he met Mama and she made him settle down. Later on, because he'd been there longer than anyone else, the company promoted him to Administrator."

"Your adventurous father settled for a nine-to-five job?"

"Heavens, no! — No nine-to-fives in the tropics, although one did develop a rhythm for living, an ecstasy, a thrill of expectancy. Whatever you do, Olaf, when you get that diploma next year don't dig yourself a rut."

"What do you mean?"

"You know. Those poor creatures who go to work every day, hate what they do, buy a house, furniture, cars, vacation homes, get trapped by the pride of ownership, drinking cocktails, talking about hospitalization and retirement, thinking they're living, when they're simply marking time waiting to die."

Olaf twitched his mustache, grinned his grandfather's devilish smile. "Are you talking about Mom and Dad? With a law degree, I'll end up like that, too."

"No! No! Backpack through Europe! Climb the Alps! Cross the Sahara! Live a little."

He laughed ruefully. "They expect me to be a lawyer."

I detected despondency, a reticence. His future already mapped! He'd join his father's prestigious law firm, make partner, earn lots of money, marry a nice girl, be tremendously successful and never know life.

"Well, if you don't want to be a lawyer, don't do it — rebel! Sow a few wild oats. Look for love until you find it. Don't stop until the feeling fills your heart to the point where you think it will explode. Love makes life worth living. It's life's true redemption, the best and only revenge."

"Gramma, you're too much. Everything is not that simple. Things get complicated."

"Life falls into place when you follow your muse. What is it that excites you?"

He laughed outright. "Working on the Studebaker, but that's not going to cut it."

Tinkering with motors was a mechanic's job. Did I understand my grandson would rather be a mechanic than a lawyer? So like my Olaf who refused to go to college and settled instead for adventure! He ended up running company plantations — a difficult life, a different life. He craved the challenge. Sowing, reaping, packing, shipping from seed to a product on the shelves, the journey fulfilled him. The trip turned him into a rough, rugged man, but never an unhappy one.

I ran a dry tongue over my dry lips. All the sap in my body had dried up — a miracle the blood still flowed. I wanted to give Olaf some advice, but I had difficulty connecting coherent words.

"You want a little water?" asked Olaf.

"Yes, thank you. You don't know how blessed it is to be able to open a tap and drink. Water was our constant problem — drought, bacteria, disease. The company constantly struggled to keep water pure. Have you ever been thirsty, Olaf? Gone hungry?"

"Can't say that I have — "

"Nor have I, but hunger is a terrible thing. The poor came to our kitchen door, women with sunken cheeks and hollow eyes, holding out their hands for our left over scraps. I've seen death in the eyes of children living on the streets, rummaging through trash scavenging for a morsel."

This wasn't what I wanted to say. This wasn't advice. My mind was barreling down a different track impossible to rein.

"Gramma, it's okay. Don't get agitated. It's okay."

"No, it is not okay!"

Olaf sighed and clicked off the recorder. "Gramma, I want the story of your life, not a lecture on social conditions. It's all politics. There's nothing an individual can do. It's called fighting City Hall. It gets you nothing but ulcers."

"Is that what they teach you at Tulane? That you don't matter — that you can't make a difference?"

"No. No. They encourage us to do a certain amount of *pro bono* work."

"*Pro bono* my ass! — " My voice rasped as though an iron file had scraped my vocal chords. Exhausted, I sank back and breathed pure oxygen through the thin tube attached to my nose. Olaf had to understand. "This isn't about social morals. This is about love — loving your fellow man." A strange wheezing echoed in my head. Was that my voice?

"I didn't mean to tire you, Gramma." Olaf sounded contrite. "I'll go now."

"Olaf, you must care." I lifted a shaky hand and tapped my heart. "From here."

"I do, Gramma. Really, I do." He crossed and uncrossed his legs, undecided whether to go or stay.

"Caring is not enough. Caring without doing is like faith without works, no good. Look at your opportunities! You'll be practicing law. You can correct injustices. Instead of representing corporations or rich Mafia crooks, you can help those poor ones who can't afford a lawyer."

"They have public defenders."

"Bah! — Young punks straight out of school who haven't landed a job yet, or old men worn down by drugs and drink."

He looked me straight in the eye and asked, "Who defended José?"

The question took me aback — "Why, nobody."

"He was maltreated and injured. You and your classmates nearly killed him and all the punishment you got was to stay in after school?"

"For one whole week — "

Olaf shook his red head. "That's incomprehensible."

"Well — " How to justify the action? There was no good excuse. "Workers were expendable. Mama often said the company took better care of their horses than they did their laborers. If a *campesino* quit or died, a hundred stood by ready to take his place."

"That colonialism ethic — "

Katherine entered carrying two ice cream bowls, one in each hand, and saved me from having to rationalize the company's actions in a former, far away life. In the context of its time, colonialism seemed right, just as in their era Plantation owners thought owning slaves was okay. Change evolved, sometimes peaceably, at other times brutally violent. Time and events were never static.

Katherine dressed in a sleek black dress that skimmed her hips and touched the floor leaned over my bed. The light caught the diamond sparkle of her rings and bracelet.

"No-sugar kind," she said, holding out a bowl.

What the hell difference did it make at this stage if I ate a spoonful of sugar? *'Sugar makes the medicine go down...'*

"She's singing," Katherine said. "Mama, you're singing." She held a spoon to my lips. I drew the coldness into my mouth. By the time I took three swallows, Olaf had finished his bowlful. "Do you owls know it is past midnight?"

If I looked out the window and saw light, it was day; if I saw dark, it was night. In this broad time spectrum, this cocoon I lived in, hours and minutes were irrelevant, had no meaning.

"It's time to get some rest, Mama. Here, take these — " she held out her hand, three pills nestled in the palm, " — for your blood pressure and to help you sleep."

I took the pills. My daughter watched me as I put them in my mouth, then she held a glass to my lips and I gulped water. Sometimes when Katherine or Surviva turned around, I hid the pills under the pillow. I didn't want all these ailments controlled. I wanted the system to go haywire, the command center to short circuit, the pumps to quit pumping and the cells sloshing up and down my blood vessels to jam

Cuba on My Mind

up like a monumental traffic gridlock *and be done with it – amen.*

High blood pressure, diabetes, emphysema and the latest blow, the one that closed my house and brought me here, lung cancer — there was no beating that combination. What upset me was that I didn't do this quickly, neatly the way Olaf did, a round of golf, a funny noise in the bathroom, a massive heart attack and presto!

Katherine kissed me goodnight, her sweet perfume tinged with party residues — smoke and alcohol. "Wayne, it's time you went to bed, too — and don't you be revving the motor in that old car. You kept us awake half the night last night."

A hard look came over Olaf's face and his eyes turned rebellious. This car was a big bone of contention.

"Goodnight, Gramma." Olaf collected his little recording machine. "Sleep tight."

"'Night — and don't forget what I told you."

Katherine was on the alert. "What'd she tell you?"

Olaf shrugged — "Nonsense, mostly."

Chapter 3

Olaf was young — as my sun set, his rose. I had crossed the sky. His morning glow lightened the horizon. Life was so fragile, a breath. Why did he bother me with my past? What good was it to him?

"Tell me about your mother." He had a picture, an old black and white, Daddy with his arm around Mama. She was holding a baby — me.

Would he believe it if I told him my mother was a saint? That's what the people called her, *Santa Caridad*. Her name meant Charity, and she was the epitome of that virtue.

Olaf didn't know poverty. He thought poverty was food stamps and Medicaid. He had no notion of beggars living under bridges or in cardboard boxes blocking dark alleys. He wasn't able to close his eyes and see babies with swollen stomach and haunting eyes, nose dripping snot, arms and legs withered from malnourishment.

"Every Tuesday my mother went down under the bridge."

The Banes River, a little more than a muddy stream, split Banes in two. To the north, the *Colonia Americana* had wide boulevards lined with Royal palms whitewashed four feet from the ground giving the impression the slender trunks all wore matching socks. Flaming red bougainvillea hedges defined the area as effectively as any electric fence. The profusion of tropical flowers carefully tended by a phalanx of gardeners was so startling and brilliant it looked as though a rainbow had fallen from the sky and kissed the earth.

To the south, across the wooden plank bridge spanning the dry river bed, sprawled the dirty, noisy, gaudy Cuban town, the *pueblo civil* with winding streets and narrow alleys smelling of scorched coffee beans, open sewers, diesel fuel and horse manure. Carts, trucks and laden mules worked their way through the maze. Crumbling colonial buildings, Spanish relics, leaned into each other, wrought iron balconies sagging. Paint flaking from sun-blistered facades shed like molting skin. Everything on the Cuban side was brown, gritty, tired and worn out.

Under the bridge connecting these two separate worlds, caught like flotsam on pilings, the beggars made rag nests and clung precariously to life. For them the days held no hope, except on Tuesdays when Mama came.

"Why did she go under the bridge?" Olaf asked.

"To rescue the dying – "

Olaf looked skeptical though he knew homeless lived under bridges and overpasses here, too. In the cold cities up north they slept on sidewalk grates where the steam from the underworld rose, but somehow these sad drifters were never as poor as our tropical homeless. American homeless had places to go if they so chose – Catholic Charities, Red Cross, welfare office, government shelters. They had recourse. Our destitute had nothing, nothing.

***

I went with Mama one morning.

'Be careful, Señora,' Manco said as she stepped away from the truck. 'You never know –'

Her withering look stopped him. 'These are my people.' I started to follow. 'You stay with Manco,' she said.

Manco leaned against the fender, protecting the four good tires, hubcaps, working wipers and unbroken windshield. It was a company truck, and the company kept everything in excellent condition.

When the beggars heard the truck door slam, they stirred, came alive, waiting for Mama. An old woman draped in black, bolder than the others, crept from the murky shadows into the golden haze of the rising sun, the sky already a blue mistake. She said, 'She's here.' The two little words spurred the shadowy underworld to movement.

The wretched ones watched from below as Mama descended the steep bank one careful step at a time, sturdy brown boots protecting her small feet. She slipped, caught herself. Mud stained her white skirt. She wore a white blouse; a white scarf hid her black hair.

She floated above the misery like an apparition, the way the *Vir*-

gen *de la Caridad,* Mother of Charity, soared above the Christ Child. Some mornings when the sun shimmered through the cotton skirt and white radiance engulfed her, the beggars weren't sure whether she was real or a vision. What they did know for certain was that the miracle happened every Tuesday.

She stopped at the edge of the bank where cold gray stones and black boulders worn smooth divided darkness from light. With gentle motions, she urged the people forward. She spoke with a quiet authority, the trills of her native Spanish rolling easily off her tongue, 'the children first.' The onrush almost knocked her over. Ragged women hugging bundles struggled up the river bank, the veterans ahead, knowing where the flat stones were, the sure footing. Those with swollen legs and distended stomachs dragged themselves forward on all fours. The skeletal ones, translucent skin falling away from sharp bones, staggered to their feet. All moved through dismal gray toward the light.

An unseen force drew me forward, a pull so strong I disobeyed Mama. She turned and looked at me. I thought she was going to reprimand me and send me back. 'Be careful,' she said, understanding in her eyes. 'Don't touch anything. Don't go past those black stones.'

The bold woman dressed in black reached behind a barnacled pillar and grabbed a frail girl cradling a baby. 'Hurry! — *Venga!*' As if that were the given signal, shadows surged forward, arms outstretched, the wails from their cracked, dry lips filling the black vacuum around them. 'Please. Mine. I am sick. The baby is sick. Me. Me. *Por favor.* Please, by God's grace, me.'

Like stray kittens bagged for drowning, mothers placed newborns into burlap sacks. They grabbed toddlers with worm-swollen bellies and fever-bright eyes and pulled them forward by their spindly arms. The bold woman elbowed her way, dragging along the young girl and her newborn. The girl had dark circles under big, starved eyes. Hunger hollowed her cheeks and sugar cane juice rotted her teeth. 'She's not taking my baby. I won't let her. This is my baby.'

The crone had no sympathy. 'And you not even old enough for milk! Do yourself a favor, do your baby a favor, or you both die. You understand? You both die.'

The child-mother sniffled. The baby, too weak to cry, mewed softly. The bold woman placed a gnarled hand between the girl's shoulder blades and propelled her toward the bank.

Two half-naked boys struggled with a cardboard stretcher bearing an old man. They jostled through the anxious crowd and stopped at Mama's feet. The old man's mouth sagged open, yellow gums exposed, saliva puddles at the corner of his mouth. His Adam's apple protruded as if a stone were stuck in his throat. Every bone and tendon in his neck was discernable through the parched, taut skin. Blank eyes stared straight ahead. Mama reached down and placed two fingers on the man's limp wrist, then gently shook her head.

One boy cried out in anguish, 'Papa! — My Papa!'

From a dark niche under the bridge came a verdict: 'He drank himself to death.'

A quick rebuttal rose from the dim, murky blackness. 'Don't judge unless you've walked in his shoes.'

'He had no shoes.'

Death so close smelled like wet earth, cold ashes, spilled semen. Death so close spurred the able to grasp life. With yet more determination the old woman grabbed the girl cradling the newborn and pulled her up the embankment toward the already overflowing truck, 'Hurry! — Hurry!'

'No! No! He is mine! Mine!'

Contorted bodies, one atop the other, filled the pickup bed, everyone jockeying for a more comfortable position, avoiding squealing babies, feverish ones and stone-cold ones, infants covered with oozing sores, old men and women with makeshift crutches, dead legs dangling over the truck's side.

The old crone tore the baby from the girl's arms and handed the limp child to extended hands.

'We can take no more,' Manco said. 'No more! Get off the running board!'

With a stiff right arm, his only arm, Manco held back those pressing forward while Mama and I squeezed into the truck cab through the slightly open passenger door. Manco slammed the door shut, slammed it on hunger, fatigue and the never-endlessness of it.

Then he climbed in, slid behind the wheel and turned the key. The people aboard stopped their clamor and wailing. They were moving, driving to a future.

In the rearview mirror, Mama saw the girl running, arms outstretched, a tortured supplication.

'The mother,' Mama whispered a prayer in her voice, 'The mother.'

Manco looked straight ahead and didn't answer. The vehicle sped toward the hospital. The figure in the mirror staggered and crumpled.

'Stop! — ' Mama cried. 'Go back.'

Manco objected. 'If we go back they will overturn the truck.'

'We must risk it.'

Tight-lipped, Manco made an abrupt U-turn.

Those on board, terrified that their journey had been aborted, screamed and shrieked without mercy. Their blistering grief sparked the beggars left behind. With the sudden surge like a flame stoked by a strong wind, they burst upon the truck, a hundred arms extended, as many hands beseeching.

'Just the girl,' Mama said.

Manco asked through clenched teeth, 'And exactly how will we manage that?'

'With God's help,' — Mama rolled the window down a crack. '*La niña*,' she said to the old crone holding onto the door handle.

Understanding lit up the beggar's dull eyes. She nodded and hobbled to the curb where the grief-numbed mother had collapsed. Half-dragging half-carrying the girl, the old beggar forced her way through the human avalanche about to overturn the truck.

Manco warned, 'Don't open the door, Señora.'

Mama reached through the window half rolled down. Her white-sleeved arm encircled the girl-mother's waist. She pulled her onto the running board. 'Drive slowly,' she said to Manco, 'so she doesn't fall off — how many?'

Manco — sympathetic now that the truck was a safe distance away — replied, 'Maybe twenty. You can't save them all, Señora.'

Mama placed the indigent as she thought best. The first stop was the company hospital, *Hospital Americano*. The heavy-set head nurse, Jean Dixon, came out to the truck, authority stitched in every seam of her starched white uniform. She scanned the human cargo, checked glazed eyes, felt feverish brows, examined cuts and wounds, and pointed, 'You. You! You! You stay here.' Against company regulations she sneaked them into the general ward and Doctor Ruiz ignoring consequences treated them.

When the trucked stopped, the girl-mother jumped off the running board and clambered onto the pickup bed. She wrestled her newborn from the crippled woman holding it, scooted into the furthest corner. The truck jolted to a start. Passengers swayed and lurched.

The next stop was the Flower of Charity Orphanage. Sister Maria approached the truck, reverence in the clasped hands holding the rosary, a silver cross hanging from her neck, the wimple swooping away from both sides of her head like stiff white sails, the hem of her floor-length white habit stained by red dust. Close behind her came Sister Teresa, for the nuns worked in pairs. The girl-mother couldn't avoid the kind hands. Soft religious fingers pried the baby from her arms. The girl leapt from the truck.

'Where is she going?' Mama asked.

'Back under the bridge,' Manco replied. 'She will have another baby.'

'Manco! — '

'That's the way of life, Señora.'

The old and infirm were delivered to the rest home run by the Salvation Army with the convenient cemetery near the back door.

As Mama unloaded the misery, she gave those waiting to alleviate anguish the same orders: Shave their heads. Feed them only broth at first. Bathe their wounds. Give them hope.

The last person delivered, Manco sped across the bridge into the American Colony. The truck turned into the driveway of our sprawling West Indies home. Nanny Carmen waited at the door, hands on hips, mouth puckered as if she'd been sucking a lime. She gave me a cross look and asked Mama, 'Any smallpox?' Small pox had killed half her family.

'I don't believe,' Mama replied. 'Has Mr. McAuley arrived for lunch?'

'You are saved. He is not here yet — typhus?'

'Many of them had the fever.'

'Blessed Virgin! — Hurry, then.'

In her bedroom, Mama raised her arms and the frowning servant stripped off the white cotton dress. Without a word, Carmen rolled the garment into a wad, crossed to the wash yard and dropped the clothes into an iron vat of boiling water and lye. The combination killed germs and sterilized. Only good quality white cloth could withstand the strong treatment. Though much more pleasing to the eye, printed or colored material bled and streaked. The dyes ran; the colors muddied. With angry, twisting motions, Carmen wrung the clothing. Then she carefully spread the skirt, blouse and scarf on the grass to dry.

The tropical sun bleached the cloth and restored it to the original white, a blinding white, pure and dazzling like refined sugar.

Cuba on My Mind

Chapter 4

The past few days, professional cleaners descended upon the house, waxing wood floors, mopping tiles in the kitchen and bathrooms, dusting chandeliers, polishing silver and ironing linens. On hands and knees a janitorial team scrubbed the marble steps fronting Saint Charles Avenue and steam-cleaned the circular driveway. The florist brought huge bouquets. Caterers came and went presenting menus and hors d'oeuvres lists.

The only room spared was mine. Surviva brought tales of the hectic activity. My daughter ignored any reduction I suggested. My objections to the big *fiesta* went unheeded. If I'd been healthy I'd be celebrating my birthday canoeing up the Amazon or hang-gliding in the Alps or with my easel set up in a picturesque corner somewhere — certainly not at a cocktail party with strangers. Olaf and I avoided parties as if they were a plague. But this was Katherine's idea, and arguing with Katherine was useless. Once she got something in her head, it was there to stay. And, I did appreciate the trouble and effort she put into the celebration. I wasn't ungrateful — just tired.

The morning of the party I asked Surviva to open the bedroom window wanting to clear my head and fill my scarred and battered lungs with fresh air. She waddled over and raised the sash. "There — hope that makes you happy."

The smell of newly mown grass mingled with the sickroom's dour odor. Boom box rock music filled the air. I rolled the wheelchair to the window and observed the gardeners planting new bushes and weeding old flower beds to the noisy rhythm. The harsh sounds scared the birds. They twittered and fluttered from one tree to another.

Before long, Surviva rolled the chair away from the window. "I gotta get you dressed — don't give me no trouble. There's 'nough trouble goin' on without you addin' to it. Miz Katherine says you're to wear the blue outfit."

The sheath had a bodice embroidered with seed pearls and crystal beads. The jacket had a Mandarin collar. Yesterday a hairdresser came to the house and did my hair, making the white wisps look full and fluffy.

Later that afternoon, James on one side and Olaf on the other, leaning heavily on posterity, I reluctantly shuffled into the living room. They arranged me in high wing-back chair — the Queen Mother sitting on her throne.

Next to the chair, propped on an easel was my portrait — sixteen years old, I was then, sitting on a split rail fence wearing jodhpurs, white shirt collar open, sun light playing on the auburn hair pulled back and tied with a black velvet ribbon, a riding crop across my knees. The arguments Mama and Daddy had about that portrait! She wanted a formal setting; he said, 'Let her be.'

The guests gawked at the portrait, looked at me, back at the portrait, then me, kissed my hand or my cheek, paid homage and assured me that enduring this long took talent.

I would've liked for Katherine to exhibit my self-portrait, but she didn't like it or any of my other paintings, either. She thought my colors too strident, the lines too bold; the composition too abstract. My art didn't blend well. It overtook a room, clashed with her furniture, her décor.

The birthday guests complimented me and admired my dress. I passed my hand over the bodice, touching the pearls and beads. Was this my beaded blouse Grandmother made? Or had she given it to my cousin, Sarita? Was I wearing the blouse or did Surviva steal it? She took my things. As soon as Katherine left the house that insolent woman opened drawers and closets and rifled through the contents. She probably stole my blouse. My trembling fingers fumbled with the beads and reassured me I was wearing the right blouse, the blouse my blind grandmother took years to make.

"Is my grandmother here?" I asked Katherine. "Has anybody gone across town to fetch her?"

Katherine said, "Relax and enjoy your company, Mother."

"Grandmother? — Where is grandmother?"

Cuba on My Mind

A little crowd surrounded my chair. They leaned toward me, eyes as big as full moons, baffled and respectfully pitying. What was the matter with them? What was there to be sorry about?

"It's a beautiful blouse," I said, passing my hand over my shrunken chest. "My grandmother made it."

"Sure," Katherine said. "Your grandmother made it." To the others she explained, "Sometimes she slips back."

Because I was going deaf, Katherine often talked about me as if I weren't present. Though I missed the words, I caught the tenor of the voice, the body language.

Grandmother! My grandmother could sew when she was blind, that's how good she was. Every Thursday Manco drove me across the bridge. Our visits lasted one hour. She received her grandchildren sitting on the veranda swing wearing a cotton lavender print, thin white hair pulled back into a bun, diminutive feet shod in soft leather barely touching the floor. She held onto an ivory-handled cane, clouded gray eyes staring straight ahead no longer discerning. We thought her ancient. She was younger than I was today.

"Come, have some refreshment." Katherine herded the guests toward the dining room. "Wayne, stay with her a few minutes. She'll be back."

My grandson moved my legs over and sat on the ottoman at my feet. "What about your grandmother, Gramma?"

Grandmother...grandmother...grandmother...grandmother couldn't see and barely heard. Once, she knew who approached by the footsteps. She said Eugenio shuffled, Gloria tripped as if her feet were too much for her to manage and Hector had slow, ponderous steps. She was convinced he was a thinker. Nobody ever had the heart to tell her he was killed in the mountains. She said I took quick, flying leaps, two steps at a time. When all sounds carried the same dull thud like heavy objects striking a soft surface, she said 'eh?'

"Eh? Eh? Eh?" Each little explosion shook my wobbly head and coughed me back into the room filled with people, laughter and tinkling dishes. Bright spots whirled within my vision range. Moving streaks formed colored shapes. Symmetrical patterns shifted like tinted kaleidoscopic mirrors.

"Gramma, what is it?" Olaf rested his hand on my knee.

I leaned forward so he heard me over the party noise. "Olaf, do I say 'eh?' a lot?"

"Yep, a whole lot — "

"Oh, dear — " I sympathized with Grandmother now. Then, I was impatient when I had to yell. "Do you get impatient if you have to yell in my ear?"

"You have a hearing aid. I get impatient when you don't turn it on."

"There is static. Do I have it on now?"

"Of course, you do. You can hear me can't you?"

"Eh?"

A voice said, "I hope when I'm your age I'm in as good a shape as you are — happy birthday, Catalina."

I trapped the extended hand in mine. Sometimes feeling something solid, tangible, held me in place. "My grandmother's name was Catalina, did you know that?"

"That's nice." The woman gave a silly cackle.

"Daddy agreed to let Mama name me after Grandmother, an honorable gesture she took to heart, the way I was flattered when Katherine named Olaf after his grandfather."

The woman looked baffled.

Olaf explained, "I was named after both my grandfathers — Wayne and Olaf."

"Sometimes I wish Olaf had been your first name instead of the middle one," I said, "then everyone would call you Olaf."

"Olaf sounds so foreign," the woman said, "like Wayne could belong to the Gestapo or something." She cackled again and moved away.

When overwhelmed, I simply closed my eyes and removed myself from the present. The perceived impression was that lacking stamina, old age's inherent weakness, I fell asleep. The truth was I checked out because these people bored me. I had nothing to say to them. We were moons apart.

A new arrival bent down, her face close to mine, and yelled in my ear, "Beautiful dress, Miz Cata!" The hearing aid wheezed and crackled, protesting the decibel.

Katherine's good friend — I recognized her — too much perfume.
I ran my fingers over the crystal beaded blouse, plucked at the collar. "My Grandmother made it. She worked for years sewing these
beads."

"You silly little goose — " she pinched my cheek as if I were a child
— "that's a Bill Blass. I helped Katherine pick it out at Lord & Taylor's
last week." She flitted like a butterfly to the next flowery group.

Goose! She was the goose. *Abuelita* had worked on my blouse
for as long as I remembered. Days when Grandmother felt well, *Tia*
Adela placed different textured baskets in a predetermined sequel at
Grandmother's elbow. Each basket contained different colored beads
and sequins — red, purple, orange, blue, white, green, black. Grandmother felt the baskets, reached in, ran the needle point through a
miniature bead hole, smoothed the cloth between her fingers, and
slowly sewed in place a small, shiny spangle. Her fingertips followed
the design she created.

On Thursdays when my cousins and I visited, Grandmother kept
her hands busy. I threaded needles for her. My cousins! They'd know.
They'd set the perfumed one straight. "Olaf, are any of my cousins
here? Is Sarita here?"

"I don't know. I'll go find out."

He left to inquire and I snatched a passing sleeve. "Where did my
cousins go? Are they coming to visit Grandmother today?"

"Everybody is coming to visit you today," the voice replied. "You
are Queen for the Day."

Olaf was back. "You cousin Sarita isn't here. She's — "

The expression on his face betrayed him.

"Dead."

"Yes."

"How long? — "

"More than ten years, Mama said."

"No wonder she hasn't kept in touch."

"Her daughter is here. I'll go find her."

Grandmother's veranda faced a patio filled with blooming plants,
an orange flamboyán tree and a trickling fountain. When the grand-

children visited, we sprawled on the tile floor at her feet, perched on the railing, or sat on worn cane-bottom chairs. For a time, after she couldn't see us, she could hear us, and when the silence rolled into her head like a dense fog, she identified us by smell — Hector smelled sweaty, Gloria like her mother's kitchen. She said I was sweet-smelling like a *mariposa*. When she could no longer breathe our scent, she encouraged us to come near. She ran her hands over our faces, her fingers through our hair. Touch had not yet failed her.

On good days, when she gathered her faculties about her, she compared us to a flower garden, colorful and vibrant. She said she felt our energy, our vibrant youth. We were buds about to blossom and she loved us. Maybe she loved us more because she wasn't distracted by her senses. Probably she loved us because she didn't have to tend the garden. Weeding took its toll.

"Sarita was Tia Adela's daughter," I said. "We were cousins." These strangers walking back and forth, holding plates and drinks, had I known them before? "Sarita and Tia Adela lived with Grandmother because Uncle Ramón died with the typhoid, did you know that?"

Nobody cared.

Uncle Ramón's picture hung in the main hallway of Grandmother's rambling house, a solemn looking man with a thin mustache. A votive candle forever burned beneath his black and white photograph. Flickers from the eternal flame danced on the gray face, making the eyes look as if there were alive.

A voice replied in Spanish, "No, but I bet Julio from Miami remembers your aunt and uncle. He's up there in age. Hang on a minute. I'll find him."

The man who came and sat beside me had such a huge frame, he made me feel shrunken. Before the flesh sagged away from his bones, he must've had a corpulent physique, the remnants yet visible.

"I'm Julio," he said, "with USSCo transportation. I was Mr. Broussard's clerk." He offered the information as if he were presenting rank and serial number. "I was there when your father told him to hire Manco. I found the blue uniform — remember the gold trim — and taught Manco to drive. I knew Sarita. She lived in Coral Gables.

Many Cubans lived there. You could tell our houses."

"How? — "

"We took off those cheap veneer front doors and installed carved mahogany doors. A little thing, but it gave us a sense of home. Sarita grew very fat, obese. She ate her way through unhappiness. At the end she looked like a shapeless loaf of self-rising bread."

"So much sadness," I said. "So much distress — "

"Yes. After Castro took over and the pretense fell aside, Cuba was a disaster. We didn't know how to deal with the new reality. The situation was impossible. We feared for our lives, so we left, jumped overboard like rats leaving a sinking ship." Julio placed a hand on my shoulder as if he needed to brace himself from painful memories. "We left behind our property, our conscripted sons." Even after these fifty years, unshed tears brightened his eyes. "We took only memories," he said, "and the clothes on our backs. I was a lucky one. I boarded the last Continental flight leaving Havana. Others left by ship, and when that was no longer possible, they built inner tube rafts and lashed together floats and cast off to the Florida Keys, the closest haven, 90 miles away."

"What happened to Sarita?"

"Remember Sarita lived with her mother, Adela, in your grandmother's house? Well Adela wouldn't leave Banes. She said she was too old and communism couldn't be any worse than U. S. Sugar. She'd stay put and deal with whatever happened. Years later, Sarita, her husband and daughter — she's here today — went to Venezuela, New York, and then Miami. They left their son behind. We all did. Able-bodied young men weren't allowed to leave. They were placed in government run schools or drafted into the military. Sarita's sorrow was so deep, her mind was affected."

"I saw Sarita every Thursday when Grandmother received her grandchildren. Tia Adela served fresh coconut cookies and Fanta orange drinks to all the cousins."

Every detail was as clear as a Technicolor movie. Manco dropped me at my grandmother's then left to do Mama's errands. One day our car almost hit a boy running beside it, hanging onto the door handle, saying, '*Gimme, gimme, gimme,*' his face pressed against the glass. At the

Chinaman's Café, the police were there. Something had happened. Manco said it had to do with the black woman who dangled from the light post and beckoned people.

Tia Adela was cross with me. She was always cross with me. When I told her about the running boy and the confusion and the black woman, she replied, 'Welcome. The little princess has come across the bridge.'

Grandmother loved me best and that upset the others, Tia Adela most of all.

I was Grandmother's namesake, the child she'd never seen. A hundred times I'd described myself for her benefit: auburn hair, hazel eyes; freckles. Yes, freckles, Grandmother, and tall — taller than all the cousins.

'So you must look like your father,' she said. 'But you have your mother's energy. I feel the force when you enter.' She made me sit by her side.

Tia Adela said, 'Sarita, sit yourself, too.' Sarita and I sat on the swing on either side of Grandmother.

Grandmother's hand was withered and dry. She felt the surface and edges of my new bracelet. 'And what is this?' she asked.

'A new silver bracelet, *Abuelita*,' I replied. 'Daddy gave me the bracelet on Santa Catalina's Day.'

Sarita reached across Grandmother's lap and said, 'Oh, I wish I had a bracelet just like this.'

That made Tia Adela unhappy. 'We can't afford those extravagances.'

'Here,' I slipped off the bracelet and handed it to Sarita. 'Put it on. Maybe Daddy will buy you one, too. I'll ask him.'

Sarita placed the silver bracelet on her arm, sliding it up and down from the wrist to the elbow. 'It's magnificent.'

Grandmother asked Adela to bring the beaded blouse.

'It still needs to be ironed,' Tia Adela replied.

'Bring it anyway.'

Tia Adela left and returned with the blouse, shook out the wrinkles and held it up for inspection.

'It's beautiful, Abuelita,' Sarita and I both said at once.

Over the years, we'd followed Grandmother's slow, tedious progress. The blouse was blue, not turquoise like the bracelet stone, not robin-egg blue, not baby boy blue, but a dark purple-blue, like the ocean when the water deepens and the depth is measured in fathoms.

'The cloth has to be a deep, deep tone,' Grandmother had explained when she first started the blouse. 'Sequins and beads shine best if the color is true. Paleness doesn't do justice to sparkles.'

Tia Adela placed the blouse in Grandmother's hands and Grandmother ran her sensitive fingertips over the intricate design. The blouse had a V-neck, outlined by seven rows of beads and sequins. They were placed in a geometric design. Miniature copper-colored tubular beads set at an angle on the first row; pale violet sequins, the second; then another row of copper, followed by red sequins; more copper; then a blue that picked up the cloth's midnight; and the last row again copper.

'Odd numbers are more artistic,' Grandmother said. 'Three flowers, five candles, seven dwarfs. You know about the seven dwarfs? Seven is a great number. Seven veils, seven seas, seventh heaven, lucky seven — '

I peered anxiously at Grandmother. 'Is she all right?' I asked Sarita.

'Her mind wanders,' replied Sarita. 'She talks gibberish.' Sarita handed me the bracelet. 'I love this bracelet.'

I gave it back to Sarita. 'You can wear it.'

'Be still,' Grandmother said. 'You are like jumping jacks.'

'The blouse is truly beautiful,' I said.

Grandmother shared her secret. 'Begin and end with the same color. It gives the design a finished look. Does it look finished?'

'Very much so,' I replied, ignoring the spots where the lines ran not so straight.

'Good — and the bow? How does it look? Do you like it? Really like it?' The beaded work ended in a magnificent bow, a huge bead and sequin splash that covered the bodice front like a sparkling fireworks explosion, the tendrils drifting downward in colorful sprays.

'I love it, *Abuelita*. It's wonderful,' I said.

Sarita raised her arm and gazed at the joy encircling her wrist. The silver bracelet gleamed against her brown skin. 'I'm not giving this back to you. I'm stealing it.'

'We may be poor,' Tia Adela snapped, 'but we are not thieves. Take that off.'

We rose from the swing and moved away from Tia Adela. A few minutes later, we were back, standing before Grandmother. I leaned over and my lips brushed Grandmother's ear. 'Who is the blouse for, *Abuelita?*'

The question, long unasked, brought a sudden silence. Tia Adela looked up sharply. Grandmother didn't hesitate. She felt Sarita's arm then my arm. She encircled our wrists and slid her sandpapery hands over our smooth skin and long, hard bones until her fingers touched the turquoise stone.

****

The girl who leaned over me kissed me on both cheeks. She was here! Sarita was here. "Hola, Sarita," I said overcome with joy.

"Gramma, this isn't Sarita. This is my fiancée, Barbara," Olaf said.

Fiancée — he hadn't mentioned a fiancée! The girl giggled and flipped her blonde hair. A golden strand fell over one eye.

"Is Manco here?" I asked — maybe the girl would know.

"What's she talking about? Who's Manco?"

"Somebody — she gets the past and the present confused sometimes." He patted my shoulder.

So condescending! I did not get things mixed up. They were very clear. "Olaf, did we cross a bridge? I don't remember crossing the bridge."

"You've crossed lots of bridges, Gramma."

I asked the girl, "Am I wearing a bracelet?"

"Yes, you are — a beautiful bracelet."

"Does it have a stone?"

"A stone? — No — It's a flat, gold bracelet." She raised my arm and took a closer look. "Your initials are on it."

Katherine hurried by and I clutched her sleeve. She had to know about this. "I wanted to wear my silver bracelet with the turquoise stone. The one Daddy gave me on my Saint's Day. Was it in my jewelry box, or did Surviva steal that, too?"

"It was never in your jewelry box, Mother." Her gay laugh was for the benefit of the others. See with what patience and good humor she put up with all my idiosyncrasies? Brushing my concern aside, she opened her arms wide and embraced the girl. "Oh, — Barbara! Barbara! What a joy to have you home!"

"I'm glad to be back," Barbara giggled again, reaching for Olaf's hand and pulling him close, a possessive gesture that didn't escape my notice.

"Wayne's happy you're back. He's missed you so! Welcome home, my dear! Welcome! Welcome!" Katherine was blustering all over the girl. She stopped long enough to ask, "Wayne, have you seen your dad?"

Olaf shrugged. "Try the bar on the patio."

Katherine pursed her lips. "Fine — that's fine. We're getting ready to cut the cake — let me go check. You and Barbara help Mama into the dining room." She leaned over and straightened my jacket collar. "What in heaven's name are you doing?"

Doing? I had no idea. I was just sitting there.

Wayne replied, "She's rubbing her arm up and down and fiddling with the gold bracelet. She thinks she's wearing a beaded blouse her grandmother made and a turquoise bracelet her father gave her."

"Heavens — Wayne, spare me. If I ever get that senile, do me a favor — "

"Sure, Mom, I'll shoot you."

Chapter 5

Amazing, the way Katherine managed to locate my cousins and second cousins — distant relatives, younger folks who had kept in touch long after my aunts and uncles had died. They came to my party from Miami, New York, Madrid and Managua. Those who didn't come because of distance, finances, or health reasons sent exotic tropical flower bouquets that must've cost a fortune.

My birthday party turned into a Cuban reunion. With joyous shrieks long-lost cousins embraced each other, their faces wreathed in smiles, their eyes teary. They meandered through the local guests, looking for one another, eager for news, for the touch and warmth of a long-ago world.

Fifty years now, maybe more, Fidel Castro had ruled the island. This younger generation had never set foot on Cuban soil, yet they'd made this special effort to come see me. That touched my heart, invigorated me.

"Who are you?"

"Maria Eugenia, Sarita's daughter, Adela's granddaughter."

"Ah! Adela! — " My oldest aunt gone many years now. "Where do you live?"

"In New York — you look beautiful Tía Catica."

"And you, too, my love. I'm so glad you're here. You'd come to my funeral, but this is so much nicer." I held both her hands in my feeble, blue-veined ones. "This is special. Don't bother coming back for the other."

"I own your fish painting. I bought it from a gallery on Fourth Avenue. I love it. It has such movement! It looks like the fish are actually swimming!"

"Oh, yes — " bright slashes — orange, gold, green and yellow slicing across blue water — my first free form piece. Instead of conventional shapes, I translated bold lines into meaning, a liberating moment. "I'm glad you have it."

Each painting was like my child, conceived in passion, nurtured with time and patience, birthed when it reached artistic maturity, a precious moment captured on a canvas and trapped by a frame.

We were interrupted by Elisa from Miami. She kissed both my cheeks and left Gorgio Armiani lingering on my clothes. "Mami always talked about the Rolls Royce," she said. "She never forgot the day the *barbudos* came down from the mountains — " she stopped herself. This happy occasion shouldn't be marred by painful reminiscence. "She was there, you know. She said she was glad you were not."

"That was a long time ago," I said — like yesterday. The nostalgic bond of those who couldn't return to their native land descended like a mist around me and closed my throat. I had a coughing fit.

Olaf bent over me, solicitous. "You want some water, Gramma?"

"I can't go back." My vocal cords weren't working right. The voice didn't sound like mine.

"Where do you want to go, Gramma?"

How could he understand? His movements had never been restricted or denied.

But Elisa knew. "Mama died moaning to go home. We draped a Cuban flag over her coffin thinking that would give her comfort."

"It's changed," I said. "It wouldn't be the same."

Yet we didn't acknowledge Cuba's aging, refusing to admit the island's demise as we knew it. Like the famous who died young and were eternally frozen in our mind vibrant and beautiful, so Cuba was forever the shining star she was when we looked over our shoulders that one last time.

The photographer arrived and took over. Everybody backed away while Katherine stood on one side of my chair, Olaf on the other — three generations of Van Nuys. At my age I should have many grandchildren, but that wasn't happening — only Wayne Olaf Kennedy. The Van Nuys name had fallen from the tree like a dead leaf in winter. James came and stood by Katherine, then relatives, then a group picture, stand this way, move over, short ones in front, look here, say cheese — tiresome procedure, essential ritual.

The camera flashed silver-edged blue spots before my eyes. The scented tropical flowers and old friends with their tales triggered a melancholy so strong it was like nausea. I yearned for Olaf, his sweaty, smelly old shirt, his big, clumping boots, his rough beard against my cheek, the salty tasting kiss. My heart ached for my love and I wanted to go where he was, anxious to hear his gruff greeting, eager for his easy laugh. Why am I here without him? Last night thinking about this hullabaloo today I couldn't sleep, and I saw him, sitting in his old wicker rocker, swaying back and forth, his far-seeing eyes staring at me across the impossible void. I had to go there. He was an impatient man. He wouldn't wait forever. I struggled to rise from the chair. Olaf had ceded his post and it was Katherine who restrained me.

"Is this too much for you, Mama? Are you all right?"

"I need to go."

"You want to go back to your room — to the bathroom?"

"I need to go...need to go..." I fell back in the chair. The distance was too far, the walk too long.

"Wayne, help me get her up."

I shook my head. "I'm fine — fine." Shrill laughter, music, babbling voices, rattling cups and saucers — the noise tumbled and echoed in my ears, tilted the world. I closed my eyes to clear my head.

"Barbara, bring her some water, please," Katherine said.

A few sips and I felt more stable. Maybe Katherine gave me a pill. I didn't want to make a spectacle of myself, disgrace my daughter. This party had cost her too much time, effort and money.

There wasn't enough breath in my lungs to blow out so many candles. Olaf held my hand while he did it for me. Those gathered sang Happy Birthday, first in English, then in broken Spanish. I was touched that for my sake they had learned the words. The cake had pink icing and white sugar flowers. I ate two big slices. My diabetes went haywire, off the meter. I spent the next two days comatose, but it wasn't my time to go, because I revived and was still here.

Now Olaf sat once more by my bed with his tape machine, badgering me anew. "Gramma, the woman from Miami said your family had a Rolls Royce." Eagerness vibrated in his voice. "You didn't really have a Rolls Royce, did you?"

Cuba on My Mind

"We most certainly did. People in the tropics did crazy things. Daddy bought the car in London. The day the machine arrived at Port Macabí it created quite a stir."

I closed my eyes and pretended sleep. Where would I find the energy to tell him the whole truth?

***

A hydraulic crane lifted the Silver Wraith off the S. S. Preston's deck, the rainy season it was, September hurricanes lashing the island, every road impassable, muddy ruts and water-filled potholes everywhere. The yellow and black car with the chrome flying lady on the hood swung from the guide wires overhead like a golden bird in flight. As the crane pivoted, dock workers argued how best to place the Rolls on a railroad flatbed normally used to transport cut cane. Finally, they ran chain loops through the axles and secured the car aboard.

Daddy climbed the flatbed. He pointed to burlap sacks piled on the dock. 'There. Get those. Spread them on the floorboard. Are they clean?'

'Very clean,' the worker replied.

To protect his white linen suit, Daddy wore a loose, beige-colored canvas coat. He opened the car door and slid sideways across the saffron-colored leather seat, both legs straight out. The overcoat hadn't spared the white trousers. The cuffs were mud-encrusted; a splat on the maroon bow tie. He rolled his pants legs to the knees. His white shoes dripped mud. 'Take off my shoes.' He had big feet and white silk socks.

He placed both hands on the steering wheel, his fingers tapping the surface softly, gentle touch like a lullaby. Underneath his white pith helmet his sunburned cheeks were pomegranate pink, as if excitement had pumped every ounce of blood into his face. 'Don't scratch it,' he said to the workers tugging at the moorings.

One man wiped his forehead with a red bandana and waved a tattered straw hat. 'Ya! Bien! Vamos! Vamos!'

The engine chugged away from wharf's bustle and confusion; away from the hiss and spit of the sugar mill's grinding and crushing machines; away from the dark bagasse residue smoke belching from tall chimneys. The noxious particles hung in the air then drifted down, dusting the roof, the fenders. 'There!' Daddy pointed. Black specks on the car's golden hood! 'Look there!' The homespun shirts were too rough. The men pulled off their soft cotton undershirts and wiped gray particles.

The locomotive slowly worked its way from the port and past the mill, traveling beyond the corrugated tin warehouses and the concrete block Custom House. Agent Juarez left his post and joined the others gaping at the yellow canary, at the austere *patrón* looking through the arcs created by the windshield wipers, a seldom seen smile on his flushed face. After the big snaking curve, the train left the sea behind, climbed into the green, dark Yaguahay Mountains, and rumbled through undulating sugar cane fields flowing in places where machetes and sweat labor had triumphed over jungle.

At crossroads, peasants ran out of their thatched huts trudging through yard mud and road slush, whooping and hollering. They kicked chickens aside and tripped over mongrel dogs that rushed the locomotive and attacked the iron wheels. A woman with a naked baby draped around her neck ripped a parasite orchid from a low limb and cried out '*Mr. Hoo!*' The purple splash landed on a fender.

'Keep them off the track!' Daddy ordered. He wanted to arrive at the railroad yard before dark. 'Shoo! Shoo!' He waved away the barefoot boys and girls who ran alongside. They pointed and giggled, reached out but dared not touch.

Runners carried the news from village to village. Through the mountainous jungle trek, through dark switchbacks and sunlight patches, through lush Technicolor environs where bananas, oranges, lemons, guavas and mangos hung from branches like bright Christmas ornaments, awe-struck peasants again and again blocked the narrow gauge rail. The journey became a parade, as if the flatbed carrying the automobile were a gay carnival float, a spectacle to be welcomed with dance and song, guitars and music. No one had ever seen such an automobile.

The Silver Wraith was a fifteenth wedding anniversary gift for Mama, a celebration of the day when she stood on her tiptoes and whispered, 'yes' in Daddy's ear. The registration papers in the glove compartment gave her title to the vehicle, a surprise that overwhelmed and confused her. 'An affront to my people,' my Cuban mother said and refused to ride in the car.

Daddy built a metal shed with a metal roof, a wooden plank floor and a door that bolted shut.

Mama inspected the air-tight building. 'Much better than any *guajiro*'s hut,' she complained to Nanny Carmen. 'This extravagance rubs salt in the wounds of the poor. How could he do such a thing?'

'Because he loves you,' Carmen said.

'Because he doesn't care,' Mama countered. 'Have I ever said I wanted a car?'

Carmen reasoned with her. 'He builds the workers huts. He pipes them water. He makes sure they have latrines. He's the best thing ever happened here.'

'Sure — the same way you feed a dog because of a sense of duty but have no feelings for it.'

'You expect too much. He's not one of us.'

Mama was adamant. 'Already there are three vehicles in the garage. Why do we need another one?'

'This one is yours.'

The Rolls didn't have USSCo branded on its side, as did everything belonging to U. S. Sugar.

'You know I don't drive,' Mama fumed.

Carmen had little patience. 'Maybe it's time you learned, then. You never know when knowing might come in handy.'

After a month of hurt feelings and bad karma, Daddy said, 'Oh, bloody hell,' and drove the car into the garage better than any peasant's hut, bolted the door shut and double padlocked the hasp.

He locked up the sky. The dry season came and lingered months past its allotted time, stayed so long that first thing in the morning and last thing at night everyone looked to the heavens, hoping. The drought that began in January burnt its way through the months. May came and went and still not a drop: June; July; August. The cane fields faded from lush green to yellow to crackling brown. Lacking water the stalks turned *piojota*, the black nodes omens of hunger.

Company workers burned fields that couldn't be harvested. Dry cane leaves caught fire and flames leaped high. The burnt smell clogged the air. A gray haze hung over the mountains and the valleys. Field workers coughed and choked. Their clothes smelled smoky. Water became a precious commodity and the company rationed it, the east side of the colony in the morning; the west in the afternoon; the golf course, always. Peasants carried buckets to the trickling stream that six months ago flowed like a proper river.

Some afternoons a cooler breeze blew in from the sea and rippled through the crisp, brilliant air. Then people stopped whatever they were doing, lifted their eyes to the billowing clouds gathering in the horizon, and followed with longing and expectation the white masses drifting across the blue. They watched the mirage until the clouds broke and scattered, dispelled into thin tails and worthless wisps. Roads became dust. Dust painted brown the yellow colony houses. Thatched huts bristled like dry tinder. Immobile old men, cheeks sunken, teeth a memory, sat in doorways, blank eyes staring straight ahead, dust to dust, ashes to ashes. Lethargic children, feverish, covered with sores, struggled for breath. Dogs dwindled to skin over bones. The world turned brown, an easy burn.

One unbearably hot August day Sister Maria from the Flower of Charity Orphanage, rosary hanging from her waist, hands clasping a missal, Sister Teresa at her side, came to see Mama.

'Welcome, Sisters. What can I do for you?' Mama asked.

'A favor, very big — we are having a procession for rain,' said Sister Maria.

'We need it,' replied Mama.

The nun said, 'We will invoke the *Virgen de la Caridad* to bring us rain. We will take the blessed statue of the Holy Mother to the hill halfway between here and the beach. You know that high point where you can see the ocean three kilometers away?'

'I know the place.'

'It is a far walk but we are willing, but the Holy Virgin — she deserves better.'

'Better?' asked Mama.

The nun clutched the silver cross hanging from her neck. 'Our

Blessed Mother should not be dragged through the dust. She needs to go in comfort, with the love of God.'

'What are you saying?'

'What I'm saying,' the nun fidgeted with her rosary, 'is that she needs to ride the big car locked in the garage.'

Mama was silent, mulling over the request. 'Why didn't Father Juan Antonio come ask me himself?'

'Ay, he wanted to, but you know how your husband doesn't have much use for us Catholics since that business with the Pope. Church rules,' sighed the nun, 'sometimes do more damage than good.'

'You understand I must consult Mr. McAuley.'

'Naturally, but it is your car — a gift, no?'

'Yes, but I have not accepted the gift. I will let you know.'

And so it was that the six-foot tall plaster Virgin of Charity, baby Jesus in her arms, divine look on her face, paraded through town strapped to the back seat of the yellow Rolls Royce. Father Juan Antonio sat in front, outfitted like the Pope himself, white cassock, jewel-encrusted chasuble, silk stole on his shoulders, crosses embroidered in gold, and a four-cornered biretta protecting him from the scorching sun. He waved to the crowd who ignored the billowing dust cloud trailing the yellow-rimmed tires and walked alongside, pressing alarmingly close. Manco, overwhelmed with emotion, proud as any general entrusted with the entire well-being of his country, looked straight ahead. Wearing his spotless uniform, washed and pressed the day before by Carmen, the one-armed chauffeur slowly drove the Rolls through the city streets, past the hospital, past the railroad yard. The car turned onto the dry, rutted road to the seashore.

Directly behind the Silver Wraith walked two priests holding high Pope Pius XII placards, faded, dust-covered; next came the altar boys, lace-clad angels trying not to wriggle and bounce, carrying the fourteen Stations of the Cross. They were followed by parishioners hoisting patron saints' statues and placards. Whole families — gray-headed grandmothers, husbands, wives, children, aunts, uncles — carried flower bouquets limp from too much heat and too little water. The worshipers held white flickering candles, fireflies of hope. Shoes covered in dust, the choir trudged along, chanting a Latin liturgy. The white-robed nuns with their swooping wimples, they who had been the first to ask, came last. The procession started after the eleven o'clock Mass. Everyone marched to a single drum beat. The noon sun diffused a hot silver light that dried every liquid drop, saliva even. When the last straggler reached the summit, the petitioners knelt and prayed toward heaven, prayed toward the mountains, prayed toward the mocking blue sea, faced the Vatican and prayed to the Pope. By sunset, the Rolls Royce was back in its garage.

That night the rains came.

There was no keeping the Rolls confined after that. The Banes mayor begged it for his daughter's wedding. She rode to the cathedral with the top down and her white tulle veil floating behind her. All parades and procession now required the Rolls.

Manco worshiped the car. Being its driver elevated him to a status that in his wildest dreams he never imagined. Every day he brush-cleaned the interior, wiped the tufted leather seats, polished the wooden dashboard, straightened the glove compartment, and made sure the hand straps hung straight. He positioned the rear-view mirror exactly so, opened the trunk and checked the spare tire; raised the hood, stuck his head into the machine's innards and spent hours under there. He washed the car daily. Who more deserved it than the one that had carried the Virgin to the mountain and brought the rain?

Nanny Carmen, in order to participate and have some say-so, saved for Manco old rags and soft towels. When Manco finished polishing the car to a blinding shine, the chauffeur leaned over and kissed his reflection on the hood.

Daddy drove the car Sunday afternoons to "keep the engine tuned." I rode with him. We drove up and down the colony's four paved streets. Sometimes we ventured into the civil town. Daddy allowed the street boys who ran after the car to clamber into the back seat. They squirmed and giggled, noisy, barefoot, wiping their dripping noses on tattered sleeves. When the car returned to the garage, a frowning, disapproving Manco took it apart. Affronted by the quality of the back seat riders, he scrubbed and polished the interior, inch by inch.

Cuba on My Mind

The Rolls Royce was no longer an isolated extravaganza. It was encased in holy splendor, blessed by the *Virgen de la Caridad*, a car of hope, a vehicle of magical powers, a symbol of a better future. As more and more families asked to borrow it for this occasion or that, it became the people's car. Whenever it passed through the Banes streets, the citizens clapped and cheered. Everyone remembered the day the Virgin rode the Rolls and brought the rain.

Mama had yet to ride in the car. Daddy never again invited her to do so, though at times when he returned from a spin and sat on the veranda drinking a beer, he looked at Mama long and hard, waiting, expecting her to say something. And one day about a year later, during an afternoon deluge when lightning split the sky and thunder rolled, when blessed rain fell in mighty sheets, she did.

She said to Daddy, 'Mr. McAuley' — she always called Daddy Mr. McAuley — 'I am this afternoon invited to a tea honoring Mirta and her little boy, a welcome home party given by her friends. Mirta has had a terrible time of it, abandoned in Havana. Fidel is not a good husband. Her father's heart is broken. He has convinced her to come home and bring the baby. The honeymoon is over and she must face reality. Fidel is more interested in politics than marriage.'

Daddy was curious why Mama wanted to arrive at this particular party in the Rolls Royce after her steady refusal to ride in the car. Mama had a ready explanation. 'Mirta is a cherished person, a beautiful young girl crushed by hardship and weighed by disappointment. She is one of us. It is important we welcome her with our very best, and the Rolls has many redeeming qualities' — she smiled with her eyes — 'Would you, please, request Manco to bring the car tomorrow at four?'

Papa never flinched, but the joy in his heart danced in his eyes. 'I can do that.'

He drove the Rolls to the front door himself.

Mama's hair was swept into a bun. She'd powdered her face, glossed her lips and smelled faintly of lilies. She held her chin high as though that increased her stature, a mannerism Daddy found endearing. He tucked her ample skirt around her slim ankles, the ankles that had first caught his eye and the feet, tiny, as if they were Chinese-bound at birth. 'You are beautiful, my love.'

'Thank you. Perhaps you are prejudiced.'

He started the engine. The powerful automobile responded to the slightest pressure of his foot and the merest turn of his wrist. After waiting months and months for Mama to accept the gift, having her next to him now gave him untold pleasure. He placed his big hand over Mama's small, delicate one. Jointly, they engaged the gear shift.

Beggar boys loitering on the street saw the Silver Wraith leave the driveway and caught up with the car. Their grimy hands touched the yellow fenders. Daddy gave them a severe look and tromped the gas pedal. The car swept forward.

'Careful!' Mama cried, turning, looking over her shoulder, extending her arms in an enfolding, caring gesture. Thinking she was urging them forward, the ragged, barefoot boys ran faster. The spinning wheels splattered them with mud.

***

The rustle I heard was Olaf rising from the chair, tip-toeing out of the room.

"I wasn't asleep," I said to his back.

He half turned. "Well, you were giving a good imitation of it."

I justified my action. "The Rolls is a long, long story. It was in the garage almost a year before my mother rode in it."

"Why?"

"She didn't like the car."

"How could anyone not like a Rolls? — "

"She disliked the excess it represented. Daddy was happy the day she finally recanted and rode in it see Mirta, Fidel's wife."

"Fidel — the Fidel Castro?"

"The very one — He spent a lot of time in Banes courting Mirta. She met him at the University in Havana, where she studied psychology. One of her brothers introduced them. The Diaz Balart boys were all captivated by Fidel's idealism. He has — or had then — a magnetic personality, the type person who entered a room and immediately dominated. He swept Mirta off her feet. Her social standing was much above his. Her father and step-mother were aghast when Mirta insisted on marrying a share-cropper's son. Mirta was a *mariposa*, delicate and fragile, with translucent skin and the pale luminous eyes of one predestined to suffering, born to tragedy. The newly weds lived in Havana and Fidel supposedly had a law practice, but he didn't spend much time working at it. He was always leading a protest or planning a revolution."

"You really knew him?"

"Everybody in Banes knew Fidel. He was all over the place chasing after Mirta. Her father was U. S. Sugar's Cuban lawyer and the company people were invited to the parties and wedding."

"Was there any sign of what he would become?"

"Not a smidgen, though I did hear someone say that when he walked down the aisle to the altar, he had a gun in a holster under his tuxedo. He was a big, good-looking fellow, very charismatic, filled with kinetic energy, but he didn't win over the town. Back then, he wore slacks and shirts and was clean-shaven. Later, he adopted army camouflage and grew the beard. His followers did the same, and the guerillas were called '*barbudos*,' bearded ones. Dictator Batista was born in Banes, and the town remained loyal to him, regardless of documented atrocities. The dictator had relatives and many friends in Banes, former schoolmates, business associates and government people. In Oriente Province, Mirta's father took care of Dictator Batista's legal affairs."

Olaf had done his homework. "It's not Oriente Province anymore."

"I know, renamed Holguin, but that can't eliminate the place or the people."

"You heard what the official Cuban guidebook for tourists says about Banes?"

"Julio told me: 'an insignificant little town of no consequence.' Castro wanted to erase the town from the mountain valley. He wanted not one trace of U. S. Sugar left standing. All the yellow houses were converted into apartments for the homeless."

"Why do you think he hated Banes so much?"

"Simple. It had the strongest American presence on the island.

The company represented the plateau Fidel Castro wanted the country to reach without foreigners involved in the outcome. He wanted Cubans to own the mills, cane fields, businesses, shops and have the profits equally distributed. He started out Socialist, which wasn't a bad thing. The disparity between the rich and poor was appalling. When the economy turned sour, Ché trumpeted communism. The Argentine was Castro's best friend until he grew more popular than Fidel. Before Russia became involved, something could've been salvaged. After that, it was all downhill."

Our little Eden overrun by peasants and guerillas! Paradise despoiled! Perfection marred by gloating conquerors that triumphantly tromped through our garden and wrecked our idyllic life.

Thinking about the destruction was too painful. I closed my eyes and dropped a dark curtain over bougainvillea hedges and palm tree fronds twirling in the breeze; over the yellow school house and the rambling dwelling that was home; over my Nanny, my wonderful, obstinate Nanny. I couldn't think about Nanny Carmen now — not now — maybe later.

Chapter 6

The girl Olaf brought to my bedside looked twelve years old, a little bitty thing with bony shoulders, slight breasts, no hips and long legs. When she bent her head to better hear me her glossy blonde hair swung over her face, a gesture vaguely familiar to me from someplace, somewhere.

"Gramma, how are you feeling? This is — " I didn't catch the name. "Did the birthday party do you in?" Olaf was holding the girl's hand, playing with her fingers.

"I met you at your birthday party," the girl said.

When was that — yesterday — a week ago?

"Wayne talks about you all the time."

"Wayne?"

"You're the only one calls me Olaf, Gramma."

"Is Olaf here?"

"I'm here."

"No, not you — my Olaf — what's your name?"

The silly girl giggled. "Who's on first? I'm Barbara." She goosed Olaf's ribs and he goosed her back. They tussled like two puppies, the way my cocker spaniels, Jack and Jill, once romped and played with each other. It broke my heart when I gave them to the cook. Bringing pets into another country required health papers, veterinary certificates, quarantines — endless paperwork. Daddy didn't have time to fool with animals. He had to shut down the company in a great big hurry and evacuate the humans.

I laughed a thin, hollow sound. The ability to laugh from the pit of my stomach had left me. Nothing worked right anymore, and if it did, it hurt. I waded in shallow water no strength or breath left to swim deep.

"We're engaged." Barbara kissed Olaf on the lips. His mustache was gone! His beard shaved off. He looked absurdly young without the facial hair. She nuzzled his ear, was all over him, no restraint, no decorum. She held up her left hand, fingers splayed — "No ring, yet. We're going to Antone's Jewelry tomorrow to pick out one. I want a great, big diamond. I love diamonds."

I wanted to tell Olaf about the time Jack swallowed Mama's diamond ring. The servants looked everywhere, unable to find it. Then Nanny Carmen went into a Santeria trance and pronounced that Jack had eaten the ring. Poor Jack! He was whisked to the hospital and Dr. Ruiz X-rayed his stomach and sure enough, there was the ring. He said, 'Feed the dog bread. He'll pass it, and if he doesn't, bring him back and I'll cut him open — ' everybody in the house following the dog, waiting for him to crap — comical, but telling took too much breath. What came out of my mouth was, "You can have my ring."

When Olaf died, I took off my wedding ring. His life wrapped around my finger was more pain than I could bear. It gave me pleasure for my grandson to give his girl my ring. "Open the top dresser drawer."

Olaf's hand fumbled over folded underwear and silk stockings. "This?" He held up the little velvet box.

"Open it."

He undid the miniature latch and flipped back the velvet top. A perplexed look came over his face.

I squinted to see the three-carat diamond from the Debeers mine in Africa, where Olaf went to work after Fidel Castro triumphed. Art Cleveland had a connection there and he got Olaf a job in a hurry while Olaf could still leave.

The fouir emeralds surrounding the diamond came from Bolivia. Olaf went there, too, I can't remember why. That was before we were married. "Do you like it?"

Barbara whispered something in Olaf's ear. He shrugged, placed a finger across his lips. "Shh."

"It's yours," I said.

Olaf protested. "This is your ring, Gramma. Grampa gave it to you."

"I can't take it with me."

"Grampa must've loved you very much to give you a ring like that."

"He did." However, love didn't prompt the gift, common sense did. If I had breath, I'd explain to him that residents of unstable countries accumulated valuable gems, so when one faction took over from another and nullified the money or recalled the currency, jewelry was the sole salvation. Precious stones, the bigger the better, were the passport to freedom. It was easy for an émigré to leave the worthless paper behind, grab the little velvet bag and flee. 'Enough,' Olaf had said, 'to keep us a year if we have to run.' The explanation was too long, too complicated. Neither Olaf nor his girl would understand.

"This is the most beautiful ring I have ever seen," Olaf said. He had a baffled look, probably because he'd never laid eyes on such exquisite jewelry.

The romantic thing for Olaf to do was to slip the ring on Barbara's finger, but I noticed that he simply placed his closed fist over the palm of her outstretched hand and I thought, oh, oh, she was his mother's pick, not his. The girl rubbed her palm with curled fingers and burst into an innocuous giggle that blossomed into an offensive laugh. What was so funny?

Olaf said, "That's enough, Babs."

Of course the ring didn't fit. It had to be sized. I extended my hand. "May I see it?"

My grandson looked sheepish as he snapped closed the velvet top and put the box back in the dresser drawer. "Not now, Gramma — later. We have to go now. We'll talk about the ring tomorrow and you can tell me about Grampa."

Next day when he returned, I asked, "What happened to your beard?"

"Babs didn't like it. She said it tickled and scratched. Look, I worked on our family tree." He held up a paper with lines and brackets and names inserted in slots. "Your father was Scotch and your mother Cuban right?"

"Yes. And my grandfather was an Isleño from the Canary Islands, the most hard-headed of all Spaniards. Olaf was Dutch. And Katherine married an Irish-American, so you're quite a mixture, my boy, which is good. Fresh blood aids the intelligence. No ingrown genes in our family."

"How did you meet Grampa?"

"Oh, I always knew the old Dutch rascal. He came in the fourth grade. The Van Nuys moved into the construction house down the street from ours."

"Construction house? — "

"Mr. Van Nuys headed construction. When a new family arrived USSCo assigned them a house, depending on their job. We had a transportation house, administrator's house, construction house, accounting house. The houses were furnished and staffed. They had assigned cars, daily food deliveries and drinks."

"U. S. Sugar paid for it all?"

"Yes, perks to get employees to stay."

"Sounds like paradise to me."

It was, but paradise was sometimes hard to swallow. Only a half dozen Americans lived there, mostly Southerners from Georgia, Alabama, Louisiana and Mississippi, cotton growers who'd bankrupted financially or emotionally and gravitated south to grow sugar cane. They bore the heat better than Northerners who'd appear and disappear in six months. The majority of USSCo's employees who stayed the course were British. They were the best colonizers. They recreated a little piece of Britain wherever they went — tea and scones at five and they were happy. We had Germans, French, Dutch, Finns — a community of exiles. The students had to learn all those national anthems. "You know something? There's not one national anthem about love and peace. They're all about war and conquering."

"I hadn't thought about that."

"The Company had one special office that did nothing but keep the paperwork straight for the non-citizen employees. It's very complicated being an alien — papers to fill out, visas to extend, documents to validate — insurmountable red tape. The company families were guests of any country where they lived."

"You sound like nomads."

"Not really, more like world citizens, at home anywhere, nowhere home. Then again, you might be right — nomads in one way, totally liberated in another."

"Not at all like the South."

"No. Not like this at all."

Every person in the South was a leaf sprouting from a branch attached to a tree with roots deep in the past. Inevitably, the first question a newcomer was asked was — 'are you related to so and so?' The trouble Olaf and I had with that! The year we came from Maui and pineapples to grow sugar cane in South Lousiana to be near Mama and Daddy, we tried but found it difficult to connect to the ingrown culture. After my parents died, one right behind the other — what a blessing for them — Olaf got a job with Standard Fruit and he and I and our baby girl moved to Honduras to grow bananas. We liked the climate better; we missed the sea.

If a Southerner wasn't able to "trace" you, the conversation stalled. Related to no one? Why, that's mighty impossible to believe! No aunts? No uncles? The questions asked in a sing-song drawl like slow music. Then they catalogued their relations, this generation connected to the previous one, to the one before that.

"The neck bone connected to the spine bone, the spine bone connected to the hip bone, dem bones, dem bones, oh hear the word of the Lord!"

"Are you singing?"

"You know that song?"

"It's an old Negro spiritual."

Ex-pats seldom discussed their family history. They were where they were because they had chosen to be free and unfettered, leaving behind the ties that bound. "Is that why you want my history — to connect and become a true son of the South? You'll never get that from my side. Work on your father's family. They go way back."

"I know, but they're so stable and ordinary — so predictable. And your side is adventurous and flamboyant and I don't know a thing about them."

My grandson's paternal relatives were New Orleans people, one generation founding the Cotton Exchange; another, the Boston Club and the Krewe of Rex. Down through the years, a male descendant had been King of Mardi Gras, crown, scepter and leggings a trademark, face imprinted on a gold doubloon flung from the two-story parade float into a million outstretched hands reaching for a souvenir. Everyone said Katherine made a remarkable union. She'd never lack for anything.

James Kennedy didn't build Katherine a castle. He placed her in a gilded cage, insulated her from reality. She lived in a world of spas, shopping, vacations and entertainment. She had a degree. She was a teacher, but James frowned on his wife working. He provided handsomely for her. She managed his philanthropic endeavors — lavish parties for cancer, 10-mile runs for diabetes, fiestas for heart funds, elaborate balls for AIDS relief — hard for me to understand, but that's the way Americans raised money, and they were generous with their donations, no doubt about that, but the system seemed so cold, so remote. Did Katherine really care about the dying children in Africa? Would she ever go into the misty darkness under a bridge and cradle a starved baby in her arms? Help an old woman burning with typhoid up a steep bank? Would James?

"You miss not having aunts and uncles and cousins?" I asked.

Olaf was honest, "Sometimes."

"It's up to you, then, to correct the lack. You must find a nice wife and have a dozen children."

He laughed. "That's ten times the national average. You were an only child; Mom is an only child; I'm an only child."

"It's a family curse," I said, "makes us special."

How her daddy loved Katherine! I closed my eyes and saw Olaf standing in shallow water teaching his little girl how to swim; swooping her up onto the pony's saddle; nestled under his big arm in the wicker rocker, reading to her, holding the book upside down, making up the story as he went along. She stole Olaf's heart from me, and in later life we both vied of his attention. 'Were every man to be this lucky!' he'd say.

Katherine came to say goodnight. She looked very chic in a little black dress, classic pearls and matching earrings. She and James were on their way to an important dinner. They never stopped — cocktail parties, business meetings and getaway weekends. If they ceased the frantic activity, they might hear a still, small voice.

"Mama, you listen to Surviva. Be a good girl — take your medicine. Don't give her any trouble. Surviva leaves at ten. You sure you'll be here, Wayne?"

"Babs is coming to sit with me. We'll be here."

"Wonderful! I'm so happy about this. She's perfect for you."

Olaf turned his head and looked away. He did that frequently when his mother was talking to him.

Katherine was halfway to the door when I asked, "Do you miss your father?"

The question stopped her. "Of course I do. He's been dead so many years."

Fifteen years, seven months and three days — his spirit never left me, was closer now than ever before. "But a breath — Olaf wants me to tell him about your father. Do you ever think about him?"

"Occasionally — I have good memories."

And so life passed, a pebble thrown into a pond, rippling from the center outward, concentric circles losing strength, eventually disappearing. How long would my ripples last?

Katherine handed Olaf a Post-It note. "Here's the restaurant's phone number, just in case — they check cell phones at the door." She blew me a kiss. "See you in a little while."

After she left I said, "Olaf and I were always getting into trouble together."

"What kind of trouble?"

So much mischief — not a day went by that we didn't do something strictly forbidden — rode horses into the surf until they lost their footing and began swimming and ruined the saddles. Stole the laundry woman's soap and lathered the barn's tin roof, sailed off on a coconut pod, landed on the hilly slope and skid down to the no name stream. Hung a rope from a tree and swung high into the sky, then dared one another to jump mid-air. We held our breath underwater until we almost passed out; swam with the dolphins until they neared the reef; sailed our little skiffs over the roiling foam arc to the other side where the ocean turned purple and the big liners moved across the horizon. Crossed into the civil town, went to a forbidden basketball game and returned crawling with lice. Carmen poured turpentine on my head. Olaf came to school the next day with his shaved.

Nobody entertained us. We didn't know what boredom meant.

***

Every Sunday Olaf's mother forced him into a church outfit he utterly despised: navy knickers, knee-high stockings, white shirt with a string tie at the neck, a loose, rusty silk vest and a dark blue cap. 'Oh,' she gushed, sipping her morning gin tonic and making an imaginary adjustment to his embroidered suspenders, 'You look like all the fine boys at home.' Gin moved her tongue. She didn't know what she was talking about. The Banes American Colony was Olaf's home. He was most comfortable wearing a *guayabera*.

His mother never went to church and his father played golf every Sunday morning, but both agreed Olaf could profit from a weekly religious dose. Since there was no Dutch Reformed Calvinist church in our town, Olaf was sent to the only non-Catholic service available, the Seventh Day Adventist.

Everywhere else in the world the Adventists met on Saturday, but in Banes they had given up Saturdays long ago. Religion couldn't compete with the fiestas and balls held on that day, nor with the beaches that beckoned from sunrise to sunset. I went there, too, since the Catholics didn't let the McAuleys in the door, something about Mama marrying Daddy, a Presbyterian heathen.

Reverend Juarez preached at the Adventist church every Sunday. He had bright, sharp eyes bulging from a face shaped and colored like a dried coconut. During the week he was the custom clerk. On his off time Reverend Juarez did forbidden, revolutionary work. Revolution was a sport, like football in the States. Everyone talked about it, took sides, made plans, bet on the odds. Every six weeks or so, a new revolutionary leader sprouted ready to save the island and free the peasants.

I imagined Reverend Juarez would lead the next freedom movement.The preacher did his utmost to convince his non-Catholic congregation that there was no revolutionary figure greater than Christ and that all must follow in His footsteps. He truly believed there was not one pacifist bone in the Son of God.

On my way to the chapel, I walked around the great banyan tree with the tattooed trunk that split Calle Iglesia in two. On a dare, Olaf had carved our initials on the wide, gray expanse and drawn a heart around them. The etching, one of hundreds tattooed on the tree, would've been forever had I left it alone, but as soon as the others told me, I went right over and chiseled away his sentiment and left a lasting scar instead.

That Sunday, dressed in that ridiculous outfit his mother loved, Olaf caught up with me.

'Little Dutch Boy! Stick your finger in a dyke.'

'I'll put my finger up your–'

'Watch it, Olaf. Did you forget your wooden shoes?'

He ignored my jibe. 'I'm not going to service.'

'Where are you going?'

'I have my quarter for the collection. Do you?'

'Yes.'

'I'm going across the bridge to the Chinaman's.'

My curiosity spiked, 'What for – ?'

'Cigarettes, y'wanna come? – '

I considered. One hour sitting on a hard bench listening to Reverend Juarez rave on about Jesus, or one hour smoking cigarettes. The latter was much more appealing. I'd been dying to smoke a cigarette.

Daddy had gone to check an outlying plantation and Mama was at Mrs. Corman's doing their Sunday Christian Science lesson. Mrs. Corman, from Boston, was somehow related to the religion's founder. The study books came on the sugar freighter every other week. Banned from the Catholic cathedral, Mama joined Mrs. Corman in the study of God, Christ, mind and body. Old grumpy Carmen would smell the cigarettes right away, but chances were that she'd go to her *Santeria* session, the forbidden Voodoo religion, in my thought the best religion ever. Carmen, a true *Santeria* disciple, knew how to go into a trance, talk to spirits, divine the future, wring a chicken's neck, splatter the blood and bring back the dead, something neither the Catholics nor the Adventists came close to doing.

The Chinaman's café was the first flaking blue building across the Banes River Bridge. It opened onto the sidewalk. The 20-foot high doors never closed. The protective grillwork seldom came down.

Ceiling fans stirred the air heavy with stale cigar smoke and the dank smell of spilt liquor. Since ancient times, men drinking beer and rum from brown bottles had propped their elbows on the long bar and worn golden spots on the red mahogany surface. Men played dominos and talked; leaned against the walls and talked; swatted flies and talked. They talked about women, revolution, politics, and their despised employer, U. S. Sugar Company, USSCo. When they talked, to emphasize a point or underscore a friendship, they touched each other on the shoulders, on the chest. Daddy once said tying a Cuban's hand was equivalent to cutting out his tongue. The only women at the Chinaman's were the ones who walked over from Hotel Campana looking for business.

Clear apothecary jars filled with jelly beans, gum balls, Chiclets, peppermints and rock candy sat on a glass case facing the sidewalk. Displayed inside the case in open wooden boxes were Partagas, Upmann and El Fino cigars. The cigarettes were kept somewhere out of sight. The Chinaman lurked behind the candy jars. His rimless spectacles framed slanted eyes constantly darting here and there, making sure no street urchin lifted a lid and helped himself. 'Yes? Yes? Vat you vant?'

'Camels,' Olaf said over the loud music coming from the jukebox inside the building. 'Two packs.'

I hung back and waited on the sidewalk blocked by tables. A platoon of pigeons flapped into the air. A lottery vendor waved gray tickets splayed like a winning hand and cried out: 'One thousand two hundred forty two! Today's best number! Win a million! Win another million! One thousand two hundred forty three! A house on the beach! A Cadillac! Okay, my friend.' In exchange for a few coins, he tore off a ticket and handed it to a burnt-looking *campesino*. 'This is your best chance to give up cutting cane from dawn to dark. This is your path to a better life.' A man with one foot propped up on a wooden chair plucked a single string on his guitar. The black woman leaning against a lamp post counted a few silver coins and excepting one, dropped them into a little pouch she slipped into her bosom. She flipped the withheld mite into the crippled beggar's tin bowl. It clinked when it hit the bottom. He raised his sunken eyes, '*Gracias*

— Dios te bendiga.' Dirty barefoot boys drifted down the sidewalk, eyes sharp and bright, looking for opportunity.

The Chinaman had only one Camel pack and Olaf took it and gave me the Kools. 'They're more for girls,' he said.

We quickly re-crossed the bridge to the American Colony side, climbed the steep Calle Iglesia, the cigarette packs burning holes in our pockets. We had a mission, a purpose, and only one hour before church dismissed and the faithful and the penitent rose from their knees. Once through the turnstile that kept the cows from entering the golf course and churning the sod, we broke into a run.

'No. 9! — ' cried Olaf. The remote green was the furthest from civilization. The wind billowed over the dry cane field on the other side of the boundary fence. The dry leaves rippled like ocean waves at low tide. A short distance way, crowning a hill top sat a big concrete cistern, reservoir for precious rain water. I collapsed on the plank bench inside the caddy shack.

'Around back! — ' Olaf yelled.

We sat on the dry, warm ground, leaned against the yellow wall and lit up. The blazing sun scorched the dry, rustling cane field and turned silver the barbed wire surrounding the reservoir. On the velvet surface of No. 9 green, the light made bright puddles. The bells tolled for 11 o'clock Mass.

The Kool tasted like menthol. I threw the cigarette on the ground. 'Yuk. I hate the taste. Light me a Camel.' Olaf placed two cigarettes between his lips, struck a match and lit them both. He flicked his wrist and doused the flame.

I tasted the sweet nicotine, inhaled the smoke, lungs about to burst, choking and coughing, cancer not even a speck in the horizon.

The wind whipped the brown cane leaves and they swished and crackled softly whispering a fine tune. The sky was so blue the eyes sought rest in the white pillows drifting past.

We lit one cigarette after another, inhaling, exhaling, spellbound by the thin blue rising smoke, entranced by the trails dissipating into the shimmering, sun-lit air that sparkled and danced over our heads.

I saw them first, little red snakes wriggling through the dry grass.

We both jumped at the same time and stomped on them, only to have them twist and slither through the parched rough and resurrect a few feet away. Olaf pulled off his blue cap and beat the flames to no avail. He removed his silk vest and flapped at the fire.

'Stop that!' I cried. 'That just makes it worse! Watch out!' His vest was aflame. He flung it a distance. 'We need water — the reservoir!'

Climbing the barbed wire fence was impossible. The dry season had lowered the water level below the halfway mark and anyway, we didn't have a bucket. A new line of flames flickered red, orange, yellow. Heat scorched my shoe soles and burned my ankles as I stamped the ground. The fire fanned out with incredible speed. One minute a spark on the grass, the next an unstoppable blaze, crackling, turning, spitting in every direction, reaching No. 9 green, the precious mound tended daily by men on their hands and knees, watered even in the dry season when the colony turned to rationing.

In seconds, Olaf's cap and vest curled up and turned black. He passed a hand over his eyes, wiping sweat and leaving a dirty smudge on his cheek. 'We're in big trouble. We need the fire brigade.'

At that moment on No. 8 green, Olaf's father, who played golf every day and never went to church, set his ball on a tee and took a wide practice swing. His partner, Mr. Corman, looked with keen concentration across the fairway. What he saw made him drop his club. Both men and their caddies stared for a confounded moment, then scattered.

We heard the fire engine. We knew we had to make ourselves scarce. 'Run!' Olaf cried. His father had a devil temper and Mr. Corman treasured the golf course more than he did his wife. They'd cut us no slack.

The firemen arrived, unrolled a hose and dragged it toward the reservoir. Two men flung it with great effort over the wire fence, a clamor arising when they discovered the hose wasn't long enough to reach the water. One scaled the fence, the barbs piercing his hands and ripping gashes in his pants and shirt. He dripped blood as he grabbed the nozzle and pulled it down hard. The hose made a long sucking sound as it drew water. Men filled buckets from the fire truck tank and passed them hand over hand. Others set a counter fire around the perimeter and the flames leapt wildly inward, consuming each other. From our hideout behind the reservoir high on the hill, we followed the firemen's frantic activity.

The flames engulfed the caddy shack, flared above the roof and consumed the building.

'Papa will kill me,' Olaf said.

Sunday sinners struck dumb by the unexpected blaze froze over their putters while their caddies gathered in knots and looked solemn.

The fire hissed when water hit the flames. Smoke rose in gusts caught by breeze and spread like gray fog. By the time the fire brigade extinguished the blaze a knot of onlookers surrounded Mr. Van Nuys and Mr. Corman, the director of Recreation and Entertainment under whose jurisdiction the golf course fell. The men stood on the ground charred black. Mr. Van Nuys shook his head and Mr. Corman, hands on hips, raised his chin and sniffed the air like a dog.

Olaf muttered, 'What are they doing?'

I suppressed a nervous giggle, 'Checking the damage. Mr. Corman will die if he can't play golf every day. Oh, oh. Look who's here.'

Karl Heinz, the Company police chief, joined the men. The German, short and squatty, was built like a Panzer tank. People whispered he was a former Nazi. His military stance and cold, aloof air lent credibility to the rumor. He was the only man in the colony allowed to carry a gun, a Luger in the holster strapped to his waist. He and his wife had no children and they stayed to themselves. We didn't know them well, but we knew their two Doberman Pinschers, attack dogs trained to kill. Olaf and I harassed those dogs every chance we got, waving red meat at them from a safe distance away, watching them hurl themselves in a howling frenzy against the wire fence.

Chief Heinz walked around the spot where No. 9 shelter once stood, scraped the dirt with his boot.

Olaf muttered, 'What's he's doing?'

'Looking for clues,' I replied.

Olaf's voice rose to an anxious pitch. 'He'll find something. You know he will.'

Our agony was frightful. In whispered tones we debated whether to stand up and meet our doom, or remain hidden. Better to have burned down the sugar mill than the golf course. The golf course was the colony's life saver, the men's touchstone to sanity. We knew the right thing to do, but were afraid of the consequences. It was like causing a wreck and driven by terror, leaving the accident. Better to admit the fault, confess the guilt and take the punishment, yet we hesitated, thinking that by some miracle of God we could outwit the Chief, knowing we would not. My nerves brought on uncontrollable hiccups. My mind was busy fabricating excuses, dredging alibis.

Chief Heinz squatted low on his heels and peered at the ground, as if the ashes could speak, whisper a tale. The sparkle left the sky; the hour grew hot and humid. Even the tree limbs stilled, waiting. We were sweating like dock workers. Out of that penetrating silence, that bone-chilling stillness, Olaf rose to his feet. 'I bought the cigarettes,' he said. 'You stay here.'

'I'm coming with you.'

'No!' He was impulsive that way, bullheaded.

He stepped from behind the concrete reservoir. As he descended the hill instead of growing smaller and smaller, he appeared to me he grew larger in statue, bigger through the shoulders, straighter, his footsteps sure, the wind ruffling his flame-colored hair. He reached the inevitable consequence.

The church bells tolled twelve times.

***

When I woke up I had church bells on my mind — clear, crisp sounds and deep resonating gongs coming from a cathedral. "Do you hear the church bells, Olaf?"

He cocked his head to one side. "No."

"Do you go to church?"

"Not often."

"I'm not a big churchgoer, either. There's too much politics in religion. But I do believe in God. Do you?"

"That depends on how you define God."

Interesting, how a word or a scent can awaken the music asleep in my mind, not in a fragmented way, cut complete and full-blown. I sang out, "King of Kings! Lord of Lords! Hallelujah — Handel's marvelous chorus from the *Messiah* — that God. Have you ever listened to it?"

"Can't say I have — "

"That's too bad. Music is food for the soul. You read poetry?"

"No."

"People in the tropics read the Bible and they read poetry. Poetry embodied their native country's soul and they brought that with them. Shakespeare?"

"C'mon! Are you kidding? I tinker with cars, Gramma. I find poetry and music in the whine and purr of an engine."

Those who chose to be pilgrims left behind family and friends, but carried with them their land's literature and music. A samba or a rumba had no effect on my father, but if by some remote chance he heard bagpipes, he went into a Scottish fling. Once, a servant misplaced his Bobby Burns poetry book creating a major crisis. My mother brought to the States her volume of José Martí poetry and her Perez Prado records. Music and literature connected the spirit to home like no other art forms.

"Your grandfather was a voracious reader — knew the Bible by heart — had a quote for every occasion."

One whiff of smoke, rum or old leather and Olaf stood before me, his Panama straw hat low on his forehead, a fat Partagas clamped between his lips, fingers curled around a glass. "He loved a stiff rum drink, classical music, and a good cigar."

"I don't smoke cigars."

"Some mornings I'd kill for a cigarette."

"I don't smoke cigarettes, either. They give you lung cancer — you should know. I smoke pot sometimes."

"Marihuana? — "

"Yes."

"I hear say it is good to ease pain. I've never tried it."

"Would you like to?"

I'm so close to the end, it's foolish not to try everything, and I did have legitimate pain, valid reasons. Katherine wouldn't like it. She was very concerned with drugs and dope in the world today, though one peek in her medicine cabinet made that hard to believe. In this house there were drugs in bathrooms, on kitchen shelves, on every bedside table — a mind-boggling medicine clutter. There was a magic pill for every ache and pain, and sometimes the medications cancelled one another, or reacted negatively and produced side effects, diarrhea, shortness of breath, difficulty swallowing. Many nights I felt like swiping the bedside table clean, sending all those vials and bottles crashing to the floor, and hollering for Nanny Carmen to bring me hot orange leaf tea.

"I'll bring you a joint. Don't tell Mom."

"I'll get you Handel's *Messiah*."

He bent over the bed and kissed my withered cheek. "Sounds like a deal."

Chapter 7

Doctor Jonathan's nurse came today, prodded and pushed on my withered body, looked into every crevice, checked my pulse and heartbeat and listened to my lungs. Her pronouncement threw the house into a tizzy. My overall health had improved — my breathing came easier, my heart beat steadier, and my kidneys — well, skip kidneys, bladder, intestines — messy, disgusting body parts that still managed to somewhat function.

Was the news of my improvement received with joy and relief by my daughter — or with a sigh of resignation? Personally, I'm ambivalent, not struggling to stay alive, not catapulting toward death, no longer dwelling in the past or focusing on the future. At my age, one accepts whatever happens.

Tomorrow, if there was one, would take care of itself — my diminishing mind had no room for great, marvelous worldly happenings and events, only for small nuggets, valuable little treasures of love and care. My soul was calmed and quiet, returned like a child for comfort at a mother's breast.

I did want to finish telling Olaf my story. He pulled the chain I had avoided these many years, not wanting to be imprisoned in a past that was and is and shall be. Answering his questions forced me to follow each memory link to its original source, a painful journey, a joyful trip.

Hopefully, my Olaf waited while I lingered on. What a reunion we'd have! Fireworks and effervescence! More and more in my sleep or coma or semi-conscious state, whatever the limbo, Olaf reached for me. The touch of his fingertips opened my eyes, the sound of his voice came to me in the still nights.

"When Grampa took the rap for the golf course fire, is that when you knew you loved him?" asked Olaf.

I swirled through a dark memory tunnel into the dazzling sun-light, the cerulean sky, the sea breeze. If I talked slowly, caught my breath, I could let my grandson know. "Oh, no — long after that." My mind spun in widening circles, a whirlpool of turbulent waves — a perilous place where I shouldn't go, where I must go. "Olaf and I were always buddies." Strong currents dragged me down, down, down. "I knew the exact minute when things changed and were never the same after that."

Olaf leaned over my bed. He had good eyes, slate gray like his grandfather's, a kindness and gentleness in their depth lacking in my Olaf's. My grandson placed his little recording machine on the pillow and pushed a button. "Talk slowly. Catch your breath. We have lots of time."

Kind lies and fiddlesticks.

He prompted me. "You were telling me about you and Grampa, when you first met."

Olaf's family moved to Banes when he was in the fourth grade. We became instant buddies. We went everywhere in groups, but Olaf and I always ended up together in some mischief or other. We could swim farther, ride faster, hit harder, climb higher. We competed with each other.

"There were cliffs. We were forbidden to go there. Lots of places were off limits. We scaled the red clay walls, crawling over cracks and crevices, finding footholds, handholds, working our way up, past a honeycomb of crumbling caverns. At the rim where the trade winds whipped in from the sea, the trees all leaned westward. We'd wrap our arms and legs around the long lianas hanging from the branches, push against the trunk with our bare feet and shove off, miraculously transformed into birds that soared through the sky. We swung through the trees the way Tarzan did in the movies; swung over the pasture with straight-line paths like parts in green hair; over the empty concrete trough."

Under the sheet my crooked toes twitched. I curled them around the vine thick as a cable, swung out and back, let go one hand, one foot, imitating the trapeze artist who once came to Banes with the Barnum Circus. The wind whooshed into the legs of my red silk pantaloon. I extended an arm, a leg, bent backward from the waist, then forward, fingers touching toes, showing off.

"She's curled in a fetal position." Barbara had glided silently into the room to lure Olaf away. I smelled her predatory scent. "Should we straighten her up?"

"No. She's resting. She'll come back. She won't remember your name, but isn't it amazing how she recalls every detail of the past?"

"I hear old people do that. Your mother says she's better. My grandfather was that way — got better for a few days then died in his sleep."

I wasn't asleep. I was gliding through dark waters. Their voices were like sunlight shafts penetrating the deep. I opened my eyes. It took a few seconds to focus. Olaf had his arms around the girl and they were kissing. She was bewitching him, hitting him with a bolt from Aphrodite, stronger than fire, brighter than stars, a passionate explosion that catapulted him into an emotional turmoil. I closed my eyes, gave them privacy. When I opened them again, I had not the faintest notion what we'd been talking about. I couldn't remember the first word — so aggravating. Was it important — trivial — of no consequence? I didn't know.

Olaf disentangled himself from Barbara's clutch. "Gramma, you were telling me about flying through the treetops like Tarzan."

"Tarzan? Who's Tarzan?"

"He swings from tree to tree on long vines. You called them lianas."

"Oh, yes — lianas." The word filled in the blank, brought back the context. Other times, days or weeks passed before the unuttered word at the tip of my tongue took form and popped into my mind. "We swung out over a pasture."

The memory came to me like a television re-run, current but faintly familiar. I seized the recognizable blip and held onto it before it disappeared again like a will-o'-the-wisp.

****

I spotted a beggar and pointed her out to Olaf. The woman stood by the cattle trough, removing a white cotton cloth from her head.

Long, black hair fell from her shoulders to her waist. She was waiting for something or somebody. We swung back to the cliff, let go the lianas and tumbled to the ground. 'Look,' I whispered. 'Here comes Eduardo.'

The gardener walked briskly through the pasture gate, a burlap sack under his arm. He came near the woman, strutting a little, head cocked to one side.

He withdrew white shoes from the bag. My sandals! They were too tight. Nanny Carmen had put them in the giveaway box. Eduardo offered the shoes to the beggar, one in each hand. She took the shoes, turned them over and inspected the soles. Then she did something that absolutely astonished Olaf and me, the both of us, left us mute. She climbed into the trough and stretched prone on the concrete bottom. Eduardo dropped his trousers in a crumpled heap and climbed in behind her. From our vantage point high above we stared, mesmerized.

'We need to go,' I said.

'Yes,' agreed Olaf. Neither of us moved.

Eduardo's buttocks lifted and lowered like pounding waves spilling upon sand. The breeze came and went, waxed and waned; the palm tree fronds dipped and swayed, the entire world dancing to a whispered, cosmic music. Beyond the pasture loomed the dark, mysterious forest, the limbs and branches moving incessantly up and down, right and left. Out of sight, but within hearing, the waves surged in, sighed out. The limp lianas swung forth, came back like pendulums on a grandfather clock. My chest rose, fell, breathing in harmony with time, pulsing with nature, part of the universal movement.

A lifetime passed before Eduardo got out of the trough, pulled on his pants and hurried back to the house. A few minutes later, like a genie rising from a bottle, the woman appeared wrapped in a white tunic, draping the cotton shawl over her head. She waited a proper measure then departed.

Every day Olaf and I spied on the pair.

The blind rush to climb the cliffs and settle into place before the woman and Eduardo arrived became a compulsion, an event not to be missed or afterward discussed. The routine never varied: the beggar woman came first; the gardener arrived later with the burlap sack. She inspected the contents and upon approval climbed into the trough.

Mama's old dress changed hands; so did the brown, fuzzy teddy bear that slept with me until recently; an old aluminum kitchen pot; next day towels and a roll of toilet paper.

'Bathroom day, today,' Olaf said. Toilet paper was a big luxury.

Daddy's underwear! Olaf stifled a laugh. 'Tonight some peasant will be wearing Mr. *Hoo's* jockey shorts.' The thought was too much. He snorted out loud.

I shushed him. 'They'll hear us.' When a tin of Libby's fruit cocktail changed hands, I whispered, 'His goose is cooked. Mama makes Margarita account for every tin of that. She orders it from the States and it's very expensive. She only serves it when we have important company.'

Just when Olaf and I thought there was nothing else the gardener could pilfer, Eduardo came bearing my red pantaloon. I had snagged the pants on a root and asked Carmen to mend them. How had Eduardo gotten my favorite outfit — surely not from Nanny Carmen. I resented the big, satisfied smile on the beggar's face. The other items didn't matter much, but these pants were my favorites. I was attached to the soft silk, the rhinestones sprinkled across the waistband. Wearing the pantaloon made me feel as if I'd stepped out from between the pages of *Ali Baba and the Forty Thieves*. Eduardo was a ten-cent robber baron and the woman the receiver of stolen goods.

'I'm getting those back.' I stood.

Olaf pulled me down. 'Don't be crazy.'

What a burden knowing the unknowable was! What a burden to keep a secret — to bury feelings so deep I couldn't find them or forget them. Knowing the forbidden colored my every waking hour. I went through the days, numb, distracted like a sleep walker. Nights I lay wide awake, the gardener's heaving buttocks and the beggar's long, black hair a vision that wouldn't vanish. Something unexpected happened, too. The way Olaf and I perceived each other changed. It was as if suddenly we realized that we, too, were of different sexes, capable of performing the same act as those in the trough. The awareness caused shyness and awkwardness between us that had never existed before, our bodies sending impulsive, unexpected messages we were not emotionally prepared to receive.

I was scared that Olaf wouldn't keep his mouth shut. 'Don't tell anybody.'

'I won't' he promised. 'Cross my heart and hope to die.'

What a confusing time that was for me! My baby fat melted away and I developed breasts and a waistline. Nanny Carmen gave me the birds and the bees lecture and I had a hard time swallowing my guilt. I already knew about that and didn't want to discuss it. My prolonged silences affected my sunny outlook and my appetite. I couldn't look at Mama or Nanny Carmen in the eyes. Those two could read minds and discover hidden secrets. At dinner time, I stared at my plate. Mama took me to Dr. Ruiz. He said don't worry about it. It was my age. I'd get over it. No medicine. No vitamins. Let time be the healer.

The day Eduardo arrived at the trough empty-handed, bearing no brown sack filled with stolen treasures, the woman was furious. She refused to get into the trough. An angry Eduardo yelled an obscenity. She shrieked and slapped his face and he knocked her to the ground, pounced on top and ripped the white wrap off her back. She kicked him and he jumped to his feet, howling and cupping his crotch, cursing and spitting, lunging again. They rolled over and over, kicking and fighting, biting and tearing their clothes, getting covered with dirt. When he finally released her from his grip and got back on his feet she lay whimpering on the ground. He gave her a vicious kick.

The kick revived the beggar and she uncoiled like a striking cobra, spit in Eduardo's face, grabbed a rock and hurled it with deadly aim. The stone struck his head and his legs wavered and crumpled. She stood over him, wrapping what was left of the torn white cloth, of her dignity around her body. Before fleeing, she repaid him in kind, a swift kick to the ribs.

'He's dead,' Olaf whispered.

'Oh, my God.' This was horrible! Terrible! 'Should we call the police?'

He looked at me with intense gravity, a new, unfamiliar look as if he'd discovered I was a girl and girls didn't have much sense. 'Have you lost your mind? We're not even supposed to be here.'

An eternity passed before Eduardo moved a little, slowly hoisting himself onto all fours like a dog. He rocked back and forth experimentally then grabbing the rim of the trough, grunting with effort, he pulled himself to his feet and limped away.

That was the last time Olaf and I went to the cliffs. From then on, we avoided the pasture, the trough and each other. The secret we shared was a heavy load to carry. I toted the clandestine knowledge from dawn to dark, from home to school and back, down dusty roads winding through mountains and into the cavernous, obscure sea. All day, all night, I staggered under the wearisome load.

Early in June, the rains came — torrential afternoon downpours that made everyone run for cover. Some days, the non-stop drizzle screened the sun's hot rays, stretching rainbows across the sky. Curiosity got the best of me and one afternoon I went back to the forbidden haunt, wrapped my legs and arms around a familiar liana, shoved off through the dampness and the drizzle, and soared over the cliff into the pearl-gray sky. I swooped out and swung back, out and back, out and back, one hour, two, out and back until the sky turned pale pink and violet. I kicked my feet angling downward and passed over the trough and saw something — somebody — at the bottom. The outline of a white-wrapped body was visible through the clear rain water. My body lost its weightlessness, felt heavy. I slowed my swing and dangled closer for a better look. Suspended black hair floated all around the pale, dead face. My own face reflected in the water; my eyes in her eyes; my mouth in her mouth; distorted mirror image.

At first nobody believed me, but I persisted. 'Daddy, I know what I saw. I saw a dead woman in that old concrete trough.'

'What in the world were you doing in that abandoned pasture?' I looked away. I couldn't say. 'You have a vivid imagination, Catica. Go play.'

'I didn't make this up! It's true! Go see for yourself!'

Finally, Daddy sent — of all people — Eduardo to look. 'And you will be punished, my dear. Haven't your mother and I told you a dozen times to stay away from that pasture and those dangerous cliffs?'

Eduardo took a long time. He returned hours later — 'Nothing there, *Señor Hoo.*' His sinister stare raised goose bumps on my arms.

Next morning I rose early and went looking for Olaf. We hadn't spoken in weeks, but I knew he'd go with me. I had to know. He'd want to know, too. We always did everything together. I missed his companionship, his heckling and our constant bickering. We picked up long sticks, poked them into the trough and raked across the bottom, back and forth, back and forth, up and down, side to side, the water brown and murky.

***

My grandson adjusted the curved cushion that eased my neck pains. "You dozed off," he said. "Mama brought supper for you. She wants me to help you eat."

I waved the tray away and pushed aside the spoon he held to my lips. My body was here, but my mind was still trapped above the pasture. "Have you ever spied on anybody?"

"Not really — eavesdropped, maybe. Chicken soup — it's good. Swallow a little of it."

"Everybody in Cuba is a spy now. The ones from Miami were telling me every block in Banes has a head spy who reports if you buy goods in the black market, if you receive dollars from the States, if you go into a tourist hotel, if you trade your vouchers, if you keep your children from attending the Young Communist training meetings."

"We spy, too, but in more sophisticated ways — hidden cameras, radar guns, bugs, telephone taps. C'mon, Gramma, take a sip. Is it too hot?"

I shook my head, anxious to finish telling him what happened. He made me resuscitate past life and the unearthed memory hung suspended in air. To bury the recollection again it had to be dead, and it couldn't die until words killed it.

"Was the girl here with you?"

"Yes. She had to leave."

"Are you marrying her?"

"I guess so."

"You guess so? My, that's enthusiastic."

"Marriage is such a big step — forever, supposedly. Every friend

Babs and I have who has gotten married has also gotten divorced. I'm not sure — "

"Your mother likes her. She's beautiful."

Tanned and healthy, straight teeth, good posture, clear skin, shiny hair, educated mind. Her parents did all the right things for her as we did for Katherine. Because Katherine was our only child, our treasure, did Olaf and I go overboard? Did we give her too much attention, too many material things, made her think the universe revolved around her? Were we ultimately responsible for our daughter's self-centered unhappiness? Was it too late to fix it? Would I go to my grave bearing that cross?

"Babs was Spring Fiesta Queen — the prettiest debutante gets that title. The winner has to have it all together — school, volunteer work, fitness — all that stuff."

"*Young men's love then lies, not truly in their hearts, but in their eyes.*' "

"What?"

"Shakespeare. Did you know Romeo lusted after Rosaline before he met Juliet?"

"Not really. I don't read that stuff."

"Well, you should. You'd learn a thing or two. Sex is electric but when the electricity goes out, what you need is a dependable generator — that's what true love is, a power that never falters. Your spouse has to be your best friend, your champion, your defender. Good sex and great love combined is a sensation like no other — pure bliss. Don't shortchange yourself. Olaf and I had that and so should you. We learned about sex together, at the same time."

"You mean you — "

"Heavens no — respectable people didn't have sex before marriage back then. I'm still not comfortable with the concept, though Lord knows it is commonplace enough now. It's tawdry."

"*Tawdry?* — " He burst into laughter.

The word divided us like an iron curtain. On my side conduct rules existed, a code of acceptable behavior. On his side the rules had melted like slag in a furnace. The parameters were gone leaving no boundaries to bump against.

"Don't get married if you're not sure — "

"Nothing wrong with marrying the best-looking girl in town, is there?"

"If you love her — "

"Drink this soup. It's getting cold — "

The soup warmed my stomach, made me sleepy like a kitten that lapped milk then curled up and took a nap. Drifting off, the thought kept running through my mind that no matter how beautiful, how rich, how accomplished Barbara was, she just wasn't the right girl for Olaf.

Chapter 8

This morning Katherine gave me a warm sponge bath.

"Where is Surviva?"

"Late."

"I'm glad she's late."

Katherine dipped the washcloth in the porcelain basin next to the bed and dripped water on my body. "Mama, try to get along with her." She ran soft, gentle hands over my thin shoulders, concave chest, hipbones sticking out like they did when I was twelve. She raised one arm and then the other. "Hmm — bruises. They hurt?"

"Everything hurts."

She helped me turn over, started at my neck and ran the washcloth down my spine, over my shrunken buttocks, down each leg. "Bruises back here, too. Where are you getting all these bruises?"

"Surviva — "

"What? Come now!"

"She's rough and has bad breath and sits in my rocker and eats potato chips the minute you leave the house, but what's the point of complaining? You never believe me."

Katherine drew a big, noisy breath. "I believe you, but she's the third one we've hired. They say you're hard to get along with."

"I don't need those lazy women hanging around my bed. You know what would be a good idea? Send for Nanny Carmen. She'll take care of me."

"Believe me, I wish that was an option."

"No, you don't. I hate to be such a burden. You don't believe Surviva stole my ring and money and now my passport is gone."

"You don't have a passport anymore."

"I've always had a passport." My American passport wasn't easy to acquire. I had to memorize the constitution, go to court, swear before a judge I'd be loyal to the United States, this envied country where I am to end my days. The black-robed magistrate asked me if I wanted to change my name. He said most immigrants did. I wasn't a privileged native born citizen. I was an adopted child.

"Mama, let's not get into a senseless argument first thing in the morning. Your passport expired and we didn't renew it."

"You didn't renew it!" I had no idea where my birth certificate was, where the U. S. naturalization paper was, but as long as I had my passport, I had legal rights everywhere. "You didn't renew it!"

"You're not going anywhere."

"But I might need it — "

"You won't need it. Let's not argue, okay?"

"Anytime I say anything you say I'm arguing."

"Mama, please."

"You're so short tempered! Always uptight! What bothers you so?"

Instead of answering, she wiped my cheeks and left the damp washcloth over my face. "I'll talk to Surviva."

***

A few mornings later, Katherine arranged my frail bones in a wheelchair, put a blanket over my knees, a shawl over my shoulders, tucked the portable oxygen tank next to my feet and rolled me outside for a little fresh air. She had taken care of me the last two days, a heavy silence between us. I wondered where Surviva was, but didn't ask. If I did, we'd get into an argument. I was too tired to argue. I didn't want to argue. I just wanted world peace.

Should I ask to be sent to a nursing home? Sit with all those doddering ancients whose heads hung down, spit dribbling from their mouths and strange cries erupting from closed throats? Was I at that point?

The gardener had placed a sheet of plywood over the three terrace steps. Katherine maneuvered the wheel chair through the French doors and out to the flagstone patio. Four magnolia trees blocked the sun and shaded the area. Wrought iron chairs and chaise lounges, bright flowery cushions, tables, potted plants and a brick barbecue pit gave the patio comfort and beauty. Beyond was a pool so bright and dazzling blue it hurt the eyes.

At home we always sat on our veranda, a dozen rockers, a potted palm between each one, small tile tables and ashtrays on chrome stands scattered about, the overhead fans slowly revolving. Mama's friends came, sat, smoked and drank tall lime-rum drinks. They sewed, embroidered, crocheted or rolled bandages for the Red Cross, their hands busy as they discussed the events of the day and ways to improve their world. The west end had a nest of wicker furniture, the rocker where Daddy sat and sipped Hatuey when he came from work, the same one he brought with him to the States, the one he left to me when he died and I gave to my Olaf; the connection we carted all over the world and that now, the worn brown cushions recovered with flowery cotton cloth, anchored my bedroom. On the east side where the veranda widened into a semi-circular cupola, sat a big wooden radio. When the reception was good we received American stations from Miami or New Orleans. On those clear, starlit nights everybody present, particularly the young people were encouraged to lean into the machine and improve our English by repeating words after Helen Trent or Amos and Andy.

Katherine's patio was a pleasant place, though anyone seldom sat there. She and James were too busy. By late August sitting outside was impossible, the heat rising from the ground like steam, but today was abnormal, the rain last night had cooled the earth, and the day was clear and comfortably warm.

Azaleas surrounding the yard formed a green privacy barrier. The rain revived the bushes and the leaves lost the droop brought on by heat and they looked bright and perky. Birds flitted here and there, pecking the lawn and darting about a feeder. The redbird perched on the concrete birdbath splashed water on its wings. A hummingbird, looking for nectar, hovered near a suspended glass container. A small green lizard made its way across the yard. The peaceful, idyllic scene was disrupted when blackbirds descended, cawing and croaking and flapping their wings.

"Mrs. Van Nuys, here's a little sassafras tea for you." A girl placed a bent straw between my lips, her breath like fresh mint, her touch a soft breeze.

"Who are you?"

"I'm Connie Giovingo your new caregiver."

"I don't need a caregiver. I'm going to the nursing home."

"No, you're not. Nobody is going to warehouse you somewhere to die. I'm here to take care of you. Your daughter tells me you're feisty and impossible, full of grit."

"She said that, did she? Did she also tell you I'm a burden, a millstone around her neck?"

"No. She said she loved her mother and wanted you to have the best care possible."

"Where is Surviva?"

"I don't know. Who's Surviva?"

"The other one — I sent her packing and I'll get rid of you, too."

"We'll see. I have a lot of stick 'um."

"Are you from the same agency?"

"I'm a temp. I work day time," Connie said. "I'm taking a night course at the vocational school to be a nurse's aid. Then I'll become a nurse, then a doctor."

Her abundant black hair was caught in an old-fashioned net and held away from her face. Her strong jaw line was softened by a soft, pointed chin. The light played upon arresting coal-black eyes. She was so slight she didn't look strong enough to push the wheelchair. Just like the agency to send a child to do a grown woman's job. "How old are you?"

"Eighteen."

"And you have it all planned out?"

"Oh, I do! I do! I'm passionate about it."

When was the last time anybody I knew was passionate about anything? Fidel Castro was passionate about taking Cuba in a new direction; Evita Peron about rescuing the *descamisados*; Adolph Hitler about conquering the world. Beethoven was filled with musical passion; Van Gogh gloried over sun flowers; Alicia Alonso had to dance or die.

What happened to my passion? When did it disappear? When my joints hurt too much to hold a brush? When Olaf died and took my heart with him? When I moved into this house, looked out the front windows and saw the streetcars on St. Charles Avenue, put up my easel and smeared paint on the unforgiving white carpet?

My fingers curled around a long, flat brush — bold strokes, primary colors, energy, force. Critics said that about my paintings.

The girl grasped my cold hand in her warm one and pried my fingers open.

"What are you holding?" she asked.

"My paint brush — "

"I could tell you were an artist."

I looked at her with new curiosity — "Really?"

The black birds scattered with an awful racket. Olaf and the girl at his heels walked across the lawn.

"Hey! Gramma! Gramma! What are you doing out here?" The pair stopped when they saw Connie. "Hi, I'm Wayne, the one and only prodigal grandson. This is Barbara."

"Hi y'all, I'm Connie, temporary caregiver. I'll go freshen her room while you visit, okay?" She hurried away.

Olaf turned on his heel and stared long and hard after Connie as if trying to place her, as if he'd seen her somewhere before, knew her from someplace other than here. With a slight shake of his head, he pivoted back to me. "Gramma, remember Barbara?"

I nodded. Didn't I give her my ring or had Surviva stolen it? Did I see that ring yesterday? Did I show it to Olaf? He'd found the little black velvet box in the dresser drawer, held it in his hand. Had the diamond sparkled? Had the emeralds glittered?

"Where's Surviva?" I asked Olaf.

"Mama fired her. Didn't you hear the ruckus? She was yelling and arguing, threatening to sue — sent Mama to bed with a headache."

Barbara said, "I was there yesterday when you showed us the ring."

"You were? I did?" What a relief!

"Yes, but there wasn't — "

Olaf interrupted her with a stern look identical to his grandfather's. One look from my Olaf shut up the most prolific blabber mouth. "Gramma, remember you told us about the beggar woman dead in the trough? Did they ever find her?"

Barbara giggled — "The beggar woman, the ring. Can't you see? Your Gramma is losing it. Maybe there was no beggar woman."

How could this silly girl know? She wasn't there, but that's what Mama, Daddy and Dr. Ruiz said, too. They convinced me that I had seen a reflection of myself in the water and I should forget the whole thing. Some months earlier, I had confided to Nanny Carmen that I could fly, not hanging onto a liana, but by jumping off the garage roof and flapping my arms like wings. I glided easily over the river and the trees and the sugar cane fields. Dr. Ruiz talked to me in a gentle, serious voice. He said the vision in the trough was the same as my flying, an imaginary flight peculiar to children who spent too much time alone.

"So Wayne tells me after the trough thing you and Olaf fell in love?" Barbara's tone offended me, as if she were goading me to confess another fairy tale.

"No. He fell in love with the Spanish teacher. Her name was Señorita Evita."

I clammed up, screwed my mouth shut tight and said no more. Barbara had no business asking me questions. She was not blood. I wasn't telling this silly girl anything. She'd never hear about Señorita Evita from me.

Barbara tugged Olaf's arm. "C'mon, Wayne, let's go. I'm bored. We haven't had any fun! Everybody's gone to Pensacola. If we leave right away we still have time to spend a day or two. Our last free week and we haven't done a thing!"

She was antsy, impatient; eager to be off. She didn't like hanging here, wasting her vacation.

"I told you, Babs. I'm spending the entire time with my grandmother."

"You meant that?" The pout that spread over her pretty face was an omen of things to come. This girl got her way and steered the ship. "You really meant that?"

I waved a weak hand. "Go, both of you." I didn't want to be anybody's albatross.

Olaf objected. "I'm not going anywhere."

"Well, I've had it! I'm getting in my car! I'm on my way to the beach — " she gave him a pointed look — you'd better come with me or else — before she flounced across the terrace and up the steps.

Olaf followed her. "Listen, Babs." They disappeared around a corner.

When he returned, there was misery on his face and defiance in the thrown back shoulders. I wondered who won the skirmish.

"You should go," I said, not wanting him or anyone else moping around me because of a sense of duty.

"She'll be all right," he said. "I hate sand."

I loved sand, missed the gritty feeling under my bare feet; missed building elaborate castles that took days to construct, only to be instantly washed away by high tide, or slowly eroded by little lapping waves; missed running over sand in the heat of the day, skipping and jumping as if walking over hot coals.

"What if she doesn't come back?"

He balanced his elbows on his knees, laced his fingers and rested his chin on his hands. He looked so like his grandfather when Olaf was glum and down that I laughed.

"What's so funny?"

The explanation was too long, required a stream of words I didn't have the energy to string together. The connection between now and then, between this Olaf and the other love-struck Olaf was too complex for my grandson to understand.

"Love — "

Love was an all-consuming affair, a constant battle to pull in the extremes and meet in the middle, a situation made tolerable because the hormone-induced emotions made sweet music that filled the heart and agitated the body, trembling jubilance mixed with unexpected hazards and deep pitfalls. When my Olaf got caught in the love net, he wasn't himself any longer. He became a different person, a stranger who hated his father, resented his mother and ignored me, his loyal, life-long friend.

"Your grandfather was so in love with our Spanish teacher that for the first time in his life, he was happy his mother made him repeat the eighth grade."

***

Our Spanish teacher was a wild, dark-skinned creature with puckered red lips and flashing dark eyes, her face framed by wiry, untamed black curls. Afternoons, after Miss Kelly left, Evita took over for Spanish classes. She always came late, galloping over the hill crest astride a Tennessee walker assigned to her by U. S. Sugar, its forelegs stretched taut, hooves glinting and kicking up sod, mane flying; horse as wild-eyed as its rider. Señorita Evita had named the spirited animal, sixty-five hands tall and broad as a molasses drum across the middle, *Amorcito*, Little Love. The horse, mouth frothing, arched his noble neck and neighed when she reined him. She swung down from the English saddle and looped the bridle over the hitching post.

Olaf's boredom at languishing in educational limbo brought him a thrilling and unexpected consolation. Newly awakened as he was, he fell in love with Señorita Evita. He day-dreamed all day and the dazzling visions spilled into nights. His desire was a concentration, a magnet, overwhelming, leaving no room for any other thought.

Every afternoon Olaf waited for her sitting on the bottom step of the school house stairway. 'You're late,' he said. Punctuality was neither a virtue nor a sin, simply something that didn't happen in the Tropics. If you got there, you got there, if not, there was *mañana*, an attitude that drove Americans crazy, imprisoned as they were by their watches and clocks. But Olaf had to say something, open the conversation in some innocuous manner that would give voice and shape to his thundering heart.

The teacher replied, 'Who are you — the timekeeper?' She bounded upstairs, taking the steps two at a time.

I felt sorry for Olaf. The sleeveless white cotton blouse tight over Señorita Evita's uplifted breasts stirred his private parts — new discovery, magnificent sensation. The riding britches curving over her hips, the jangling silver spurs, the pointed boots thudding on the wooden steps turned his ears red, made him crazy. With her woven leather crop, she tapped a steady note on the stair railing all the way up. Her perfume paralyzed his brain. Though he was careful not to talk about it, his love was no secret. For one thing, he stared after her with the same look a faithful dog gives his master.

Cuba on My Mind

After school, he hid behind the big ceiba, the trunk scarred with a thousand initials encased in hearts — love forever. He watched as Señorita Evita crossed the street and disappeared into the American Club, where men waited for her — old, pucker-faced Mr. Cleveland, Mr. Corman, Mr. Kelly, and others who came from the ship or from outlying plantations, Olaf's father, too, and sometimes mine. The men sat in wicker chairs under slowly revolving fans, drinking De-Wars, laughing, low, vibrating sounds waiting for her to come. Olaf resented the way they touched her shoulders, her hips, arms; the way she spun from one to the other like a whirling top.

At the beach he stared for hours as she stretched on the sand, the glistening sun kissing her dark brown limbs. Sometimes, her back against a coconut tree trunk, she read a book or paged through a magazine. He jealously watched the palm fronds move split shadows back and forth across her body. What she did at any given moment, whether it was teaching, or playing golf, or having a drink didn't matter. What consumed Olaf was that she *was*. He was smitten.

The other boys teased him. 'You dream about her? You see her naked legs in your sleep?'

One day when he asked me to find his pencil I accidentally opened his composition notebook. He'd scrawled her name, Evita, Evita, Evita over and over; Aetje, Aetje, Aetje, in Dutch; in English Eve, Eve little Eve — *naked in the garden*. As if an asp had bitten me, I snapped the notebook closed and shoved it into his book sack.

I felt sorry for him. What he was going through was sheer torture and the consequences showed. He became quiet and withdrawn, morose. He sighed at the most unexpected moments as if gasping for air to stay alive; neglected reading his assignment and stared out the window. The trough business catapulted him into another stage of life, and like me, he wasn't ready. I thought maybe his parents would take him to see Dr. Ruiz and he'd receive my same diagnosis.

And I hated him — hated the way he overlooked, snubbed and completely ignored me. The anguish and distress filling my heart triggered an emotional turmoil — anger and sadness, defiance and utter misery. I was no longer number one in Olaf's thoughts, his best friend. All new and thrilling possibilities involved the Spanish teacher. I begrudged his drowning interest in Señorita Evita because it created a hole in my existence, introduced me to boredom and before long jealousy and resentment crept into the vacuum. My former best friend and I viewed each other across a wide gulf, neither exactly sure how the separation came about. Nothing had changed. Everything had changed.

One afternoon Olaf raced up the stairs behind Señorita Evita. The two burst through the door into the classroom at the same time. Both stopped short.

'What are you doing here?' Olaf asked, astonished to see his father leaning against the blackboard wiped clean of yesterday's lesson.

Señorita Evita blinked thick black lashes, 'Señor? To what do we owe this honor?'

Erik Van Nuys said, 'I need to speak to you,' and noting the students' expectant stare, the question in our eyes, he added, 'In private.'

Señorita Evita waved us outside. 'Go play — early recess. Twenty minutes.' Turning to Mr. Van Nuys she arched an eyebrow and flipped the mass of tangled hair over one shoulder. 'Will that be sufficient?'

As we trooped outside, Olaf asked me. 'You think he's here about me?'

'I hope not.' I worried that Mr. Van Nuys had found out about Olaf's crush on the Spanish teacher. He was an irrational man who went into uncontrollable rages and threw magnificent temper fits. He was still ranting about the golf course, long after everyone else had put it aside, laid it to rest.

'I bet he's going to tell her I have to graduate this year.'

'You have to, sometime, you know. You can't stay in the eighth grade forever.'

'I'm not going to Amsterdam.'

His older sister, Birgette, had left for Amsterdam four years previously and instead of a high school diploma got into troubles only talked about in whispers.

We sat on a playground bench and Olaf was so down, I put an arm around his shoulders. 'It'll be all right.'

Dejected, he propped his elbows on his thighs, chin resting on

Cuba on My Mind

his closed fists. He was taller than his father, with the same slate gray eyes, unruly red hair and identical, crooked eye teeth, as if they'd been genetically implanted. As my physique had changed, so had his, and he'd grown broad through the shoulders, wide chest tapering to a narrow waist. Anxious, curious, we looked up to the second-floor windows, the green working shutters flung open on this sunny day, and saw only the ceiling fan slowly turning.

'Do you hear anything?' he asked.

'No.'

'I'll kill him.'

'C'mon, Olaf — he's your father.'

He said something truly shocking. 'He's a son of a bitch.'

At the end of our time out, Mr. Van Nuys hurried down the stairs, his florid face flushed redder than usual. He motioned for us to return to the classroom. As we passed him on the steps, Olaf's father smelled of turpentine and something else... something else — perfume?

Señorita Evita wasn't at her desk. The door to the janitor's closet was ajar, hanging from the ceiling the 45-watt light bulb constantly left on to discourage mold. Olaf grasped the knob to close the door on the lingering, noxious smell of damp mops, chalk dust and turpentine, definitely turpentine.

'Olaf! For heaven's sake! What are you doing in the closet?' Señorita Evita was back at her desk.

Red-faced, Olaf mumbled, 'Nothing,' and took his seat, but he knew it wasn't *nothing*. We all knew it, the way kids instinctively knew without being told. It was *something*, only we didn't know what.

'Your father,' Señorita Evita said, as if Olaf needed an explanation, 'is a very respectable man.'

Olaf muttered to me, 'He's also a mean bastard who makes my mother cry.'

I didn't say anything, because after all, Olaf also made his mother cry. It was common knowledge that since arriving in this tropical paradise five years ago. Mrs. Van Nuys wept constantly. Everything upset her — the weather, the bugs (she shrieked when she saw a cockroach and fainted if an iguana found its way into the house), the isolation, the lack of society. The servants whispered tales — how when the bed-room went dark and she thought the help had retreated to their quar-ters and the children were asleep, she screamed at her husband about many things, women included. 'Bitches — Latin whores! Jezebels! All of them!' Their quarrels always ended on the same note. She wanted to go home where the weather was dismal and the people civilized.

Señorita Evita rapped her desk with the leather crop. 'Eighth grade history — come, please.'

Because Olaf repeated the eighth grade, Elise Corman and I had caught up with him and Dwyane Corman. The four of us left our desks, walked to the front of the classroom and sat on the green bench facing our Spanish teacher.

'We will start with the History of Cuba, Chapter 6, Spanish Revo-lution, Mr. Teddy Roosevelt and San Juan Hill. You have five minutes to read the first page and then we'll discuss.'

Olaf raised his book and looked over the rim at the teacher. She cooled her flushed face with a cardboard fan; gazed out the window absent-mindedly, fingers playing with the leather whip. When it was time to discuss the history assignment she asked, 'Where were we?' and he had to remind her.

I made up my mind we might as well hear the verdict, find out what had happened, shake it out and get it over. I asked the teacher, 'Are we in trouble again? We haven't done anything.'

'Nobody is in trouble.'

Jealous that his father had the power to make Señorita Evita take time just for him, Olaf asked, 'Then why was he here? To make sure I graduate?'

'What?' Señorita Evita said in a distracted way, 'Oh, you! You are graduating, Olaf. It's way past time. We can't keep you in the eighth grade forever.'

That was the same thing I'd said.

'I'm not going away,' he said stubbornly.

'Yes, you are. Everybody goes away.'

'Not me. I'm never going away.'

Back and forth went this ping-pong of words until Señorita Evita changed the subject. 'The Preston docks tomorrow. Your father says the ship has a new captain, Captain Jack King from Georgia. Look on the map, Olaf. Where is Georgia?'

The arriving sugar freighter eclipsed all other events. The ship docked every other Thursday, loaded with supplies and necessities, news from abroad and fresh faces. Late Sunday afternoon when the sugar-laden ship sailed away after endless parties and entertainment, it left in its wake a physically exhausted and emotionally drained colony.

'What happened to Captain Nicolaus?' Dwayne Corman asked. The grumpy Greek with the walrus mustache and bad disposition had been docking the Preston as long as we remembered. While the mates came ashore to drink, dance, gamble, and find women, the captain left his quarters only when necessity demanded it, and neither fiestas nor sinful pursuits came under this category.

'I suppose he retired,' Señorita Evita replied. Her shoulders twitched with a little rumba movement. 'The new captain is young and your father says he can dance, light on his feet as a cork bobbing on water and I am to entertain him and make him feel welcome.'

Was that why his father had made an appearance? To pass Señorita Evita on to the next man, to give her away like a homecoming gift. Here, *she's yours while you're ashore, then she's ours again.* Ours! Who was *ours*?

'There will be a full moon for the dance Saturday night,' Señorita Evita said dreamily, 'a full moon.'

When the moon was full, tides responded, farmers planted crops, crime increased, coyotes howled, lovers embraced and women gave birth. The sun brought daylight, shimmering heat and misery. The moon cooled hot souls and warmed cold hearts. The rays like golden swizzle sticks, stirred hidden emotions. Whatever was impossible by day became a reality at night.

'Yes!' Olaf's eyes shone bright with anticipation and hope. Anything was possible, *anything*. His breath caught in his throat, 'a full moon. Yes!'

I knew it in my bones, right then and there. Olaf was in water way over his head. In a spiteful, jealous fit, I hoped he drowned.

Chapter 9

Katherine expressed amazement how Olaf's visits had revived me, given me a second lease on life, not physically because my eating hadn't improved, swallowing was a chore and my breath came irregularly at best, but mentally.

"You're much more here," Katherine said.

I cackled. "He's cleaning out my closet."

"In a few minutes Connie will give you your bath." Connie had an angel's touch. "What would you like to wear — the pink silk gown?"

I thought about it — "My birthday dress." Katherine frowned unsure as to whether or not I was in one of my continuous mental slides. "Why can't I wear it one more time before you bury me in it?"

"I'm not going to — "

"Heaven's sake, please do. Don't go spend a bunch of money on another outfit when the birthday one is perfectly good."

My daughter had a deep, throaty laugh, seldom heard. "You're something else, Mama. The blue dress it is — today and whenever."

After Connie had bathed me and dusted my body with sweet-smelling talcum, zipped the blue dress, and combed my wispy hair, exhaustion overtook me — very poor judgment expending what little energy I had left on one trivial, self-indulgent act. If it didn't take so much effort, I'd take off the dress.

"Ah, you look like a queen. Here, let me do this." Connie rubbed my lips. "Gloss."

Even those who loved me most avoided physical contact, fearful to cause harm or stumble in death's way, but Connie didn't seem to mind. She patted my shoulders, rubbed my back and dropped quick little kisses on my head. Frailty had a repulsive ugliness — bones crumbling, skin wrinkling, basic organs malfunctioning, and the mind fading. The body developed a foul, repelling odor that neither perfume nor deodorant could disguise, yet this slow decay didn't disturb Connie. Dying young was a tragedy of unfulfilled potential, but over-staying your welcome was a bore, like a guest who lingered too long and wouldn't go home.

"This is what we're going to do," Connie said. "You're going to lie there — " she knew exactly how to wrap her arms around my torso and help me into the hospital bed that Katherine had delivered yesterday so I'd be more comfortable — "and I'm going to hook that oxygen so you can breathe easier and fill those baggy lungs and then when you regain your pep, I'll roll you outside and we'll have lunch by the swimming pool — how's that?" She acknowledged my wan smile and weak nod with a pat on my shoulder. "This house is so beautiful — like a palace!"

"Where do you live? — " My voice a notch above a whisper.

"We have an apartment on the other side of town — across the tracks."

"You're married?"

"No — I live with my dad. My mom died."

"I'm sorry."

"Cancer — I took care of her until the end. Dad fell apart. He couldn't handle it."

I grudgingly admitted, "You're gentle."

"Every person I take care of, I think this could be Mama." She gave my hand a little squeeze. I wanted to return the sentiment, but my fingers had no strength left. "Is your grandson coming today?"

"Yes. He's taping my old life. He wants it all on record before he leaves next week."

"What will you talk about?"

A good question — what deep, dark secret should I share? "Maybe I'll tell him about Art Cleveland."

"Was he an old beau? I bet you had boys swarming around like bees after honey."

"No. He was an old scar-faced bachelor who loved our English teacher."

Connie draped a light blanket over me. "You close your eyes and think about that Cleveland fellow. Get it all straight in your mind. I'll be sitting over there if you need anything."

She looked right in the wicker rocker, as if she belonged there, her legs curled under, a book in her lap, not at all like Surviva who insulted my senses — fat hulk spilling from the chair as she crumbled potato chips into the cracks between the cushions. Connie's shoulders duplicated the arc created by the back rest; her thighs followed the curve of the arms. Against the wicker's coarse texture and weave, the white cotton uniform appeared as smooth and cool as fresh milk. Her black hair drawn away from her face, her luminous black eyes, the black book in her hand — all formed a harmony, a natural line for the eye to follow. My fingers twitched.

She peeked over her book. "You're not sleeping."

"I'm thinking."

"That's good. Think about your beaus."

***

As I dozed off, I saw Art Cleveland standing on the American Club veranda, one muddy boot propped on the railing, motionless, on one leg like an aging crane drink in hand. He was absorbed in thought, watching rain drip off the eaves onto the shiny green leaves and slide down the center veins to the ground.

The others would be there shortly, gathering for their afternoon drink. Once they arrived, the conversation invariably turned to endless complaints about the heat, the sugar crop; the unreasonable demands from Boston headquarters.

Mr. Cleveland drained his glass and set the empty tumbler on the veranda railing and walked across the deserted ballroom with resolute step, a trail of red plantation mud in his wake. He found Miss Kelly in the library, exactly where he knew she'd be, sunk deep into a leather chair, one leg crossed beneath her, a book halfway to her nose. Across the room, sitting in a high-backed chair facing the fake fireplace, I was lost in Moby Dick sailing the seas. The tropics had no need for heat, the climate generated enough of its own, but those who came from colder regions felt more at home relaxing before a fake fireplace. The company's motto was anything to make the personnel happy, make them stay.

I heard Mr. Cleveland say, 'What are you reading?' and peeked over the side of the winged chair, curious. Miss Kelly brought her leg out from under, long and shapely, gently curving from ankle to knee.

'*The Hunchback of Notre Dame,*' she said, impatience edging her voice. We students knew Mr. Cleveland perturbed her. She ducked and avoided him whenever possible. Instead of feeling grateful that he was at her beck and call anytime, anywhere, she resented his dependable solicitude. 'I'll be studying Victor Hugo this summer.'

'Will you sail on the Preston?'

'Yes — on Sunday.'

He pulled a wooden chair closer, straddled it, one muddy boot on either side. His feet were enormous. He rubbed the jagged line running up the side of his crocodile jaw, up his left cheek and into a tuft of damp, pinkish hair, a habit of his when doubt or nerves assailed him. 'Have I ever told you about my scar?'

'Yes, I've heard.'

We had all heard. The favorite colony pastime was telling yarns, recounting adventures and near escapes: colossal hurricanes that blew away entire villages; earthquakes that split the ground in two; volcanoes that spit lava and cooked the world; man-eating cannibals; storms at sea; malaria-carrying jungle mosquitoes big as helicopters; boa constrictors that strangled elephants; plagues, epidemics; demagogues and dictators they'd helped to topple — incredible deeds related with matter-of-fact relish — we did this and this and this. These stones had been turned so many times, we knew them by heart, knew the hieroglyphics etched into each hard surface, until sometimes we thought we'd been there when the carving took place, though we had not.

'You've never heard it from me,' Mr. Cleveland said.

'From others.' She looked down and concentrated on the book she was reading. Her fingers traced the words across the page.

Her absorption didn't bother him. He wasn't the least discouraged or put off. 'My red hair got me into trouble — '

Miss Kelly sighed and crossed her arms over her chest.

'That African queen loved my hair. Jesus! She must've been seven

feet tall. She ran her big-knuckled, black fingers through my flamin'
orange hair. Grabbed it by the roots and yanked it playfully up and
down. I should've suspected something, her subjects all looked so
happy, big grin on their black faces, like carnival was right round the
corner. She set me up in a hut, sent over a banquet like I'd never seen
before — '

Miss Kelly interrupted, 'Your last supper.'

He mistook her sarcasm for wry humor ' — a great big meal and a
tray of diamonds — twinkling little stars — my jackpot.' Rumor had it
he had a hundred diamonds in his office safe. Changing the subject
abruptly, he asked, 'Have you ever been to Africa?'

'No. Be nice to go, though. Erik Van Nuys once worked sugar
cane around Cape Town. He said it was wonderful.'

'I'd like to sail up that same river to that same village if it's still
there — see if they'd try to boil me like a lobster again.'

'That was a long time ago. I'm sure they're more civilized by
now.'

'I don't know so much about that. Those heathens came after me
shouting and leaping straight up in the air like they had springs on
their heels. When they grabbed me and started dragging me to that
cauldron, I got the picture quick. I managed to cut loose and bolt.
Threw diamonds at them, except for a few down deep in my pocket,
hoping. Those savages didn't even look down — plenty more where
those came from. They came after me slinging spears. I can still hear
the zing of the one that bounced off my skull and ripped my face.'
He rubbed his deformed cheek. 'Herr Schmidt had this little trading
post down river. He sewed up the gash — blood streaming down my
face — the German pulling the skin together, hands blood red and
slippery, daylight from one cheek to the other, lucky to have missed
my eye — with a big sewing needle and black thread, best he knew
how and I thanked him for it, though he left me puckered for life.'
His fingertips traced the latticed scar. 'Damn stitches like railroad
crossties.' Mr. Cleveland recoiled from his own rumbling voice. Miss
Kelly sat straight in the chair. The puzzled look in her magnificent
eyes reduced him to a schoolboy, clumsy and awkward.

'The scar isn't so bad, really. After a while one doesn't even notice it.'

His face turned beet red. 'Margo?' His hand touched her bare shoulder. 'I'm so glad this old scar doesn't bother you because...because — ' the old man was tongue-tied.

She made a little moue of a mouth, 'Doesn't bother me in the least. Why should it?'

'Because...because — ' He reached for her hand and she let him hold it without movement like a warm, dead bird. He had the same hang-dog look in his eye that Olaf got whenever he mooned after Señorita Evita.

Something in his expression, his obsequious demeanor, scared Miss Kelly and she said quickly, before he could utter another word, 'I must go.'

Her words stopped him, left him in a confused state of enamored affliction. He had to say something quickly, do something immediately to keep Miss Kelly from standing and walking away. 'Did you know your father was the first to invite me to tea?'

'Yes.' Her slim hand was trapped between his big, coarse fingers, the square nails lined with dirt from the cane fields.

'Five years ago.'

Mr. Cleveland came on the same boat with the Van Nuys. The new arrivals had been awed by the houses all painted the same egg-yolk color, red tile roofs or corrugated tin, green shutters, the residences surrounded by bawdy, stiff bromeliads and fire red caladiums.

'Time flies. You played the piano for us. Your mother worried about the piano keeping its tune, getting shipped from one country to another.'

'Mum says you were astonished to find chintz curtains, oriental rugs and blue willow china that didn't have USSCo stamped on it. She still laughs about it.'

'And the pale pink tea roses by the front entrance — so wonderful, you know, the way Abigail recreates a piece of England wherever she lives.' In a sudden rush, Mr. Cleveland asked, 'You sail for sure on Sunday?'

'Yes — making the loop — Limón, La Ceiba, Puerto Barrios, a few days in New Orleans, then on to Boston. Mum gets more excited than I do when I board the ship to go north. She doesn't put much stock on the educational worth of a summer at Boston University, but she is forever hoping I'll find Mr. Right and bring him home to meet the family.'

'Mr. Right may pop up right before your eyes.' Words cascaded from Mr. Cleveland's lips like a waterfall, a quick, nervous stream denying silence. He cleared imaginary phlegm from his throat. 'Margo, would you – ' his voice husky. 'Would you consider – ?'

Oh, my God. He was doing it! – popping the question. I leaned so far out of my chair I almost toppled over.

Miss Kelly glanced at him quickly, curiously. The flame in his eyes turned her face red and she looked away from the embarrassment. The hand he held wriggled free and she busied itself dropping books in the tote bag, cramming them in, pushing them to the bottom.

'Would you marry me?'

The awesome silence that followed the question filled the room to the brim. In the ensuing stillness, the book-lined walls seemed to expand, take over – leave no breathing space. The plants appeared waxen, every glossy green leaf awaiting the answer.

'No,' her lips curled around the word, as if she were blowing a soap bubble.

The two-letter rejection stung like a powerful slap across his face. He sagged in the chair and looked like the old man that he was.

'I'm not ready to marry anybody.'

That wasn't true. Like the other single women in the colony, Miss Kelly was forever searching, but eligible men were few and far between in Oriente Province, unless a girl settled for a short Cuban with a mustache, a saint's medal or a cross dangling from his neck, and a mistress on the side.

Mr. Cleveland salvaged what he could, clinging to any remnant of possibility, 'How about the dance Saturday? Shall I pick you up around nine?'

She spoke softly, gently, anxious to spare his feelings. 'Captain King telegraphed ahead and asked me to go.' Kindness exacerbated his wound.

The lift in her voice aged him, counted the years between them. He shuffled his mud-encrusted boots, leaned down and picked aimlessly at the leather shoe laces. He became aware that his battered, sweat-soaked clothes smelled sour, his armpits stunk, and the humid, rancid tropic odor enveloping him taken so much for granted and never before noticed, was offensive. He was no match for the debonair young man with a spring in his step, sun-bleached hair and a sailor's clear, far-seeing eyes. Jack King had adventures to tell, exotic places to talk about and stories to entertain. Mr. Cleveland had been like that, too, before he began repeating himself.

His hands fumbled as he helped her lift the heavy tote. 'May I carry this for you?'

'No, thanks — I can manage.'

'Have a good time at the dance.'

'Oh, I will! I will! I'm so excited! I'll see you there!'

She waved a casual goodbye and walked away through silver rain drops, jumping over puddles, yellow umbrella over a yellow sun dress, sun light in motion. He watched her until she disappeared around the corner, then took off his work boots and sank into the chair she'd vacated. The cushions held the warmth of her body.

***

Somebody gently shook me. "Wake up, Sleeping Beauty. Your grandson is here."

Sometimes coming back was like returning from another dimension or Mars or the Moon or Atlantis. I saw Olaf standing behind Connie, looking concerned.

Connie said, "Wayne is worried about you, the combination of the closed eyelids and the birthday dress." She pulled a chair near the bed. "Sit here, close by." she said to Olaf. "Her voice is fading today." She pushed a button and the hospital bed headrest rose until I was sitting up. "We won't go outside today. We'll do it tomorrow."

Olaf came near. Grease smudged his denim shirt. Little wrenches and screw drivers bulged in the pocket. He had an oily red rag tucked in his belt. He reeked of gasoline. I wrinkled my nose. "You smell."

"I was working on the Studebaker."

Connie said, "Olaf smells like dollar signs to me. My dad owns a garage."

Olaf looked at her, a curious spark in his eye. "Where's the garage?"

"On Magazine Street — "

His brow frowned with concentration, placing the business. "He works on foreign cars?"

"Mostly — "

"That's it! I know where that is! I took a Jaguar there one time." He looked at her intently, a new curiosity in his eyes.

Connie smiled. "Everybody brings their Jags to Papa."

"And you were behind the parts counter — "

"I might have been. We took turns helping Papa in the shop after Mama died. Now Paolo does it. He's my sister's oldest son."

"You came out from behind a huge stack of tires."

"Really — " one word filled with laughter and good humor. "You have a good memory. Pay attention to your grandmother."

Olaf nodded and set his little machine on the bed. "Gramma, how are you feeling this morning? You were going to tell me about falling in love with Grampa."

"I told you, didn't I? Olaf fell in love with the Spanish teacher."

"No."

"Did you know Mr. Cleveland asked the English teacher to marry him?"

"No."

"Did I tell him, Connie?"

She slipped off my slipper and massaged my foot. "I don't know," she said. The pressure brought back the circulation, and the numbness subsided a little. A pink tinge crept into the blue skin. At one point the doctors conferred with each other and with Katherine, deciding whether to sever above the ankle or below the knee. Limping, I fled the consultation room. Nobody was cutting off my foot, not then, not now, not ever.

"Why don't you tell him something else?" Connie prompted. "You have lots more you can tell him."

My eyes closed, the lids heavy, a frequent occurrence.

"She can't dredge it all up," Connie said. "Be happy. Take the bits and pieces. You are a lucky one. You have a terrific grandmother."

"And you?" asked Olaf.

"No grandmother."

"You have brothers, sisters?"

"Oh, yeah, four sisters and two brothers — they're gone, married. I'm the last one at home. They all come on Sundays, bring the kids to see Papa. He cooks spaghetti and meat balls for them. They love it."

"But you're here on Sundays."

"I know, and I do miss the gathering of the Mafia — that's what Papa calls it — but it's okay. This job is important to me. Do you think I'll get to stay? I do like your cantankerous grandmother."

"Well, a week has passed and you're still here. That's a good sign. Mom hasn't interviewed anyone else." Then abruptly, as if the idea popped into his head unsolicited, he asked, "Can I take you for coffee or a drink sometime?"

She turned and looked directly into his eyes, her lashes flickering in amused acknowledgement. "I'd love to, but I can't. When I leave here I go straight to night school, no break in between."

"In the morning, maybe? — "

"I can't, really I can't. I'm here at six, but you're sweet to ask. Barbara?"

Olaf ignored the question. "Some day, then — when you graduate maybe?"

She laughed. "That gives me something to look forward to."

Chapter 10

"*On the night in which he gave himself up for us he took bread, gave thanks to you, broke the bread, gave it to his disciples and said: 'Take, eat; this is my body which is given for you. Do this in remembrance of me.'*"

The Methodist preacher, a young assistant pastor — I didn't know his name — knelt by my bed, reciting the communion liturgy. My attempt to grasp the thin wafer he offered failed. My gnarled fingers wouldn't bend the right way. The sacramental host fell on the bedspread. He silently handed a second wafer to Connie. She tapped my lips with the white disc and I obediently let my jaw drop and gaped like a nestling waiting to be fed.

Somewhere from the disoriented entanglement in my mind, from the sluggish cobwebs that confused my thoughts, the knowledge surfaced that if the preacher was here, it must be the first Sunday — what month — August or October? Was Olaf still here? Had he finished taping my life or had he put me on hold?

"*When the supper was over, he took the cup, gave thanks to you, gave it to his disciples and said, 'Drink from this, all of you; this is my blood of the new covenant, poured out for you and for many for the forgiveness of sins. Do this, as often as you drink it, in remembrance of me.'*" The preacher handed Connie grape juice in a thimble-sized cup she held to my lips.

"Take a little sip," she said. "God bless you. Amen and amen."

I slipped away, churches on my mind: the big stone cathedral across the Banes River, *La Catedral de la Virgen del Cobre*, gold filigree altar; stations of the cross edged in silver, stained glass windows with Christ nailed to a cross, Christ feeding lambs, Christ sitting at a long table with his twelve disciples; rows and rows of votive candles in red and white holders; the incense sharp on the nostrils permeating the vaulted apse; a hundred worshippers sitting on red cushions on mahogany pews; the collection baskets on long handles passed three times during Mass to give everyone opportunity; altar boys in white lace; priests in white vestments; nuns perched liked black penguins in the choir loft. How I saw it all! I went there Christmas, Easter and high holidays, pompous, ostentatious occasions. Tia Adela took me because the priest wouldn't allow Mama to enter the sanctuary. She had committed a terrible sin. She had married Daddy. Mama was crushed. Daddy didn't care. He played poker with the priest every Thursday night.

Then there was the other, Pastor Juarez's Seventh Day Adventist Church, one room with open windows without screens letting in heat and birds on the wing, lizards sunning on the sills, a dozen non-conformists worshippers sitting on plank benches without backs, one single picture hanging on the wall, a black-haired, black-bearded Christ with his hand raised, touching a perfect bleeding heart, exposed for all to see. The few spared coins clinked when they hit the tin collection plate.

Catholics, Adventists, Methodists, thousands of sermons and not one did I recall.

Running feet and a commotion at the door drew me back from the fathoms where there was no day, no night, and I swam slowly to the surface, drawn by the light, reluctant to relinquish the depths, Olaf's agitated voice pulling me up. "Last rites! — who said to give her the last rites!"

Connie said, "Wayne, he's the preacher from her church."

The Reverend raised his pious head. "It's the Eucharist. I bring the communion sacrament to her bedside."

"Reverend Juarez," I said, waving weakly in his direction.

The preacher rose from his knees and extended a hand. "Reverend Kilmer, the assistant pastor."

"Pleased to meet you — I'm Wayne Olaf, her grandson. She gets confused."

I'm not confused. "Reverend Juarez!" The preacher turned to look at me. "Do you still have the Gideon Bibles?"

"What?"

"The Bibles that Quique brought to you. Don't you remember? He got off the ship with a duffel bag full of Bibles."

The preacher asked Olaf, "What's she talking about? Do you know?"

Olaf said. "Listen. She'll tell us." He stood next to the bed and clicked on his tape recorder. "Tell me about the Bibles, Gramma."

"The sailor cussed a lot. All the sailors cussed."

"What'd he say?"

"Goddamit. That's what he said — goddamit."

"Why?"

The pieces drifted past and I tried to catch them and put them together, lock them into place. Missing parts left big holes that I fell through. There were fireworks — no, not fireworks, welding sparks. Where did they come from? Up high. Up high someplace where metal grated against metal, creaking, groaning. "A crane," I cried triumphantly. "The sparks came from a crane!" The effort left me limp and as I was about to let go and fall back into the dark river of oblivion when recollections flooded my brain like water surging through a dam that had given way.

"His name was Enrique Sanchez — Quique — everybody called him, a relative of Mama's. Daddy got him a job on the ship. He was a little dandy, his clothes starched and ironed. He didn't jump out of the way quickly enough, and a hot spark burnt a hole in his pants. He shook his fist at the goggled welder perched like a monkey above the pier and yelled, 'Goddamit!' " Good word, that word. I rolled it around on my tongue and spit it out: "Goddamit! Goddamit! Goddamit!"

The preacher's eyes widened, his neck stiffened and he backed away as if hit by projectile vomit. Connie patted my shoulder and massaged an arm. "It's okay," she said. "It's okay."

It was not okay! To be trapped in skin and bones with a failing brain was not okay. To tread water painfully, aimlessly, from habit and necessity, too tenacious to let go, too cowardly to drown was not okay. To lie prone in this bed taking up space and wasting everybody's time was not okay. "Goddamit! Goddamit! Goddamit!"

The preacher said, "I'll be back later," and reaching for his hat made a quick exit.

Connie said, "Here, Wayne, help me get her up and move her

to the rocker. Sometimes a change of position helps. Communion brings her too close to the edge."

They had strong hands and arms, good legs, fresh breath. They were young and green and full of sap. They were spring bloom and I was the dead winter. My tree had not one leaf left. Why couldn't the old trunk topple and be done with it?

Connie rubbed my legs and feet. "Think of a star," she said. "Latch onto a star." She and Olaf knelt by the chair, fiddling with the blanket, their hands crisscrossed on my knees. I saw their upturned faces filled with concern, and suddenly it came to me, as clearly as if I were in one of Nanny Carmen's Santeria trances, that these two young people belonged to each other. They were my redeeming star. I'd empty my vessel, pass the contents to Olaf who'd share the long ago with Connie and later on with their children and we'd all be connected. The thought calmed the storm raging in my mind, calmed the thunderous waves foaming and crashing in my brain and brought unparalleled peace and serenity.

"I will tell you the whole story." The coherent tone stopped their fidgeting and they looked at me with anxious, questioning eyes, not understanding the abrupt change.

"Sometimes," Connie whispered, "Right before they — they — anyway, they become very serene and collected." She spontaneously kissed my sunken cheek and Olaf, moved by her love and compassion, followed suit and kissed the other cheek and my face was between their faces, their breath warming my skin and my heart and I wanted to embrace them both and tell them this was their prophetic moment, the moment when they should know they knew, but I didn't have enough strength to raise my arms or my voice. When they backed away, I felt the change in the air, the electricity that passed between them. I had to hurry and tell Olaf everything, so that his children could step back over the stones of my life and be with me in spirit.

"I'm fine," I said. "Turn on your machine, dear Olaf." He seemed even more special to me now that I had a sense of mission, of what must be done. "I will tell you about the sailor. Sit close, so you can hear me." The young people dropped to the floor. How easily their joints folded! How graceful their bodies, well-oiled machines! Before I was through, Connie's head rested on my bony knees, a heavy weight, joyful weight. Olaf's big hand engulfed my fragile one and love encircled me and gladdened my heart.

***

Daddy was the one who crossed the bridge and negotiated to have the sailor and the reverend released. 'The Guardia threw them both in jail,' Daddy told Mama, swallowing a chuckle. 'Imagine their surprise when those two found themselves in the same cell.'

Daddy sat on the veranda drinking his beer, and I was there, all ears. I was that kind of child, always snooping and hearing things I had no business knowing. I assembled the patches I overheard into a pattern that made a whole, much like sewing random squares together to make a quilt.

'How about stepping out from behind that potted palm and pulling off these boots for your old, tired dad, Sugar Plum?'

I ran and gave him a big hug, crouched and unlaced the leather thongs, listening to him tell Mama about his day. Before long, I knew exactly what happened on the dock:

After the welding spark burnt a hole in the sailor's bell-bottom pants, he was much upset. He walked faster, fussing aloud. The navy whites slung low on the hips were for shore leave only. Aboard the S. S. Preston, for wrestling banana stalks and sugar sacks, handling davits and cranes, the crew wore old khakis and cut-off jeans. To Quique's way of thinking, his pants were now ruined. Even if he took the trousers to a girl in town to mend, the patch would be visible. The hole about the size of a quarter, charred brown around the edges, upset him much more than a squall at sea or a fist fight on shore. Those things went with the job, with the territory. But not a hole in his pants! His only white pants!

The heat in Port Macabi was atrocious. The sun reflected on the water and bounced off the concrete wharf and tin warehouses, no shade anywhere. The fiery temperature baked the burlap sacks stacked high on the dock, ready to load. The smell of melting sugar gagged. The sailor walked past vultures devouring a bloated dog, tearing into the flesh with razor beaks. A sharp claw sent carrion flying and blood spattered his white pants. He kicked air. The buzzards cawed and flapped their wings.

He carried a duffel bag and a heavy cardboard box. At the custom warehouse, he passed through the door marked *Aduana* into the immigration cubicle. Reverend Juarez, the Adventist preacher who worked during the week as a custom agent, sat behind a wooden desk. I knew the place well. We, too, stopped there whenever we arrived or departed the island, presented our passports, let him look though our bags, gave him the little gift he anticipated. Behind the desk hung a Cuban flag — three blue stripes, two white, red triangle with white star in its center; Dictator Batista's solemn portrait; and a poster of a curvaceous girl clad in a skimpy, two-piece suit advertising Hatuey beer. A sub-machine gun stood carelessly in one corner. Cigar smoke and freshly dripped coffee smells mingled with floating dust particles and accumulated grime.

'*Buenas tardes*, Señor Juarez.' Quique presented his passport. 'I have no luck today. I am cursed. A welder's spark burnt my pants and the vultures spattered me with their shit. I come off my ship all turned out, and before I get to the end of the pier I look like I've been wallowing in a pig sty. How am I supposed to get a girl looking like so much trash?'

'*Bueno*, Señor Quique.' Reverend Juarez replied, 'the girls don't care about your looks. All you sailors look alike to them. They care how much is in your wallet.'

'I admit that's so, but my pants are my lure, my bait. It's like fishing, Reverend. The white attracts them, the sharp crease draws them in, I catch their eye and we make contact.' He pointed to the hole in his trousers. 'Look at these pants now! Ruined! I might as well turn right around and go back to the boat.'

Señor Juarez had little sympathy. 'You worry about a little bit of nothing on your pants and our men in the hills are running barefoot, in rags. How can we do revolution with sticks and stones?' He threw up his hands in disgust. 'We have no money! We cannot buy bullets! We need rifles!'

Quique glanced over his left shoulder, then his right. He leaned closer, punched the custom clerk on the chest with an extended finger. 'You watch it, Reverend. These walls have ears. You never know who might be listening. You know U.S. Sugar doesn't want anybody involved in that guerilla movement up in the mountains. We have all been instructed to stay clear.'

'The *gringos*,' Reverend Juarez extended his arms wide, taking in the surrounding world, 'can tell you what to do because you are on their boat, but they cannot tell me what to do. I do not — ' he shook his head emphatically — 'work for USSCo.' He pronounced it *Uzco*.

'Of course you don't. This office isn't on their dock — '

The reverend cried, 'This is Cuban soil!'

Quique asked, 'And where does your pay subsidy come from — angels in the sky?'

Reverend Juarez replied with passion, 'I am a Cuban government employee!'

'You think that's safer? What if a Batista soldier or a *guardia civil* hears you endorsing guerilla fighters? It won't mean your job, man. It'll mean your head.' He made a throat cutting motion across his neck. 'They'll whack it off or stand you blindfolded before the *paredón*.'

Quique slid his documents across the agent's desk, listening to the preacher's mumbled complaints. 'Stealing gas! Burning cane fields! What good is that?'

'Why don't you tell the rebels to steal that machine gun in the corner?' Quique pointed.

Señor Juarez held the passport under the circle of light provided by a goose-necked lamp. He gave it a glance and stamped it. 'You know that's not possible.' A steel tag, USSCo255, was attached to the machine gun's butt. Every item the company owned, from ocean-going vessels to household spoons, was labeled and numbered. If anything disappeared, big or little, it didn't take Chief Heinz, the company's police captain, long to find the missing item as well as the culprit.

'Well,' Quique said. 'I have something that will make you happy. I have a gift for you.' All officials expected a *mordida*, a bite, to ease the paperwork. The sailor knew the system. He had no trouble with it. He set the heavy box on the desk.

With eager fingers, the preacher dug under the cardboard flaps. His eyelids flew up and his mouth dropped open. 'Where did you — '

'Don't ask. The less you know the better.'

'The revolution will be grateful.'

'I understand.'

Weighing the sin against the gain, the preacher said, 'You broke the eighth commandment. But this is what we need. Without this, we are nothing.'

'I know. You've told me.'

'The answer to my prayers — God works in mysterious ways! Where did you get them?'

'In New Orleans — '

'You stole them in the United States?'

Quique was offended — 'Negotiated for them, Reverend.'

The custom official stared into the case — 'How many?'

'A dozen — '

'Bless you,' he said.

'You know I'm not a religious man,' protested Quique.

'But you are a Christian man.'

'Not me, but I hope these do the trick for you, and if they don't — ' he opened the duffel bag, dug around clothes, cigarette cartons and magazines. 'Maybe this will be more help.'

Overwhelmed with gratitude, the customs agent embarrassed Quique by jumping up and throwing his arms around him and kissing the sailor on both cheeks. Quique gathered his passport and was almost to the door when Señor Juarez called out. 'How can the revolution ever repay you?'

'Win,' Quique said breezily. 'Win.'

The sailor hadn't been gone three minutes before a civil guard materialized before the custom agent's desk. 'Hand it over.'

Reverend Juarez pushed the cardboard box closer to the desk edge, withdrew a red soft-cover book, Holy Bible written in gold letters across the top and Gideon on the lower right hand corner. He looked up at the rotund, overweight guard and said meekly, almost prayerfully, 'Bebo, they are Bibles. He brought Bibles for my church.'

Bebo snatched the holy book and rifled the pages as if he were shuffling a deck of cards. 'In English!' He threw the Bible across the room. It hit the cracked plaster wall between the president and the pinup. 'Your parishioners now read English, my friend?' The same thought had occurred to the preacher before he decided the writing didn't matter. The men would derive comfort from the soft leather covers, the paper-thin pages, the uneven black lines of texts familiar in any language. 'Answer me! Do those heathen non-Catholics who sit in your pews read English?'

'A few — '

The guard snorted: 'Hugh McAuley and his daughter and the Dutch boy and who else?'

Reverend Juarez shook his head. His Adam's apple slid up and down as he pumped saliva into his dry mouth 'No one else.'

'This is contraband literature, you know that.' The guard placed both hands on the Reverend's desk and leaned his fat hulk on them. 'This crap you could keep, for all I care. Who gives a shit about this? But the other — the other is a serious offense. Let's have it.'

Reverend Juarez reached for the submachine propped in the corner. 'It's a company weapon.'

Fat fingers clamped around the preacher's throat. Bebo snarled, 'Do I look stupid? The one under the desk — '

The preacher's face slipped from purple to blue. His eyeballs bulged from their sockets. The guard's grip strangled. Reverend Juarez couldn't rise from the chair. He moved his legs in sweeping motions from side to side until his boot touched the rifle butt. With the tip of one shoe and the heel of the other, he dragged the weapon out from under the desk.

Bebo released his grip and reached for the Remington, on his face the satisfied look of a man who did his job, knew how to get results. 'How close are you to God, Reverend?'

'Close — very close — ' a raspy, bloody whisper.

'Good. You're going to need God and a multitude of angels. Come with me.'

A great feeling of loss and deprivation enveloped Reverend Juarez. Arguing was pointless, dangerous. He pushed back the wooden chair, stood up slowly and walked around the desk.

Chapter 11

I had talked too much, exhausted my supply of words, but I wasn't finished. There was more to tell. My face was stiff and my jaw hurt and the memories were wearing. I was back in bed. Who moved me from the rocker? I was tucked beneath the covers, my legs straight, my heart beating in odd little jerks, my breath short quick gasps. My hands felt cold and anxiety engulfed me. What if there wasn't enough time to finish telling Olaf? I must find the strength to tie him to our history, weave my thread into the tapestry that is his life.

"The preacher was dragged off to jail, and not long afterward, so was the sailor. Nanny Carmen and I were there when that happened."

My nanny had a back pain. We crossed the bridge to the civil town to the *curandero's* place, a smelly hole in the wall with wooden bins overflowing with medicinal roots, herbs hanging from the wall in ragged, uneven rows, and in the rear love and hex potions wrapped in dry banana leaves. Carmen didn't want to be sick and bent over when the ship was in port. Those were big fiesta days. Nanny Carmen knew Quique and I knew him, too. He was somehow related to Mama. Carmen said *hola* as the sailor passed the herb stall and sauntered down the block where he ran into the street woman. Nanny Carmen knew her, too. 'That's Consuelo.'

Was I talking aloud or in my head? Retained words reverberated inside my skull, echoed, grew larger, deeper, until they burst forth in sounds that shot forth like bullets, ran their trajectory, exploded and went dead.

'You see that sidewalk?' Nanny Carmen pointed to the spot in front of the Chinaman's Café. 'It's public property, but to make a living and keep the peace Consuelo pays the Chinaman a percentage and extra whenever she uses his storage room.'

Consuelo wore a pink satin sheath with spaghetti straps and a little lace swag on the bodice. Her black mesh stockings had ragged tears and crooked seams. The red plastic bag slung over her shoulder was her closet, bank and drugstore. The wrought iron lamppost was her anchor. She pressed against it, one arm extended over her head, the other reaching for the approaching sailor. She keeled to one side like a sail filled with wind.

Nanny Carmen paid a few cents for willow bark. The old *curandero* wrapped the purchase in yellowed newspaper and we left the stall.

'What will you give me?' I heard the woman in the pink slip ask. She was smiling at Quique, a smile more practiced than genuine. 'I can give you – '

'Claps,' replied Quique, 'Syphilis.'

Nanny Carmen stopped. Street business was everybody's business and anyone within earshot had the right to listen and give an opinion, or back off and stay a safe distance away. We didn't retreat.

Quique felt for his watch, intending to remove it from his arm to his back pocket. It was gone.

'She's good,' Carmen said.

The sailor yelled, 'Give it back!'

'Give what back?' the woman cried.

'Give back my watch before I call the police!'

'Don't do that, my love. Of truth, you don't wish that.'

'Give it back.'

Consuelo thrust her pelvis forward and made a grinding motion. 'I can give you lots more.'

'My watch!' he cried.

She lured him. 'Let's have a rum right here, at the Chinaman's. We can have a little rum.'

He remained firm – 'My watch!'

'I'm hungry,' she said. 'Buy me *congri* from around the corner?'

Angrier now, he yelled, 'My watch! – this minute!'

She favored him with a long, lazy look. 'I can sew that hole in your pants for you. I can wash your pants if you want.'

'Just give me back my goddam watch – right now!' Quique grabbed her by the hair. The woman shrieked.

The Chinaman heard the commotion, left his establishment and waddled down the sidewalk, 'Move on, Consuelo — no plobems. No plobems.'

Quique abruptly let go the woman's hair.

'Who says we have problem?' she asked, shaking her head and rubbing her scalp.

The Chinaman shook a fat finger with a vulgar jade ring and one long, curved fingernail. He spoke through his drooping, tobacco-streaked mustache. 'I say plobem. Everybody, move on! — Move on!'

Rather than disbanding, the commotion attracted more watchers. We stayed.

Consuelo walked away.

Quique yelled, 'Hey! She's got my watch!'

She turned and held up empty hands, palms out. Quique jumped the distance that separated them. He grabbed her by the shoulders. She kicked his shins with high-heeled, pointed shoes and bit his arm when he thrust his hand into her bosom and ran his fingers over her right breast and her left breast and there was nothing there.

'You see?' She leaned over and straightened her fishnet stockings, now ripped from knee to ankle. 'There is no watch. *Imbecil!*'

'Here!' he said. 'Here!' and with an angry swoop he tore the red bag off her shoulder, yanked it open, and dumped its contents.

'*Cabrón!*' Spread on the sidewalk were her pitiful belongings — a soiled handkerchief, a leather pouch with a few coins, a crushed box of *chiclets*, a set of underpants, a gray silk garment rolled up, a comb, lipstick, a condom in its foil wrapper.

Carmen said, 'He had no right — '

A dark mustached man looking mean and ugly emerged from a cantina, belching garlic and clutching a beer bottle in his hand. 'Leave her alone! Look what you have done! Now, it is me who calls the police!'

Consuelo spun around. 'Please, Jorge — by God!' Summoning official brutality never solved anything. Street people were always guilty. It was simpler that way. 'Forget it! Forget it. It was a mistake, nothing more.'

Jorge raised an arm muscular from cutting cane and shoved

Quique in the chest. 'You disappear! Or you are dead.'

A roar of approval went up from the onlookers. Consuelo's macho man would rescue her.

Quique stumbled backwards, caught himself and charged forward, spoiling to punch the man's face, eager to split the jutting jaw, see blood pool under the eyes, the sockets turn black. Something stopped him.

'He knows better,' Nanny Carmen said.

'Is he afraid?' I asked.

'No. His shore leave will get cancelled if he gets in any sort of brawl. He'll be locked in the ship's brig for the next three days.'

Quique worked his tongue inside his mouth, spewed spit, and stomped into the Chinaman's Café, everyone at his heels. 'Wong,' he snapped at the hovering Chinaman, 'bring me rum.' The Chinaman waved his jade ring finger and a waiter hurried over with a Bacardi bottle.

'*Buenas tardes, Capitán Quique* — all you mariners are off the ship?' asked the waiter.

'The crew will be ashore in the next hour and I am not the Captain and I am not crazy, either.' Quique swigged rum, instant fire in his stomach. 'That watch was on my arm when she stopped me.'

'That one?' asked the waiter. 'That one was trained by the gypsies.'

'What do you mean?'

'They are fine masters of stealing. She took your watch.'

'I don't think so. I ran my hand under her clothes. I dumped her bag. I almost caused a riot out there.'

'She has it.'

The sailor stared at the waiter who advised him, 'Her drawers hold a fortune.'

'You mean — ?'

The waiter pursed his lips and nodded, 'Right between her legs.'

'You're sure of that?'

'Sure as I am standing here. If that watch were mine, for certain I would go after it.'

Quique gulped more rum. 'You're right.'

Consuelo had disappeared down the block. Quique hurried past the shoe shop, meat shop, fabric shop. The barefoot boys who loitered by the Chinaman's Café trotted after him. Several bored women waiting for the ship crew to come ashore, edged along looking for excitement. The sailor gathered a following, including Nanny Carmen and me. We ambled casually, a few paces behind, pretending we were window shopping. Shopkeepers leaned from their doorways, some yelling encouragement, others telling Quique to go back where he came from and leave the woman alone. The procession made its noisy way along the sidewalk.

Hearing the stir and buzz behind him, Consuelo's man looked over his shoulder. Pivoting on one heel, he yelled, 'You did not understand? You did not hear me? Come one step closer and you are a man dead.' Jorge cracked his beer bottle against the curb and grasped the neck.

It was one thing to threaten a man in private, quite another to bully him before a rag-tag army not of his own choosing. For Quique to discontinue his quest at this point would be a cowardly and disgraceful act, not to mention his followers might turn hostile if he let them down.

Carmen assessed the situation. 'Quique has no weapon,' she said. 'The sailors are not allowed to bring guns ashore. It will not be an even fight.'

Growing concerned, imagining we could be accidentally killed in the fray, I said, 'We should go.'

'Don't be silly,' Nanny Carmen replied. 'You want to miss the end?' She turned to me, frowning. 'Who do you think will win?'

I looked closely at the two men. The aggrieved sailor was short and wiry, tanned by the sun, recovering his stolen watch a big motivator. Consuelo's defender was more muscular, sinews as thick as ropes running up his arms and neck. A dark fury contorted his face. How far would he go to defend his woman? 'That one,' I said, pointing to Consuelo's man. 'He looks meaner.'

'Don't point, that's rude,' Carmen said. She held out her hand, a peseta on the palm. 'Put yours here,' she said. 'You can have that one — Jorge. I'll take Quique.'

I dug in my little pouch and brought out a coin. Others were doing the same, some squatting on the sidewalk or leaning against lamp posts or hitching posts. A great hub-hub rose from the crowd.

What came next took place with such lightning speed nobody was sure exactly how it happened. At one count there were ten different versions making rounds. Every story carried its nugget of truth. The consensus was that Quique had grabbed Consuelo by the waist, pulled up her flimsy dress, and yanked down the fishnet stockings with two hands; one hand; with his teeth. Consuelo's private parts were exposed for all to see. There again, the descriptions varied widely, no two witnesses in accord. Some saw a red rose tattooed on the prostitute's left buttock — no, right buttock. Not red; white. Not a rose — a dove, swore the butcher. A woman who got a close look insisted it was a dirt smudge, lack of washing. What everyone did agree on was what fell out from between Consuelo's legs. Wallets, money, bracelets, chains and holy medals jumbled in a heap around her feet. There was a universal astonishment as to how the woman managed to store so large a cache in so tight a place.

A beggar boy yelled, 'Here comes the Guardia Civil!' and as if the street had opened and swallowed them whole, the onlookers vanished, Jorge the first to disappear.

The mounted guard, slouched in the saddle, rode slowly down the street, the horse's hooves an ominous clatter on the pavement.

From the pile on the sidewalk the sailor fished his watch and slipped it on his wrist. 'This is all I want.'

'*Hijo de puta*,' Consuelo hissed and crouched next to Quique, raking her loot back into the red plastic bag. 'Now see what you've done? There's no reason for this!'

'You took my watch!' Quique thundered. 'You thief!'

'You have it back! Is it worth ruining my life?'

The guard dismounted. He loomed as big as his horse. He came closer, clicking the handcuffs open, shut, open and shut.

'She's trembling hard enough to shake the world,' I said.

Nanny Carmen whispered. 'It's the handcuffs. Bebo is the law. He's a mean pig. They say the more a prisoner screams the better he likes it.'

Consuelo cried, 'I pay you — '

'Shut your mouth.'

'He'll throw her in a jail cell,' Carmen said, 'and the guards will entertain themselves with her day and night, not paying.'

The same thought must've crossed Consuelo's mind. In a vain attempt to hide, she stepped behind Quique who jumped aside. Three big steps and Bebo stood before Consuelo, handcuffs dangling from the enormously fat hands.

'I did nothing,' she said, fear deep as bone marrow forcing her eyes closed.

'She needs help,' Nanny Carmen said, handing me a smooth rock.

I protested, thinking she wanted me to cast the first stone.

Instead, she said, 'Hold it tight and pray for her. Pray to the Virgen de la Caridad, Jesus Christ the Son and God the Father.'

'Who will you pray to?' I asked.

'The *Iyalocha*,' she replied, 'she is most powerful.'

Where had Nanny Carmen found the lizard she was squeezing so hard its slim red tongue hung out?

Consuelo edged away, her hands over her eyes.

Bebo roared, 'Gun runner!'

Consuelo's hands flew down and her mouth gaped open. She gawked at the steel bracelets encircling the sailor's wrists.

'What the hell are you doing?' Quique yelled, yanking his arms away. 'I just came off the sugar freighter! Let me go!'

Bebo raised an arm and struck Quique's head. 'We know that. You first stopped at Customs — you're supposed to check in there, eh?'

Clutching his head, Quique said, 'Yes, of course. This is a mistake — '

A greasy grin slid over Bebo's ugly face. 'Is it, now? Even if I have Juan Juarez's written confession you brought him a rifle?'

Quique threw up his manacled hands, 'A hunting rifle! That doesn't make me a gunrunner.'

Bebo wiped oily sweat off his brow. 'In our jurisdiction bringing in weapons is a punishable offense. We act by direct order from *El*

Presidente.' He grabbed Quique's arms and twisted them, forcing the sailor to his knees. His grin was sinister, '*Comprende*, amigo?'

'You're mistaken! You don't understand! It's a hunting rifle — '

The army boot struck Quique's backbone with a sharp crack.

In anguish Quique cried out to the prostitute. 'Listen! Get my Captain! Call the Company!'

She turned her back and walked away then had second thoughts. 'I'll do what you say.' Consuelo held out her hand, reaching for revenge and consolation. 'Give me the watch.'

The watch, so important minutes before, now seemed little enough to pay for freedom. 'Take this off my wrist!' he said to the guard. 'Give it to her!'

Bebo unsnapped the chrome band, deliberately examined the basket weave design, the crystal face, the numbers, the make, Timex. He dangled the watch before his prisoner and asked, 'You want me to give this watch to that prostitute? That whore?'

'Yes!' bellowed Quique. 'Yes!'

'My friend, you don't understand,' Bebo said softly, almost gently. 'A gift of this magnitude is not for a street woman. This gift is best given to the proper authorities,' and with a thin smile and an emphatic nod of his big head, the civil guard slipped the sailor's freedom into his shirt pocket.

Chapter 12

Next morning after the bathing, eating and fussing was over Connie rolled my wheelchair to the north window for a different view, a different perspective; a new landscape. The north light was always the best light to paint by, early morning or dusk.

Beyond the pool was the big utility building where the mowers, blowers, edgers and all gardening equipment was kept; gallon cans half filled with leftover paint, stiff brushes no longer of any use; and old skiff and a kayak from younger days. On the concrete apron surrounding the buildings the help parked their cars away from the main house. Olaf's Studebaker was parked there, too, the hood propped up and the doors flung open.

The driveway from the utility building went straight to the side street. I was absorbing the early morning colors, watching the gardeners getting out of their trucks, the cook digging in her car trunk for an apron. I heard their happy interchange, not yet tainted by the day's frustration. A tow truck with a big wench backed up the service drive, beeping a warning. A man jumped out, circled the Studebaker and waved to his buddy behind the wheel. "Come on back!" With swift, direct movements he hooked the wench to Olaf's precious car.

"Connie! Look! Come quick!"

She was at my side. "Oh, goodness! — " Without another word, she flew from the bedroom and reappeared on the driveway outside.

Olaf's Studebaker — the one he'd worked on all summer! I had seen Olaf lay down on a wooden trolley, roll himself under the car, and disappear for hours. Other times, his head under the hood, he tinkered with the motor until dark. Some nights, too carried away to stop, he rigged lights and continued to work. He reminded me of Manco and the Rolls. There was nothing Manco loved more than the yellow Rolls Royce.

The men saw Connie and stopped. By their gestures, they knew her. After much talking, hand waving and shoulder shrugging on their part as well as Connie's they got back in their tow truck and drove away, dragging Olaf's future behind them.

She was breathless when she returned. "I told Eddie to tow the car to Papa's shop. I had no business doing that, but they were towing it to Airline Highway — " she read the question in my eyes — "that's the graveyard. They cut up the cars and sell them for spare parts. At least if it's in Papa's shop Wayne will know where to find it and the car will be in one piece."

The magnificent row when Olaf discovered his father had the Studebaker towed was like a volcano eruption. No walls were thick enough to contain the roar and the fire; the ashes of their argument spread through the house like poisonous residue.

Connie stayed late that night. She needed the overtime and extra pay. Having her there was a comfort, her gentle calm a buffer between me and the upheavals in this house. Before she left at ten, she pulled open the curtains and raised the bedroom window. "I know you like fresh air." She stood bathed in a golden glow, one hand on each heavy silk panel bordering the white sheers.

"The moon — is it full?" I asked.

"To the brim," she replied.

"A moon for lovers — "

"You're a hopeless romantic." She had a delightful chuckle.

"Turn off the light."

Connie flicked the switch and the room went dark except for a burnished gold slash across the floor. My fingers twitched and I felt the spatula, the narrow-edged, flat kitchen spatula, the curve of the hilt, my secret weapon. Texture, the critics said. My paintings had texture. Uneven, ragged, one broad swipe through the inky black — no, too stark, much too stark. Midnight blue would be better. Blue held a bit of heaven. Yes! "I can paint that."

"You think so?" Connie turned on the bedside lamp, leaned over the bed and looked into my eyes. I liked that about her. She never avoided my gaze or looked over my head or my shoulder. Her big, sparkling black eyes looked directly into my faded ones. "Where are your paints?"

"I don't know. Katherine put them away."

"I'll find them. Tomorrow night."

The old excitement stirred in my breast, asleep but not forgotten. My mind leapt ahead and I grew increasingly disturbed and agitated thinking that an unexpected cloud might cast an unwelcome shadow or rain spoil the scene or the fickle moon on a whim grant or withhold its golden glory.

"If you start worrying you'll only upset yourself and your blood pressure will go up. The thing to do is get a good night's rest and you'll be in fine shape for tomorrow. I'll roll your wheelchair over by the window and set up your easel — don't fret. I'll find it." She smoothed the white sheet, tucked it around me and kissed my cheek. "See you tomorrow. It'll be a great day!"

"Thank you — do one more thing for me?" I could ask Connie to do things that were beyond Surviva's comprehension. Surviva would've mocked me, told me I was crazy. And Katherine was too busy. I already took up too much of her time. "Could you find a CD, Handel's *Messiah*?"

"You need music to paint? I'll get right on it."

"It's for Olaf. He has no religion. Do you?"

"I'm big time Catholic — we're Italian. Mama went to mass every morning and never let us miss on Sunday. I believe in a super power I really don't understand. But I know everybody has a Godly spark. If my spark got put in your body, I'd still be me. And if yours got put in my body, you'd be you in me. When we shed our bodies, the spark cannot be extinguished. Mama's spark dances around me all the time."

"That's beautiful."

"She said it was our duty to always keep that spark alive, to feed and nurture it so that it would light up the world like God intended for it to do." In her white uniform, Connie stood suddenly still, moonlight lighting her face and shoulders, her body in shadows like Mama on the Banes River bank the moment before she took the first step into the poverty below, the instant when the beggars looked up from the underworld and saw salvation.

"Don't hide your candle under a bushel."

"Yeah — something like that."

"Your mother was a saint."

"She was. Papa said God always took the good ones first."

"Does that mean I'll be here forever?"

"Ooops! You know I didn't mean it that way! I'll see you in the morning, old woman," and I didn't take offense because she said it with love and with caring. This girl was a jewel. Was there a way I could make Olaf see that?

Sleep eluded me. My thoughts focused on the color palette — orange, blue, purple, yellow, burnt sienna, umber — little dabs arranged in a convenient semi-circle across a mental canvas.

The grandfather clock downstairs gonged twelve times when the door creaked. A shadow glided into my room. "Who is it?"

"Wayne Olaf, Gramma — checking on you before I go to bed."

"You're out late."

"I've been to the movies."

"Took your girl on a big date?"

"No. She's off to Florida. I went with — " he caught himself — "somebody else."

"Play the field. That's good. I loved the cinema. We had a loge in the Heredia Theater, a second floor balcony with a gilded banister and red velvet curtain and chairs."

"You didn't sit down in the theater seats like everybody else?"

"No."

"Tell me about it."

"Our nannies brought us and we sat in the loges. We heard John Wayne dubbed in Spanish and laughed at a mute Charlie Chaplin or the baggy-pants Cantiflas. More than the movies went on inside our theater."

He fumbled over the clutter on the bedside table, found his recorder and turned it on.

Bed-bound, time lost meaning. I slept during the day, stayed awake at night, took long naps in the afternoon and opened my eyes at 4 p.m. waiting for breakfast. Days ran into each other. Today might be Tuesday or was it Sunday? What did it matter if it was midnight? I was wide awake and happy for company, glad to talk with my grandson or was I talking to myself?

***

One night we were watching Jorge Negrete, a big Mexican star. Women jumped from balconies when he died. Negrete, wearing a big silver-studded sombrero was about to rescue the heroine when he vanished and the numbers 8 ... 7 ... 6 ... 5 jerked across the screen.

'The film broke,' I said to Nanny Carmen.

'No,' she replied. 'It's time for Albertico Limón.'

The house lights came on. Below, couples were entangled – kissing and groping and making love in their seats. My heart jumped when I spotted our Spanish teacher. 'There's Señorita Evita!'

Wait 'til I told Olaf! Tattling about Evita was a personal triumph. Seeing her at the movies with a man was better than a knife in my hand. I'd wound Olaf in his heart.

Curses rose from the crowd. *Mierda! Carajo! Cojones!*

The man put his arm around Señorita Evita's shoulder and slipped his hand under her low-cut blouse. Evita removed his exploring fingers and tugged her blouse back into place.

Nanny Carmen ushered Elise Corman and me outside the theater. Teatro Heredia faced Dominguez Park. The townpeople had gathered to listen to the latest episode of Albertico Limón's tragic life blaring over loud speakers installed on the theater eaves. The radio soap opera stars filled the air with their resonant, emotional voices.

In the park kiosk, the off-duty firemen ceased playing their band instruments. Vendors stopped hawking flavored shaved ice, pork chitlings and Hatuey beer. Feet stilled and heads tilted, the gathering listening intently, upturned faces concentrating on the tragedy transmitted over the airwaves.

Albertico, a young, handsome, hard-working, dedicated doctor, was being two-timed by a wife he loved dearly. Last night he'd found out the depth of her treachery and tonight he was out to get the lover. At 9 p.m. everywhere in Cuba, the entire population stopped whatever they were doing, turned on CMQ radio station and listened with rapt attention to what would happen next.

'He will kill him!' a man confided to Nanny Carmen.

'Verily, he will not,' she countered. 'He is a doctor.'

'Yes,' agreed a nearby fan. 'He has taken the oath.'

'Can Elise and I walk?' I asked Nanny Carmen. 'We don't care about the soap opera.'

'I'll be right over there.' Carmen joined the chaperones sitting on the wrought-iron benches. The women focused on the radio tragedy, relaxed their watch.

Evita's friend took her firmly by the elbow and steered her into the straggling line of girls circling the park perimeter. Elise and I slipped into the promenade behind them.

The men walked in one direction; the women in the other; when a man found a woman to his liking, he changed lines and joined her and the two concentric circles continued to move in tandem, enveloped in music, laugher and glowing cigarette tips. The soap opera interruption caused the *paseo* to lose rhythm and the movement's flow was ragged and uneven.

Evita's companion said. 'Such damned foolishness!'

Spotting us behind her, Evita said, 'Hello, girls. This is Victor.'

Elise whispered to me, 'Victor from the post office.'

Victor sold stamps, sorted letters, and marked envelopes Air Mail, Certified or Registered. He placed the ones for local citizens in one bag, the ones for the American Colony in another. The postman took the town pouch. U. S. Sugar sent their own man to retrieve the company's mail, as if the local delivery wasn't to be trusted. Glue and ink — government perfume — clung to Victor's clothes.

Victor didn't acknowledge us in any way. His face was one big frown. 'This soap opera is an insult to my intelligence! To the intelligence of every Cuban! No wonder the world thinks we are ignorant, backward! How they must be laughing at us now! The entire country shut down to listen to a soap opera!'

We circled the park twice, giggling and listening to Victor grouse. Señorita Evita ignored his outbursts, straining to hear the resolution to Albertico's plight. On the third round, the loud speakers crackled and went dead. The people turned away in disappointment. Nothing much had taken place.

The woman walking behind us said, 'Because it is Wednesday.'

'Just wait until Friday,' her promenade partner agreed. 'The big things happen on Friday.'

The band straggled back to the kiosk and picked up their instruments. The moviegoers disappeared from the sidewalk into the darkened theater. Nanny Carmen stood and waved for us to join her. We tarried, eavesdropping on the argument between our Spanish teacher and her companion. Evita wanted to return to the theater. Victor had paid good money for the tickets and she was entitled to the ending. 'Shall we go?'

'No,' replied Victor, resenting the movie's interruption and the people's stupidity. 'What we need is a revolution.'

Evita laughed, 'Again? Didn't we just have one?' She pressed her head against his shoulder and drew his arm closer. Holding hands they resumed walking.

The Municipal band played *Cielito Lindo*. What the firemen lacked in skill, they made up in volume. The strollers slid into the clockwise and counterclockwise lines, the flow now moving like a shadowy stream dappled by moonlight and animated by sound.

Elise and I ignored Nanny Carmen's summons and stayed close to Señorita Evita and Victor. Tomorrow at school we would have lots to share with the others.

'You think it's funny, do you?' Victor asked.

'Oh, calm down,' Evita replied. 'Don't make an ass of yourself.'

His anger at the film stoppage stirred old rancor. He was mad at everybody, particularly the company people. 'The gringos dominate our world. They pull the strings and we dance like puppets.'

She reasoned with him. 'It is the Heredia Theater manager who stops the film, not the gringos.'

'How can you stand to work for them?'

'You would work for the company, too, if Mr. McAuley would hire you.' At the mention of my father, Elise giggled and elbowed me in the ribs.

Evita smiled at a matronly woman seated on a bench, '*Buenas noches*, Señora Rodriguez.'

' — *Buenas noches, Evita. Buenas, Victor.*'

Victor nodded curtly, jammed a cigar between his teeth, cupped his hands and struck a match. The flare revealed his face from below, pencil-thin black mustache, distended nostrils and dark circles under burning eyes. '*Imbeciles* — I would never work for them, not if they begged me.'

'Never say never, Victor. Saying never always brings bad luck and next thing you know you're doing what you never were going to do.'

Victor refused to be appeased. 'Clerking in the post office is not my destiny. A position of greater merit awaits me in the future.'

'I know, Victor, I know.' Evita sounded resigned. She'd probably heard his complaint a hundred times.

'Someday I will be instrumental in an event of great importance.'

'Sure you will,' Evita replied.

Victor said with conviction, 'What the republic needs is another José Martí.'

That was too much for our teacher. A sarcastic edge to her voice, she asked, 'Shall I go kiss his bust and make a wish?'

A bust of Cuba's poet-liberator, a man with sad eyes and a droopy mustache, stood in the center of the park, immortalized in bronze. His bust or statue marked every municipal building, school, park and hospital. Martí was the touchstone every would-be liberator measured against.

Victor reminded Evita, 'Martí's politics have stood the test of time.'

'And so has his poetry,' she replied in a bored voice.

We'd memorized dozens of Martí's poems.

'Listen,' Evita said. 'I don't want to get into a political discussion. I just want to go back and see how the movie ends.'

A disgruntled Victor didn't cease arguing. 'That American School that makes you so proud has no bust of José Martí.'

'You're right. But I do teach them Martí tried to free Cuba from Spain — he failed, but we gloss over that — and about their Teddy Roosevelt charging up San Juan Hill, and Machado killing thousands, and Batista stealing the treasury, and Grau San Martín bowing toward Miami as if it were Mecca. Nothing ever changes, Victor

— different men, same program. Can't you see it?'

'Some day it will not be so. A man will rise with the charisma of Jesus Christ and the steel of Adolph Hitler. He will stir the people and ignite a spark and we will have revolution.'

A young girl with tousled black hair and big hoop earrings slipped into the moving line. Her fluttering eyelids sent Victor an invitation.

Evita laughed outright. 'Isn't she a little young?'

'I don't even know that girl.'

Victor's habits were an open secret. Nanny Carmen discussed them with Margarita, the cook, as they banged pans or stirred pots in the kitchen. At noon, after Victor sprinkled sawdust and water on the post office floor, swept the litter into a flat pan and dumped it into the trash bin, he locked the heavy wooden doors and retreated to his apartment for a prolonged siesta where a selected señorita shared his rumpled bed. His machismo was talked about, admired and accepted. Had Victor had no women, people would've questioned his manhood.

'She seems to know you pretty well.'

'Not as well as Captain King knows you.'

'Ah! Is that what's been eating at you all evening?'

'Yes! You throw yourself at the foreigners — the town talks.'

'The town always talks. Shall we compare notes?'

'They say you and the Kelly woman are making fools of yourselves over that sailor.'

'Oh, glory! They must be running low on fodder for their gossip mill.'

'Where is your dignity?'

'My dignity, old friend, is intact — how about yours?'

Elise and I walked half a step behind them, so close that if they stopped suddenly, we'd crash into them. Eavesdropping, hearing first hand details to be doled out like precious nuggets tomorrow at school was exciting. How Olaf would suffer! His freckled face would turn crimson! The hurt would show in his eyes and they'd glaze over so I couldn't read the pain and sorrow.

As if the bickering was more than the warm, glorious evening could tolerate, a cloud drifted over the moon, leaving only the glowing red and green Teatro Heredia neon sign to relieve the darkness. A warm breeze swished through the trees. When the moon reappeared in its full and wondrous glory, Nanny Carmen stood next to us, demanding we go back and view the film's end. At that moment, Art Cleveland popped up and blocked our path and all of us were so astonished, everyone stopped dead still.

Directly Mr. Cleveland shook Victor's hand, and being a man who went straight to the point, said, 'I need to talk to Evita.' Seeing the couple's questioning eyes, he added, 'Privately.'

'Sure,' Evita raised her voice over the music. 'Is something wrong? What has happened?'

Mr. Cleveland didn't address her questions, dismissing Victor instead. 'I'll take her home.'

'Never!' protested Victor.

Evita placed a restraining hand on Victor's arm. 'It's all right, Victor. Mr. Cleveland has a problem.'

'I can smell his problem,' Nanny Carmen whispered, so intrigued by what was taking place she forgot about the movie.

'Go on, Victor,' Evita said, "we've missed the film, anyway.'

Mr. Cleveland motioned Evita toward a bench. 'Shall we sit?'

Victor thrust back his shoulders and said in a smoldering voice. 'You think because you are a gringo, you can walk right up and take my woman without so much as by your leave?' He reached roughly for Evita's arm. 'We're walking.'

'Stop it!' Evita drew Mr. Cleveland to her side. 'Come,' she said. 'Walk with us.' She looked around and saw Elise and me standing, gaping, all ears. 'We are blocking the others. The fresh air will do you good. What brings you here?' She placed herself between Victor and Art Cleveland, her hands resting lightly on the men's elbows and drew them back into the moving line.

Mr. Cleveland said, 'Jack King will be here Thursday.'

Evita replied, 'I know that.'

The trio began to promenade. They took a few quick steps and so did we. They slowed down; we slowed down; their pace picked up; so did ours. It was like running up and down a piano scale, the left hand following the right hand, fortissimo and then pianissimo, acrimonious melody.

When they walked next to a light standard, the lamp revealed their faces: Mr. Cleveland's serious, the scar running up his cheek and into the hair over his ear making him look like Dracula; Victor's face dark as a thunder cloud about to burst; Señorita Evita's reflecting concern.

'Is there a problem?' she asked Mr. Cleveland.

'The dance at the Club Saturday night,' he said.

Mentioning the American Club in Victor's presence was like waving a red flag before a bull, 'Your American Club! On Cuban soil! Off limits to Cubans! Guards at the door! What gives you the right? Who do you think you are?'

Caught by surprise, Mr. Cleveland replied automatically with the quiet assurance gained from years of confronting the same issue. 'I know who we are. We are guests of the Republic.'

'Perez Prado will be at your American Club Saturday night and my woman — '

'I am not your woman — ' protested Evita.

' — dances inside and we mambo on the street because we're not allowed to enter!'

The face Mr. Cleveland made wrinkled his scar. 'The functions are for company employees and their guests, Victor. You know that. Evita knows that. I didn't make those rules. They were here long before I arrived.' He hesitated and we stepped closer not wanting to miss a word. 'Evita, Jack King must take you to this dance.'

Evita's trilling laugh drew the attention of several men strolling past. 'I'd have no problem with that.'

'I want to take Margo myself,' Mr. Cleveland said.

I slapped both hands over my mouth to suppress a laugh. How could old man Cleveland be so obtuse? Only yesterday at the club library, I had overheard him propose to Margo and she'd turned him down with a resounding No!

Nanny Carmen muttered, 'Margo will never marry him. He's thirty years older than she is. She's not that desperate — yet.'

Though the Spanish and English teachers frequently compared notes on the few available men in the colony, they never discussed

Jack King. Captain King was a real possibility, a happening. He brought fun and light-heartedness. He came from the land of plenty and had the self-satisfied look of one who'd never lacked an essential or skipped a pleasure. With Jack King poverty didn't exist, revolutions weren't possible and life was a pleasant and delightful trip.

Evita flashed Art Cleveland a winsome smile. 'I'll do my best. Who knows?' A coquettish shrug caused her hair to dip over one eye. Her gaily embroidered peasant blouse slipped down.

Art Cleveland's gaze fell on Evita's smooth brown shoulder. 'I can make it worthwhile.'

'I will not allow this!' exploded Victor. He reached around Evita. His right arm shot out. His fist crashed against the old man's jaw.

The Spanish teacher screamed. 'Victor! Victor! Oh, my God! What have you done! — '

Instinctively, we jumped back. Nanny Carmen snatched me, pulled Elise by the arm and pulled us away. The couples before and aft in the line, the stags in file, the curly haired girls with enormous dark eyes and dangling hoop earrings scattered in all directions like pins struck by a bowling ball. The old women chaperones sat up straight, all attention.

Victor from the post office hit a company man! Had he gone mad?

Art Cleveland grabbed Victor's shirt. The old man made a fist and drew back his arm and held it there for a second like a sling shot drawn taut.

Chapter 13

Connie came on Sundays after she and her father went to early Mass. Sometimes I felt guilty that this young girl was here seven days a week, day and night, even though she never complained about her tedious assignment.

Before the Kennedys left for dinner, Katherine tucked the sheet around my old bones and gave me a perfunctory kiss on the forehead. "Sleep tight. Take good care of her, Connie."

Connie gave her employer a bright smile and a wide-eyed innocent look and me a conspiring wink.

"We'll be back late — one of those endless affairs," resigned, bored already.

As soon as the front door closed, Connie said, "Hurry. You want to be all set when the full moon shines through that window." She helped me into the wheelchair and half buried me in pillows and blankets and rolled me to the window. "You're going to get me fired." She was probably right. "I'm leaving at ten, but Wayne said he'd be here to help you back to bed."

In the room's stillness, holding the wide brush in one hand and the spatula in the other I felt as strong as a gladiator. The turpentine smell tickling my nostrils revived me as though I'd inhaled smelling salts or ammonia. I breathed forgotten happiness.

The night was blue indigo and crystal clear, the full moon diffusing its rays through the window pane like gilded spears. The golden splendor stirred my heart. I picked up the brush and dipped it tentatively in yellow ochre. My fingers trembled. The bristles against the canvas made zigzags and squiggles. No! No! A circle! The moon was round! A circle! I willed my hand steady, forcing the wrist to turn, feeling the pain shoot upward through my arm and settle on my shoulder. The brush wobbled and nearly fell to the floor. If that happened I could never reach it. I tightened my grip. A lopsided oval appeared, tentative, without force, lacking energy. With the spatula I daubed a circle thick and viscous like an egg yolk, layer over layer, yellow, then white — tone down the yellow — too strong, not my favorite color. Each stroke brought back confidence, increased a belief in self. The wide brush swiped blue and black streaks — purple, there must be purple, blue and red to purple — white and golden yellow coming through the midnight cracks.

Window panes! White horizontal lines! White didn't work. Black! Vertical lines! Joy trapped behind bars. I worked furiously, reaching the pinnacle where a superior power took over, where I had nothing to do with the creation other than to be the medium for the art, a familiar, thrilling and totally liberating feeling, healing and restoring. What was time? What was pain? What did any of it matter when the soul rose to the next plateau? Not rose, *soared*.

Suddenly, the room flooded with light.

"Mama, what in heaven's name are you doing up? It's midnight! You can't do this." Katherine scolded me as if I were six years old.

I didn't turn my head. "Off with that light! I'm painting the moon."

"You're not painting the moon! You're painting a big yellow blob. There's paint on your nightgown and your hands — a smear on your face! You'll need a bath before we put you back in bed."

Her constant nagging fell on my ears like rain pounding a tin roof. "Where's Connie?" I hadn't heard her leave, hadn't registered her absence.

"Is she responsible for this? Did she find the paint, the easel?"

I didn't answer.

"I'll look into this! C'mon now — put down that brush." When I didn't, she pulled it out of my hand. "We're all doing the best we can, Mama. You have to cooperate."

"I want to finish this — the first coat, anyhow."

"In the morning — "

"The moon won't be there in the morning."

"Oh, Jesus — "

I didn't have strength to fight a lion. "Okay. Don't throw the canvas away — please." She might trash the painting. She never did like my work. She thought my oils were too bold and strident, disturbing, nothing soothing about them. The one she owned hung in the library, the least used room in the house.

"Of course I won't. You know better than that. Here, let me help you. Connie can clean up this mess in the morning. Tomorrow is your doctor's appointment. Where is Wayne? He said he'd be here! I don't know what to do with that boy!"

Next morning Connie was contrite and quiet and I knew without asking that Katherine had given her a talking-to.

"Don't pay attention to her," I said.

"She's the boss," Connie stood by the window staring at the canvas. "Not bad," she said. "Not bad at all."

"You like it?"

"Hmm — " She gave it her full attention. "It captures a certain confusion by taking familiar images — " she pointed to the yellow streaky moon, the starry pinpoints — "and placing them in a bewildered present." Her hand's circular motion took in the blue, purple, red, black universe. "It's strong and thought-provoking."

She was an amazing girl. "You understand it?"

"Perfectly — "

The energy I had expended on painting left me drained. Last night when Katherine helped me back to bed, I refused the sleeping pill, slapped away her hand, wanting to wallow — yes, *wallow* — in the edgy tenseness, the nervous tension that followed a creative accomplishment. Last night sleep was out of the question; today, I could barely keep my eyes open.

"Can't sleep now," Connie said. "I'm giving you a quick bath then getting you dressed. You have a doctor's appointment today."

"Is he coming here?"

"House call — are you kidding? No such thing this day and age."

"Doctor Ruiz made house calls."

"I don't know about Doctor Ruiz. Doctor Jonathan is your primary care physician and he never shows his face here."

The wet washcloth cooled my neck. "Am I going in the ambulance like last time?" That had been a scary trip, strapped into a gurney, staring at the roof, a screaming siren pushing cars out of the way. Cold! So cold! Somebody put a blanket over me, then another one and I still shivered, toes like icicles, ice water in my veins, breath a frost.

"That must've been an emergency. This is just a doctor's visit for a checkup. You're going in Wayne Olaf's SUV — he put down the back seats and there's room."

"Katherine?"

"She's coming a little later. She'll talk to Doctor Jonathan before we leave."

A rap on the bedroom door interrupted us, "Everybody decent in there?"

"Come in, Wayne," Connie called. "Gramma is almost ready."

He looked rugged, unshaven, red bristle on his chin, his hair tousled and unkempt. He came and sat by my bed, steaming, barely able to contain his rage.

"Where were you last night?" Connie asked, in her eyes a deep, thoughtful look, a veiled anticipation, expectant but a little fearful. "You didn't come put Gramma back in bed. You got us all in trouble."

"Don't ask," he replied, the brusque voice forbidding further questioning. He ran his fingers through his red hair and the cowlick went wild.

Their eyes met momentarily and the anger in his made Connie look quickly away as if she'd come upon a stone too hot to touch. Was she afraid that Olaf's negligence would cost her this job — this run on the ladder she was climbing to her ultimate goal, a full-fledged doctor? A tension existed this morning that wasn't there before. What happened?

Olaf swung roughly past Connie, slipped his strong arms beneath me and carefully, gently sat me in the wheelchair. When I was young I swung from lianas and swam through waves my body weightless. Now moving the old carcass was a major enterprise. How was it possible for these brittle bones covered by paper thin skin to weigh so much? When did every joint develop a creak and become difficult to move?

My grandson left to get the SUV and Connie arranged the portable oxygen tank, the tubes, connections, and all the death defying paraphernalia around me. Katherine entered, on her face one huge frown no plastic surgeon could erase. My daughter and grandson must've had an unpleasant meeting outside my bedroom door. Unpleasant encounters were the norm in this household.

Katherine wore a dark navy suit, a gold pin big as the moon pinned onto the lapel. Her hair pulled back in a bun had gone from black to gray-streaked to platinum, fashionable but a sad complement to brunette skin. She'd come in at midnight and was ready to leave again first thing in the morning. Her whirlwind schedule took its toll. Regardless of face lifts and hair color, my daughter looked old and tired. A day at home with her feet up, doing nothing would be a blessing, but I dared not suggest it.

"Now, Mama, the doctor will do an EKG, check your blood pressure, and see about adjusting your diabetes medicine. He'll have the lab run urine and stool tests — you got that, Connie?" Connie held up a white paper bag. "It'll take most of the morning. I'll be along later to talk to Doctor Jonathan." Nine o'clock and already anticipating nothing but multiple disasters ahead, she spoke through clenched teeth, a shrill edge to her controlled voice.

When was the last time I saw my daughter smile? Before I came, did she smile? Was I the cause of her discontent? Or was it Olaf who so upset her?

I yearned to comfort my daughter. "Relax, Katsy. I'm the one dying here."

"Nobody is dying," she snapped. "You're going to live forever." That dart hit my heart and my face crumpled with pain. "Oh, Mama, I didn't mean it that way. It's just a figure of speech." She placed her arms around my shoulders and hugged the day's first problem. Suddenly, she broke down and confessed, "Can you believe it? Wayne Olaf broke up with Barbara last night, drove all the way to Pensacola to have this ridiculous fight with her."

Ah — so that was the root of everybody's stress! "Good for him! He has a lot of living to do before he gets married and settles down."

"That's not the way we feel about it — Barbara's the perfect match for Wayne!" She shook her head and blurted, "He did it to spite his father!"

It might be the end of the world for James, for the law firm's lifetime merger, for the debutante grandchildren to be, but it was the beginning of forever for my grandson.

"They're not speaking since James had Wayne's car towed away." Insult added to injury, a dangerous combination.

No doubt existed in my mind. "He's too young to take such a big step."

"Have you been putting that notion in his head? He's not going to find anyone more suitable than Barbara — "

"Your opinion — "

"She's perfect — !"

"You said that already."

"We've reserved the Boston Club for a Thanksgiving announcement party. James is livid. They were supposed to go buy a ring — I don't know. They didn't do it. James doesn't know what to say to Monroe this morning — " worried about egg on his prominent social face, was he? "Are you ready, Connie?"

"Yes ma'am." Big, dark eyes intentionally blank.

"Where are my car keys?"

"In your hand, ma'am — "

Olaf returned, gruff this morning, unhappy like everybody else. The entourage — Olaf, Connie, Katherine and me in the wheelchair rolled down the hallway, across the kitchen and out the back door like a parade. The SUV was parked, the doors flung open, the seat so high I didn't think I could sit up there, but Olaf lifted me gently, straightened my legs, yanked the seat belt tightly and locked me in place. He closed the door with a vicious jerk, folded the wheel chair and shoved the contraption in the rear, not saying a word.

"Be careful," Katherine said.

Olaf ignored her, started the engine and revved the motor, an automotive fart.

Every maroon and chrome chair in Doctor Jonathan's waiting room was occupied. Patients in wheelchairs sat against the wall. Connie approached the receptionist behind a glass partition and gave her my name. The wall clock said ten o'clock and Doctor Jonathan was already running behind schedule.

When Olaf returned from parking the van, Connie asked, "Will you stay?"

"Yes."

The young couple stood behind my wheelchair, leaning against the wall.

"I'm glad," she replied simply, from the heart, as if the gladness extended past her, beyond me, to an entire new world that included Olaf.

"It'll all shake out," replied Olaf.

"Maybe I'll die and quit worrying everybody," I said.

Connie patted my shoulder. "You're sounding like a broken record. Nobody can kill a bad weed. You'll be here for a while, so buckle up."

If Surviva had said that, I would've been outraged; if Katherine said it, it would've hurt my feelings; but there was a lack of malice about Connie, a genuine affection for those she cared for including me, a wry twist of humor that turned any acid comment into honey, sweet and easy to swallow.

"Take me out of here. I don't want to be in this room with all these people." Their warped bodies were a reflection of mine. Did my eyes have that blank stare? Did drool ooze from my gaping mouth and slide down my chin?

"You got it. I don't like it here, either. They've got a coffee shop downstairs, but you can't eat or drink until your tests are done."

"I don't care."

She consulted with the receptionist and we left the waiting room. She and Olaf ordered coffee, apologetic because my joining them was out of the question. Olaf set his recorder on the table.

"You brought that gadget with you?"

"Yeah — we're almost done. Half the time at the doctor's office is spent waiting. What was the name of your doctor — the one who made house calls?"

"Doctor Ruiz."

"Tell me about him."

"He was a busy man. You had to really be sick to go to the company hospital. Doctor Ruiz didn't have time to waste on illnesses *curanderos* had the ability to cure. Midwives delivered the babies."

"Why were you there?"

"My appendix was about to burst, and still, I had to wait. Doctor Ruiz was in the operating room. Daddy brought me to the hospital. Mama was gone somewhere. Our phone system was iffy, and of course, no cell phones, then. We had a telegraph machine everyone was taught to use in an emergency and Daddy's secretary was dot-dashing away, spreading the word to locate Mama."

In the cubicle adjacent to Doctor Ruiz's sterile, all-white office there was a cot, and I lay there, my stomach swollen and painful, the door between rooms open. Nurse Dixon frequently checked me while my nervous Daddy paced the hallway, threatening to close the hospital and fire Doctor Ruiz if someone didn't do something immediately.

Olaf asked, "Did your appendix burst?"

"No. Doctor Ruiz removed it in time, but lots happened before. As I've told you, I was an eavesdropping kind of girl, hearing lots more than was intended for young ears."

"Tell me."

Olaf and Connie leaned forward, their heads touching, eager to hear the tale.

***

Doctor Ruiz entered the cubicle where I lay in a fetal position in a vain attempt to ease the pain. He had on a blood-spattered white coat, a paper hat, stethoscope and catheters dangling around his neck, needles and pens stuck in his pocket. He looked like a hippopotamus, a huge mountain of flesh with a gigantic head, a wide mouth, bulging eyes and permanent grooves across his forehead. He scared me when I was well; terrified me when I was sick.

He pressed my stomach and I screamed.

'Get her ready,' he said. 'Where's Caridad?'

'They're trying to find her. Hugh is pacing the hall.' Nurse Dixon inserted a thermometer in my mouth. 'Don't bite down on it, love. I'm putting the burnt girl on the veranda, making a pallet there for her. I think the cool air will refresh her and — ' Nurse Dixon removed the thermometer, read it and shook down the red mercury indicator. 'Don't look that way, boss. It's the veranda or nothing."

'Anybody knows what happened?' asked Doctor Ruiz, leaving my cubicle and crossing to the washbasin in his office. He turned on the water tap and squirted Betadine on his hands.

'A girl from under the bridge,' replied Nurse Dixon. 'Who cares? Who investigates? She either jumped into the fire accidentally or on purpose or somebody pushed her. Who knows? She's about six months.'

'Do the best you can,' he said to Nurse Dixon.

'She needs two pints of A-negative and we don't have it.'

The doctor scrubbed the top of both hands, the palms, ran the brush between each finger and across the blunt-cut nails. 'Find a relative.'

Nurse Dixon placed tight fists on her hips. 'Oh, sure — send for someone from under the Banes River Bridge and the whole contingent will show up! Who has time to deal with that — you — me?'

Suddenly, the door swung open and the doctor's wife burst into his office. He looked over his shoulder, dumbfounded. She slapped an envelope on his desk.

Nurse Dixon acknowledged the unexpected visitor with a curt nod. 'Hola, Berta — haven't seen you in this asylum in a while.'

Doctor Ruiz said, 'Give me a moment.' With a quick shrug he removed the soiled coat and threw it in a cardboard box. He took a fresh coat from a pile on the shelf. He changed ten times a day. Often he wore a rubber apron for protection. 'Me and the butcher across the bridge,' I'd heard him tell Daddy.

The woven straw runner on the hallway dampened Nurse Dixon's clacking heels. She collided with Daddy. The ex-WAC snapped an order: 'Stay out of the way.' I'm sure Daddy was shocked. Nobody spoke to him like that. People were diffident and respectful around him, courting his favor. 'A nurse is on her way to prep Cata. She's next. There's plenty of time and this isn't life threatening. Doctor Ruiz is with her. Go get a cup of coffee. Calm your nerves.'

In his office Doctor Ruiz turned to his wife. 'Something of importance must've brought you here,' he said. She seldom darkened his door. 'What is it, my love? Nothing too serious, I hope?'

She snatched the envelope off the desk top and crushed it against his chest. Under her fluttering eyelids, hot, yellow sparks blazed from her dark eyes. She flung her arm back and before he managed to grab her wrist he felt the stinging slap. Her nails raked across his cheek.

He jerked the envelope from her hand. Later on I learned from kitchen gossip that on the upper left hand corner the torn half read Universidad de la Habana, Habana, Cuba. On the lower right, same blue type:

> Dr. Alejandr
> 910 Calle Igle
> Banes, Orie

The clerk who collected the U. S. Sugar mail brought the letters to the main office where they were sorted and rerouted. On his five o'clock break, Doctor Ruiz brought home the invitations, the thank-you notes beautifully handwritten on linen envelopes, the paper thin airmail letters from abroad. Why had this letter gone directly to his house? Who was responsible for the mix-up?

He pinned his wife's arms behind her back and pressed her body against his rotund belly. 'How did you get this?'

'What difference does it make — bastard!' The word, so alien to her tongue hurt like a hot poker.

'I can explain.'

'Oh, I know all about it. How old is he? Eighteen?'

'Nineteen.'

'By God, by God, by God — a year after we married!'

'This has nothing to do with you. You're my wife.'

A cry caught in her throat. 'You come to my bed after you leave that ... that woman's bed! I can't bear to think of it!'

'You've known. You know that. She's across the bridge.'

Berta writhed in the arms clasping her tightly. 'Excuse me. I forgot. She's across the bridge. That makes it all right? Is that it — if your mistress lives across the bridge that's all right?'

'No,' Doctor Ruiz said in a tired voice. 'You have good reason. It can't be justified.'

'How many?' she asked, growing quiet and still. 'And don't lie to me. Give me that dignity.'

'Six.'

'Six! What are their ages?'

'Their ages — I don't know.'

Of course he knew! The last one he'd delivered eight months ago, a baby girl with black ringlets and big, dark eyes who looked like a doll. The others were two, five, nine, and fourteen; and the oldest, ready to go to the University, wanting to be a doctor like his father. Six survived and six died: two at birth; the three-year old with typhoid; the little boy, the one who most looked like him, smallpox. How helpless he had felt each time; how inadequate. How stoic his Trina, not blaming, not accusing, firm in her Catholic faith, each death God's will.

'You don't know how old your children proper are?'

'Bertica, I'm a busy man. I can't keep up with birthdays.'

'Couldn't you have told me?'

'What was I to say? How could I do that to you? You're my life.'

'Maybe,' she said, holding back a whimper, 'Maybe we could have kept one or two, maybe all of them.'

'And take them away from Trina — from their mother?'

'Ah, yes. Trina is a mother. Every woman is a mother.'

'Now, Bertica — '

'I am not a mother.'

'Don't start, my love.'

'I want to be a mother. I want to cradle a newborn in my arms.'

Reality was a simple, lonely cry, a truth, a history. 'Bertica. — '

She clenched her fists and with renewed fervor pounded his chest. 'It's not fair. Not fair!'

'You are everything to me. I want you and you only. Nothing else matters.'

'Doesn't matter! — doesn't matter! — doesn't matter!' She beat each denial into his chest — 'Hypocrite!'

He grabbed both wrists. 'Bertica, I don't have time for this now. We'll discuss this tonight when I get home.'

'Before or after you stop to sleep with your woman?'

'Please.'

'Am I being punished by God?'

'God doesn't punish like that.'

'If only you'd come with me to pray about it.'

'Bertica, my love, look at this place. Patients in the hallways! No blood for transfusions. We lack basic drugs. We don't admit women to give birth or children with sore throats and colds. Typhoid and smallpox we send to the nunnery and let the Sisters deal with it. We can't afford an epidemic in this American Hospital, and over there,' he jabbed a thumb over his shoulder, 'is the Administrator's daughter waiting to get her appendix out. Another delay and Mr. McAuley in a fatherly fit of anger and despair will burn the hospital to the ground.' He justified my temporary neglect. 'I'm here sixteen, eighteen hours a day, you know that.'

Berta Ruiz ignored his plight and mine, 'Except when you're with her.'

The hippopotamus roared. 'Let me tell you something. She's quiet. She's peaceful. She doesn't nag. She asks for nothing. I walk in the door and she has a warm plate of rice and beans and her legs spread — ' Aghast, Doctor Ruiz stopped himself. 'I'm tired. We'll discuss this at home tonight if that's what you want.'

Berta drew herself up to her full stature. 'That won't be necessary.'

He released his wife, squeezed into his swivel chair and rested his enormous head on his hands. He felt warm ooze on his cheek, pulled his hand away and saw his blood-stained fingers.

The loudspeaker blared through the hospital corridors. 'Doctor Ruiz. Emergency! Emergency! Doctor Ruiz.'

A young nurse entered. 'The ambulance brought a man with a machete in one side and out the other. Nurse Dixon sent me to prep the girl. She said hurry.'

'All right,' replied the doctor, turning his cheek away from the nurse, and saying to his wife, 'I must go.'

'You know what I'm going to do?'

'I suppose.' He picked a cotton wad from the box on the shelf over his desk.

She'd leave. Go away on a long vacation. Abandon the house she ran so perfectly. Leave his bed where he curled his body around hers and made a nest, unproductive, but warm. And because he had the other, he was happy.

'Doctor Ruiz! Emergency! Emergency! — '

The loudspeaker spurred the doctor to action. He erratically dabbed at his bleeding face.

'Here, let me.' Berta took the sterile cotton wad from his hand and wiped the jagged cut. 'It's very ugly — messy.' Her fingers tensed against his cheek. 'Make sure Paquito has a good suit to wear.'

That his wife knew his son's name caught him by surprise.

'Give it here.' He took the blood-soaked cotton from her, gave his face one last swipe and threw the wad into the garbage pail marked Sanitary Disposal. 'A suit for the university? — '

'For the dance Saturday night — he's your son. He'll be sitting at our table, by your side.' She rested her cheek against his heart. 'We will unite this family.'

Ignoring the loudspeaker insistently paging him, the cries coming from the wards, the sirens of arriving ambulances, my incessant whimpering, the doctor tenderly embraced his wife. 'You don't understand, my love. Paquito is black. They won't let him in the American Club.'

Berta's hand reached into the galvanized bucket. Pinched between two fingers she held up the bloody cotton ball. 'You see this?' She smeared a red streak down the lapel of the doctor's starched white coat.

'Bah! Berta! See what you've done to my coat!'

Water couldn't wash out blood.

Chapter 14

The morning sun streamed through the window, reflecting on the dresser mirror. The silver glow caught my eye and I struggled to lift myself a little higher on the pillow. Who was that horrible gray-faced creature staring at me? Sunken cheeks and skin like seersucker; black half moons under droopy eyes? How did she get into my room? Why was she laughing? Who let her in?

Connie burst through the door. "I got it!" she exclaimed.

I fell back on my pillows. "Get her out! Get her out!"

Connie neared my bed and rested a reassuring hand on my arm. "Whoa! Calm down!" Her eyes darted here and there about the room. "Let who out?"

"That woman over there! — " I raised a shaky hand and pointed toward the dresser where I'd seen the old crone, the mayor of the underworld, smiling through rotten teeth, gray hair falling in strands over her hideous face and a crackling laugh. She'd laughed. I'd heard her. That was what upset me most. She'd laughed.

Connie said quietly, gently patting my arm. "There's nobody there," and observing my astonished face, added, "She's gone now. I brought you something."

She handed me a square envelope. Printed on the flap was New York Symphony. "What is it?"

"A CD — Handel's *Messiah* — "

"What would I want with Handel's *Messiah*?"

"You asked me to get it for you."

"I did? Is it Christmas?"

"No, it's not Christmas. The *Messiah* is for Wayne Olaf. You wanted to give it to him."

"I suppose that's so." I trusted Connie. If she said I said it, I said it. But why did I want to give Olaf the *Messiah*?

"I found it at the University book store," Connie said.

"Thank you." I had no recollection. Maybe later it would come to me. "Is the old crone gone?"

"Yes," replied Connie. "She left when I came in. She's afraid of me. As long as I'm here she won't come back." She gave my hand a little squeeze. "I brought you something else — you'll love this." She hid behind her back whatever she held in her hand. "Guess."

"I have no idea. Just tell me."

"Take a guess — "

"Chocolate candy? — "

"You wish." She held out another CD.

That one I recognized. "Perez Prado! Where in the world did you get that?"

"Same place. The university music department had ordered the CDs for a study on Latin rhythms and had a couple left over."

"Put it on! — right now — right away!"

On a desk across the room sat a PC where Connie tracked my medications, annotated any changes in my health, logged her time, did her homework, and e-mailed her assignments directly to her professor. The machine had a slot where she often inserted movies for us to watch or soothing music to lull me to sleep.

She slipped in Perez Prado. "*Mambo Número Cinco*" burst into the room like fireworks exploding – *poco de Monica! poco de Erica!* A little bit of each girl made a man happy. Each drum beat stirred my heart. A country's music entered one's soul forever.

I closed my eyes and swam back through time to the afternoon of the colony's big dance when Perez Prado came to Banes and the town went wild and everybody should've been happy.

I beckoned for Connie to come closer. My voice wasn't strong enough to rise above the music. "Where is Olaf? I must tell him about Perez Prado."

"He's coming. I have his recorder, so shoot."

"Do you know he broke up with that girl?"

"I heard." She plumped the pillows. "Are you comfortable?"

"Did you know her?"

"No. Just saw her here when she came with Wayne." Connie

veered away from the subject. She didn't want to discuss Wayne and his girl. I had the feeling she knew more than she let on.

"Did you know Perez Prado?" she asked.

"I saw him once. He played at the American Colony dance. I'd spent that afternoon with Mrs. Kelly. She had recruited me to play Monopoly. She played bridge with the other ladies, but they didn't like Monopoly. It took too long, was too boring."

"So what happened?"

The events of that fateful afternoon came to my mind, full blown and clear:

***

The day of the dance, Margo Kelly waited expectantly for Captain Jack King — sitting, rising, pacing, looking outside then sitting again. Mrs. Kelly had disappeared into the kitchen to settle a crisis. I sat by myself on the side veranda, warming the dice, estimating what number I'd need to reach Park Place or Boardwalk.

Captain King came up the steps, reluctant-like, the jaunt definitely missing from his sailor's stride. He carried his captain's hat tucked under one arm, eyes hidden behind green reflective sunglasses and he wasn't whistling a merry tune.

An anxious Margo greeted him on the veranda. He kissed her on the cheek. Arm in arm they crossed the veranda and disappeared into the living room.

Zoila came from the kitchen carrying a tray with a teapot, a plate of scones, butter, guava jelly, thin china cups, silver sugar bowl and creamer, unusual so early in the afternoon.

'Who's that for?' I asked the maid.

'Margo. She wants this occasion to be formal, no casual beer on the veranda.'

'What's up?'

Zoila shrugged — 'always something.'

Margo had arranged herself in the wing chair, her hands clutched in her lap, the fingers tightly interlaced.

Captain King sat on the ottoman at her feet. She leaned forward eagerly. He took his time thinking.

When the prolonged silence became unbearable, she asked, 'What is it, Jack?'

The wing chair cover, white with twining vines in varying green shades had several large egrets, wings outspread, ready for flight. The print engulfed Margo's white slacks and sleeveless blouse, took her in, made her part of the fabric, another bird poised on a limb.

He gulped hard and yanked off his sun glasses. 'I have something to tell you.'

A soft smile touched her lips. 'Tell me or ask me?'

He looked away — 'To tell you.'

She turned sky blue eyes on him, a happy glow in their depths, 'About the dance tonight?'

'Yes — no — I mean — '

She looked at him, her eyes sparkling as if inwardly lit by an incandescent bulb. 'Is there something — else?'

Zoila set down the tray.

'I'm taking Evita to the dance,' Captain King blurted. 'I have to. I must, really.' He rose, paced up and down a few steps, bumped into a curio shelf and knocked over a porcelain figure. He looked down at the shattered pieces. 'I've broken it.'

Margo Kelly breathed in sharply. 'So you have.'

With the side of his shoe Captain King raked the fragments into a little heap.

Zoila, who'd been lurking close, eavesdropping as all servants did, stepped from her hiding place behind the baby grand piano. 'I'll take care of that.' Every day she dusted the curio shelf, carefully handling each precious piece, knowing its history, where Mrs. Kelly acquired it, how she wrapped it old newspaper, packed it in foam peanuts and carted it around the world. Zoila swept the fragments into the dustpan. Gluing them back together was impossible.

'Tea? — ' Margo asked in a deceptively calm voice. 'Or maybe you'd prefer a beer?'

'Yes, yes, I'll have a beer, please.'

'Zoila, una cerveza, por favor — '

Zoila shot past me like a clumsy ox magically transformed into a gazelle. She delivered the beer, a frosted glass and a white linen napkin, then came and sat next to me on the porch couch. Four ears were better than two.

'You see —' began Jack King. 'It's complicated.'

'I believe that.'

'Last night —'

Margo interrupted. 'Did you hear Art Cleveland and Evita's boyfriend got into a fistfight at the park?'

Zoila whispered. 'There is hope. Can you hear she's hopeful?'

I supplied first-hand information. 'Elise and I were at the park. There was this altercation. Victor from the post office punched Mr. Cleveland in the face. It's true. You can ask Nanny Carmen.'

'Why would he do that? I know already.'

Jack King hadn't poured the beer into the frosted glass. He took a long pull straight from the bottle — 'Her boyfriend? Evita has a boyfriend?'

'Of course she does.'

'Very late last night she found me at El Chino's. The mariners all go there. I'd just come from the Guardia Civil garrison — one of my sailors got into an argument with that prosti — woman — there on Tráfico Street, but Mr. McAuley had already taken care of it.' He dropped down on the footstool once again, held the cold beer bottle against his hot cheek. 'Evita and I had a talk.' He looked at his shoes. There was no good way to say this: 'I shall marry Evita.'

The ensuing silence was painful and prolonged. 'Do you love her?'

'Please.'

'Forgive me for asking.' Margo's voice went frosty. 'It seemed a natural question.'

He was on his feet again, pacing. 'You are my dearest, most cherished woman.'

'Oh, spare me.'

'I mean that.'

Zoila whispered in my ear. 'She'd better not cry. Kellys don't cry.'

Margo had a catch in her voice, 'Just go. Please, just go.'

He reached for Margo's clasped hands and kissed the fingertips.

'Margo, dearest Margo, I never meant to hurt you.'

Zoila leaned closer to me. 'Good riddance. He's a sailor. They can never be loyal to one woman.'

Margo raised her right arm and pointed. 'Go!'

The "Go!" cracked like a whip, stinging the same as her "No!" to Art Cleveland had. Captain King had the same pained look that had settled on Mr. Cleveland's face. Though the captain didn't look as dejected as the old man, he was hesitant, unsure of himself.

'What are you waiting for — a butler to open the door?' Margo's voice was cold and hard like tempered steel.

Captain King gave her a long desperate confused look then turned on his heel and fled the living room, crossed the veranda and raced down the steps without looking back.

Margo sat in the wing chair for a long time, eyes closed, heart broken, vinegar tears dampening her cheeks.

'Give her a little time,' Zoila said. 'They're not like us.'

'What do you mean?' I asked. 'They — who?'

'The foreigners — they are different, so intense! To us flirting is an art, seduction as necessary as breathing — marriage? — maybe so, maybe not.'

'She loves him.'

'She thinks she loves him — and why not? He's the only eligible man come around here in years. I'd love him, too, but I wouldn't want to marry him. Besides, marrying Captain King upsets the scheduled events that mark her orderly life.'

'What are you talking about?'

'Haven't you noticed? Americans exist — '

'She's not American. She's British.'

'What difference? They all talk English. Their lives consist of arranged waits. Wait until graduation; wait until you find a job; wait until you get married; wait until you have children — all main events in neat order. We lack such order. All that waiting has left my little Margo stranded.'

'You think so?'

'Naturally — have you ever seen any Cuban sit and wait with patience? We get angry, we yell, we fight. We do not hold back. We are sad, we weep. We mourn and wrap a black band around our arm, proclaiming our grief, our loss. We are happy, we dance. We have passion, make a baby. If Margo wanted that man enough, she would forget everything and chase after him.'

'You think she will?'

'Who knows? But I don't believe it. I have to get back to the kitchen. And oh, I almost forgot. Mrs. Kelly said to tell you no Monopoly game. The altercation with the dishwashing girl gave a headache to the mistress. She went to her room.'

I should've left, but I didn't. I stayed as long as Margo sat in the winged chair, waiting for something to happen, hoping for drama — the Captain returning and begging forgiveness or Margo leaping up and chasing after her love. I stayed until the sun set and a semi-gloom settled over the room and nothing happened.

Zoila glided into the room on silent feet, the way servants did, turned on the lamps, and said to Margo, 'I've drawn a bath for you.'

Margo didn't acknowledge the action.

'Your mother is getting dressed for dinner and the dance. If you're not ready, things will be more difficult.'

'I'm not going.'

'Naturally, you are going. You are a Kelly. You have pride. You will go and show that sailor you can have a good time without him.'

'You've been eavesdropping again.'

'Your business is my business. This family is my business. Think how much more complicated life will be if you don't go to the dance.'

'You don't understand, Zoila.'

'Very much, I understand.'

'I am defeated.'

'This is a war?'

'A war of hearts — '

'You surrendered?'

'She's pregnant.'

'He didn't say that,' the maid pointed out. 'That was your conclusion. He only said he had to marry her. That girl is too smart to get pregnant. What I think is he has no idea what is going on. You have no idea. Only Evita knows what she's after.'

'She got what she wanted.'

'Maybe yes, maybe no — come, now. Show the world you don't crumble over a thing like this. The bath water will get cold.' Spotting me lurking between two potted palms, she scolded. 'You're still here? You better fly home before Carmen comes chasing after you. And don't you dare jabber, you little parrot.'

Chapter 15

The downpour we had last night was like a tropical storm that came wrapped in thunder and laced with lightning, poured forth its wrath, spent itself and vanished quickly. By morning the sky cleared and the sun shone brightly.

Connie pulled up the window shades.

"Can you open the window?" I asked.

"You know Mrs. Kennedy frowns on that. It lets out the air conditioning."

"Oh, yes. She told me there was nothing fresh about outside air. It was steaming hot. So open the window, anyway."

"Man, if you aren't doing your best to get me fired. Must I remind you again how badly I need this job?" She lifted the sash.

A sickroom smelled stale, no matter how often the floor was mopped, the furniture wiped, or the sheets changed. Fresh air dissipated the noxious urine and vomit odor and the stink coming from the yellow chrysanthemums sent by well-meaning church ladies. Yellow was my least favorite color. I used it sparingly in my work. It was too strident, too bold, didn't mix well, liked too much to stand alone and be the center of attention. I knew quite a few yellow people in my time.

"I'm going to bring your breakfast — a poached egg, toast, oatmeal, tea — how about a little orange juice?" She turned the latch and fastened the window open.

Eat or drink all that — impossible! But I'd given up arguing about little things, saving my energies for the big battles. "Sure."

A sweet fragrance drifted through the open window. I rolled with great difficulty to one side and absorbed the morning light. Last night's rain had washed clean the magnolia trees. The waxy leaves were dark green and shiny. Beyond it, the confederate jasmine covering the fence with starry white flowers sent forth a familiar, intoxicating scent.

"I want to eat on the terrace," I said when Connie came with the tray.

"Everything is wet out there."

I shrugged. "I don't care."

If I aggravated her, she never let on. She helped me into the wheel chair and we rolled outside into the brilliant morning. She wiped the furniture dry, drew me to the table, buttered my toast and cut each slice into four equal pieces. Connie did everything with controlled grace, a minimum of motion. Her hands didn't flutter needlessly neither did her tongue wag incessantly.

From somewhere down the block a chain saw buzzed and a crash followed as something heavy hit the ground. On the avenue, the street car clanged to a stop. The carillon at St. Mary's Cathedral sent forth the morning's glockenspiel. The crouching gardeners laughed loudly and the noise disturbed the birds. They fluttered away, twittering. A woodpecker incessantly pecked a tree trunk. I raised my eyes and looked into the leafy bower. Where was that bird?

Katherine's lawn and gardens weren't as brilliant as our tropical ones, the green and blues more subdued, lacking the mirror sparkle the ocean gave a landscape. Flowers struggling to survive a humidity not tempered by sea breeze were not as large or colorful.

Olaf appeared in swim trunks, squinting at the sunlight, a towel casually draped over his shoulders. My grandson was over six feet tall, long legged, broad across the chest and shoulders. When he smiled and said, "Hi, Connie," his crooked eye tooth went back three generations. He dropped a casual kiss on the top of my head. "We've got to finish your story, Gramma. I'm going back to school Monday."

More than old stories I wanted to talk to Olaf about the present, about his Barbara. He didn't mention their break and I was reluctant to pry. Youth were curious; elders, nosey.

Olaf jumped into the pool. The big splash accidentally wet Connie and almost doused me.

"Look what you've done!" Connie stood by the edge, dabbing at her wet skirt, looking down at him, frowning.

He cupped his hands and splashed her on purpose. "Jump in."

"Wayne Olaf, I *am* working."

I did the unthinkable. I rolled the wheelchair away from the table, lifted an arthritic leg, placed my foot flat on Connie's bottom and shoved. She catapulted into the pool, a startled look on her face, an astonished yell rising from her throat. For one horrendous moment I thought what if Connie can't swim? Then Olaf had to save her. She emerged, shaking her head, her wet curls flat behind her ears, laughing and wagging a finger at me.

Why shouldn't she swim? Why should she sit in the heat with an old woman? She was young, dedicated and conscientious. She had little time for diversions, always working and studying and taking care of others.

"If you want to hear the rest of the story, the two of you stay in the pool," I said.

"Is this blackmail?" The devil danced in Olaf's eyes, ash gray and sparkling mischief like his grandfather's. His unruly red cowlick was plastered down. He and Connie hung onto the side coping.

"Oh, God — look at me! Soaked! — my shoes!" Connie tugged at her uniform collar.

Olaf splashed her face. "Take if off."

The way Olaf issued the challenge reminded me of my Olaf daring me to swing from a vine, ride my horse into the ocean until the animal's legs didn't touch bottom, smoke a cigarette, or cross the bridge. He was forever baiting me into trouble and I loved it.

For some unexplainable reason in my mind this moment became a defining one. Would she or wouldn't she?

Connie unbuttoned the blouse, stripped the wet uniform and threw it on the side. She slipped under the water and swam from one end of the pool to the other, gliding like a graceful dolphin, the bikini underwear skimpier than any bathing suit. She returned to Olaf's side. Their four elbows resting on the pool's edge formed triangles.

"Your gramma is hell bent on getting me fired. Did you see what she did?"

He looked at Connie through narrowed eyes. "I see what I see."

They both laughed. Their youthful merriment filled my heart

with a peaceful happiness. This was right.

"You want the rest of my life or not?" I asked.

"Yes, I do." Olaf reached for the gym bag sitting beside the pool and retrieved his recording machine. He pushed a button. "One, two, three, go!"

"Did you meet Paquito — Doctor Ruiz's son — at my party? He came to my party."

"Which one was he?" asked Olaf.

"The portly black man wearing a white linen suit — a brain surgeon. Can you imagine Paquito a brain surgeon? Fidel Castro's government sent him to Russia to study medicine. He returned a doctor and a communist, ready to serve his country. I asked him if he remembered the night of the dance and he said, 'How could I ever forget? I thought Perez Prado would never quit playing!' He laughed and I laughed and we recalled the night at the American Club where he and I danced while everyone stared."

"He stayed in Cuba voluntarily?" asked Olaf.

"Yes, for twenty years. He said there was so much hope at first. You could feel the expectation in the air, the dawning; the new beginning."

The foreign corporations were seized. The people rejoiced and danced in the streets. The militia walked into Daddy's office at U.S. Sugar and took over the company. Cuba for the Cubans! Their time had come! Even when the purging began, when anyone who criticized the new government was shot or conveniently disappeared, people tightened their grip on change as if were the tail of a kite that would catch the wind and soar to new heights. They'd have televisions, stereos and Cadillacs; running water in their houses, indoor toilets that flushed; wood floors over the packed dirt in their *bohios*. Instead of creature comforts the new government gave the people free education, free health care and ration coupons. That was a start. At first it was enough — to learn to read, to get a blood test, to own the house and the plot of ground beneath it — what joy! Not to hear the mill whistle's piercing summons calling them to work. Before long the plants and mills shut down. Paquito said that suddenly for the first time ever, the people were hungry, trading old shoes for meat like the

Russians did in the old days. The new management, bearded generals and commissars, revolutionary heroes, were unable to run the companies. Guerilla fighters seldom made good business men. Their forte was war and disruption. Peace soon bored them and they looked for conflict and if they couldn't find any, they incited disruptions. When an informer was appointed for every block, the educated, the wealthy, anyone who was financially and physically able defected like ants leaving a burning nest. They fled to Miami, Caracas, or Madrid, anywhere an airplane ticket was available. Fidel closed the borders and over the now government-owned CMQ ranted for hours against anything American. Albertico Limón was off the air and Fidel Castro became the new soap opera.

Mama wasn't about to abandon her country — she was very patriotic — so when Castro took over Daddy stayed as temporary adviser to the new regime. They kept Daddy because of Mama. She was anti-Batista, an advocate for the people, glad someone had finally deposed the dictator. Daddy's situation was tenuous at best. Victor from the post office, stupid Victor who hated the company, the very one who punched Mr. Cleveland in the face and who knew he was destined for bigger and greater things was the new general manager, an impossible situation. My father soon became resentful and distrustful and greatly unhappy, but he stayed for five long years. When the militia broke into Hernan's house — he was Mama's cousin — and seized him for some real or imaginary infraction and strung him up in Dominguez Plaza as an example for all to see, Daddy had enough. He was leaving while it was still possible. Whether Mama came or not was her decision."

The young people propped their chins on the palms of their hands, following the tale with fascination. "She came," Olaf said.

"Her country or her husband and she loved them both. It tore her apart, broke her heart. They came to Louisiana. I was already here and Daddy went to work at White Castle where American Sugar had cane fields."

"U. S. Sugar?"

"No. American Sugar, the rival company. Daddy considered himself lucky to get employment with them."

"Even with all the upheaval Paquito stayed?"

"Yes — for a long time."

A few months after the takeover — Paquito was barely twenty when the militia banged on the door — they hoisted his daddy, his big, fat hippopotamus daddy, onto a horse and riding between two guerillas Doctor Ruiz disappeared into the mountains, an inducted member of the free health care for every peasant movement. That's the last Paquito saw of his father. He died somewhere near Mayarí. Paquito, son of the good doctor, was drafted into the Youth Movement and sent to Russia to earn a medical degree and replace the loss. He'd become very close to Berta Ruiz, considered her his second mother. With the doctor gone and Paquito sent to Russia, Berta was left alone and destitute — the new regime took the houses, furniture, jewelry — anything they wanted. It was their due, their just reward. She emptied the medicine cabinet and swallowed every pill. Paquito was named Minister of Health. He married and had two little girls. The house assigned to him had plumbing and electricity. He waited seven years for utility service."

"Was he captive?"

"Of course not — Paquito was an important man. He had a visa to leave anytime he wanted. He was free to travel anywhere."

"Then why didn't he leave like everybody else?"

"There was one little hitch. The authorities refused to issue visas for his wife and two daughters."

He was free to go, but he had to leave his family behind. It wasn't until 1978 that he paid every cent he'd saved, boarded a speed launch and came across the Gulf. He and his family left everything behind — entered illegally — caught in a net like sardines and dumped into the immigrant compound in Miami. What a terrible time they had of it! He laughed when he told me about it. It was in the past now — over. He had no American license to practice medicine. He didn't know the language. He found work with a catering company that serviced TACA. He loaded the plastic lunch trays onto airplanes. A surgeon! Such delicate hands! He studied English at night. He connected with a clinic. A patient had a brain tumor, a complicated life or death surgery. The primary surgeon said, 'You do it.' Paquito replied, 'I have no license yet.' 'I'll sign off on the paperwork. You've done this many times before. We can't let this man die.' Paquito told me his story and laughed. What was the point of crying? He'd hit bottom and nothing could ever be as bad. It was like Auschwilz — if one survived, no evil ever compared. 'Americans are kind-hearted,' Paquito said. 'Everybody helped.'

My dredging through the past made Olaf happy, so I continued babbling about the times gone by, talking to the upturned faces with the youthful, lively eyes. "The week of the Perez Prado dance, Doctor Ruiz, Paquito's father, had lost control of his life, lost the tight grip he kept on his affairs, the precarious balance he'd maintained for years. His sins were falling around him like over-ripe guavas from a tree. The on-going argument with Berta over his mistress and the children left him drained. He was tired and overworked, not a well man."

The sun climbed above the trees, the morning coolness lost. Heat crept into the day. The warmth made me sleepy. The young people ducked under the water. Their wavering bodies disappeared and Doctor Ruiz's enormous bulk emerged before my eyes.

* * *

Faustina, the Ruiz's cook, repeated to Nanny Carmen the arguments in the doctor's house. Faustina spewed the quarrels verbatim, raising her voice to a shrill pitch for Berta's accusations and lowering it for the doctor's grumbled replies. 'They argue and fight about things of no consequence,' Faustina said, but the main reason is that Berta has no children.' Faustina sighed, genuinely sorrowful. 'Such a nice woman,' she said, 'such a terrible curse.' She mused a little, sad about her employer's barrenness, her deprivation. 'Children engulf life,' she said, 'always a birthday party or a tennis lesson or a Christmas program or something — at our house nothing — nothing. Two poodles! That's it! Two dogs! And how much bridge and canasta can one woman play?'

Carmen agreed with sympathetic clucks. She stayed busy doing things for me, watching that I didn't get into trouble, mending my clothes or taking me somewhere.

Faustina told Carmen the doctor and his wife were arguing about

Cuba on My Mind

Paquito as if he weren't sitting right there in the kitchen.

I knew their kitchen well. All company houses had the same kitchens. A wood-burning black iron stove on one side; a pitcher-pump that supplied water to a porcelain sink on the other; two rolling pins on an aluminum sheeted table; copper pots hanging from an overhead rack. Recently the company had replaced the ice boxes with electric refrigerators. A wood-burning iron stove and a white enamel refrigerator — so out of place! When the electricity failed, the food spoiled.

Most people didn't trust the new refrigerators. They moved the old zinc-lined *neveras* to a pantry or back room and the iceman continued to deliver the big ice blocks that fit in the top left compartment.

Paquito stiff in a new white suit waited leaning against the wood bin.

'Move away from there,' Faustina told him. 'You'll soil your clothes.' She opened the refrigerator and handed Paquito a cold beer. 'Drink it,' she said, 'and don't worry. They argue a lot.'

The cook and the boy could hear the raging going on in the living room.

'He's been my son for nineteen years!' the doctor stormed, 'Why now, this sudden impulse to cause him harm?'

'Harm? — you accuse me! You are the one who has deprived him — kept him and the rest of them hidden in that run down house!'

'It's not run down!'

'Unfit to live in!'

'You've been there?'

'I've been there!'

'When? — ' the one word whipped out of the doctor's mouth like a hurricane gust.

'Never mind when! Calle de Pino! — fourth house to the left — blue.'

'What have you decided? — to ruin our lives?'

'To join your separate lives — one here — one there.'

'By God! — my God! — where is my son?'

'In the kitchen — '

'The kitchen! — '

'With Faustina — he refused to come into the living room.'

'And what are your plans when they turn him away at the door?'

'They won't dare!'

'They won't dare! That's how much you know about them. They will so dare. Haven't you read those signs on the way to the beach? The ones posted on every gate we open? No Admittance. *Prohibido la entrada*. Cubanos y Negros. They dare! They dare!'

'Caridad will meet us at the door.'

'You leave Caridad out of this.'

Mama took care of all difficulties. The doctor was beside himself, boxed into a corner with no idea how to extricate himself or Paquito.

He said to Berta, 'Bertica, my love, you listen to me. I entreat you.'

She replied, 'If you got down on your knees and begged me, it wouldn't do any good.' She gathered the pink satin wrap and placed it around her shoulders. 'Please. Pin this on.' She held an orchid corsage. 'We've missed the start of the dance already.'

He crushed the flower. 'I hope we live though this. The car is outside.'

A terrified Paquito sat in the kitchen with Faustina. The cook pushed him into the hallway. 'Go! They are ready. Go and make your mother proud — '

'Proud? I know nothing about pride,' Paquito said. He simply wanted to survive, to last the evening and escape.

Another thing bothered him tremendously. He had never heard his father raise his voice. Never had he been angry at their house. He was always too tired. That was what he said most, 'I am tired.'

Faustina whispered. 'You'll do fine. You're every bit as good as they are.'

Then he was in the Buick, wedged in the back seat between Berta's big chiffon pink breasts and his father's watermelon stomach, breathing unfamiliar perfume, heart pounding, feeling much as Isaac must have when Abraham led him to slaughter. Lucky for Isaac, God intervened and that was what Paquito silently prayed for — a miraculous rescue. He didn't belong in the American Club. He had no business crossing the bridge, but still, he was excited to hear Perez Prado, see with his own eyes the famous musician and his great band. He knew every song by heart and so did I. Young people memorized song lyrics with great ease, a talent that disappeared as one grew older.

As soon as Faustina left our house, Carmen hurried into the sewing room where I stood on a stool while Mama gave the final tucks and tugs to the dress I was wearing to the dance. Carmen repeated Faustina's gossip word for word, adding her own little embellishments here and there, while Mama said 'ah' and 'um' because she had a dozen pins clamped between her lips.

Perez Prado was a big happening. Cubans danced at home, in the streets, in clubs, in music halls — everywhere. They had an innate rhythm that moved their feet and swayed their hips. One drum beat and their shoulders twitched.

Paquito had another problem. He had no dance partner. Who would dance with the scandal walking through the door? Nobody!

***

As my parents and I arrived at the American Club, Perez Prado's music burst from the two-story building and washed over the uninvited throng clogging the street. We maneuvered around people dancing, drinking; already having their own party. The company could restrict access to the Club, but they couldn't confine the music.

We went up the steps behind the Kellys, Margo dragging her feet, obviously reluctant. Her father's reassuring hand gripped her elbow, her mother a few steps ahead.

Inside, the musicians plucked guitars and shook maracas, white ruffled sleeves a blur. They bent and swayed over their instruments, faces glistening sweat, black patent leather shoes tapping rhythm. Like lightning striking a rod, the sound went through the dancers sending them into twisting, whirling frenzies.

The first person who spotted Margo was Art Cleveland. The old man hurried across the ball room. Margo moved away from her parents, lost them in the arriving bustle and confusion and ducked behind a potted palm too late. Mr. Cleveland was there, standing before her.

'Margo!' Breathless, excited as a teenage boy.

'Hello, Art.' Margo's blue crepe dress matched her eyes. An enormous rhinestone pin at the waist anchored the V-neck. Sparkling shoulder clasps held in place tulle lengths flowing down her bare back. The skirt rippled around her ankles like ocean waves at low tide.

'Why didn't you call? You look beautiful tonight. I would've — '

She looked past the scar on his face, avoiding the eager look in his eyes. 'Never mind — can we dance?'

'Most assuredly we can dance.' He put his arm around her.

Perez Prado sang a bolero backed by the white-ruffled band shaking maracas and blowing trumpets. Art's feet moved lightly in rhythm. He was remarkably spry for an old man.

Margo lowered her eyes and glanced furtively at the other dancers.

'He's not here, yet,' Mr. Cleveland said. He was a touch deaf, and talked quite loud. Everyone within earshot could hear him.

Margo's face grew warm. She rested her hot cheek on the lapel of Art Cleveland's white coat. She looked as if she wished she were dead.

Señorita Evita and Captain King arrived, she a dark, mahogany vision in off-the shoulder red; he, sun gold in navy whites; a study in contrast. They came through the door, laughing, hanging onto each other, happy. They waved gaily and glided through the crowd toward the terrace, interrupted frequently by women and men who spoke with the popular captain about one thing or another.

Mr. Cleveland's arm tightened around Margo nearly crushing her to death. He whirled her around and she glimpsed the Spanish teacher and the ship captain. What a handsome couple they made! They'd have a home, children, a life and Margo would be an old maid, living in lonely outposts, teaching students English until the day she died. Margo's eyes didn't blaze with jealousy or sparkle with anger. Sadness entered them like a veil worn by widows who bore their private sorrows. She didn't trust herself to open her mouth, afraid a sob would escape.

'She's his kind of gal,' Mr. Cleveland said, 'and you're not.'

'What do you mean?'

'He can love her and leave her — no strings attached.'

'She has a big string attached — ' and before she could bite her tongue, she blurted, 'she's pregnant.'

Art Cleveland laughed so long and loud several people turned and looked over their shoulders. 'Is that a fact?'

Gretchen Van Nuys grabbed the king's arm as he went by. 'Thanks for the electric can opener.'

He flashed his quick, genuine smile. 'No trouble at all.'

'Not even a little?' Olaf's mother looked at the captain coquettishly, gripped his lapel and pulled him close. 'I was hoping you'd gone to a lot of trouble.' Her thin, aquiline nose touched his.

The captain attempted to move away. 'No trouble at all, Gretchen.' Gretchen clung to his coat like a barnacle.

Señorita Evita whispered, 'Already drunk.'

Mama went to the rescue, the sequins on her white, form-fitting, strapless sheath blinking in the light.

My mother's beauty was striking. She looked like a mermaid who rose from the sea and climbed to the stars. Her black hair was pulled back into a figure eight chignon. The light dancing in her huge, expressive eyes was like water reflecting on a pool. She moved with such grace and elegance, no one noticed how Daddy towered over her. When she walked into a room, she gathered all the scattered energy and concentrated it on one spot. Every head turned in her direction.

'Thanks for the pinking sheers,' she said. 'They will be so useful to me,' and to Gretchen, 'Mr. Van Nuys is looking for you. He wants to dance.'

'Oh, he's such a clod.'

'Come along, Gretchen,' Mama said.

'Whatever for — he'll be chasing some young thing before the night is over. He'll probably be chasing you.' She pointed to Señorita Evita.

The slurred remark offended the captain. He gripped Mrs. Van Nuy's hand tightly and pried her fingers off his coat. With delicate but firm force he pushed her away. She teetered in her high heeled slippers like a boat without a rudder, bobbing through the dancing crowd to find Mr. Van Nuys.

'She's a real *puta*,' Señorita Evita said.

The captain raised both eyebrows, shrugged and forced a smile. Quarrels on land weren't allowed. He confessed to Mama, 'I had no idea what pinking sheers were, but the clerk knew.'

For the daughters of company employees the captain brought Toni perm solutions, Maybelline eyeliner and Revlon lipstick. To prove what a fine product that was, Dorothy Corman, Elise's older sister home for the summer, kissed his cheek leaving a red, bow-shaped imprint. The girls fawned over him, giggling and fluttering their eyelashes, flitting like colorful butterflies after nectar.

Mrs. Kelly waved at the captain to get his attention. She lifted her ample bosom and shook her mountainous breasts a little.

He mouthed silent words. 'It fit?'

She nodded with a coy wink and held up her thumb and forefinger in an O and mouthed back, 'Perfectly.' Size 42, Double D Cup Maiden Form brassiere with whale bone supports — there wasn't one to be had in the company commissary or across the bridge in the civil town.

Margo's face flushed a deep pink and her enormous blue eyes blazed. She clamped her mouth shut, her lips lost in a thin line. Her own mother flirting with that cad! Her Mum who knew Margo had been stood up! And there was her Dad talking with the captain, also. And my daddy, too — everybody courting favors as if the Captain King were royalty.

Abruptly Margo dropped her arms from her dancing partner's shoulders and let them dangle by her side. She shook both hands as if to cool them after touching something burning hot. Maybe she'd lost circulation in her fingers, Mr. Cleveland clutched her so tightly, but I think — you know what I truly think? — I think she was shaking off an overpowering urge to slap Jack King's smiling face.

Chapter 16

We were back in my bedroom. Connie and Olaf had tucked me into bed and placed multiple pillows behind my head. Olaf had changed into khaki shorts and a Tulane tee and Connie was wearing a dry uniform.

"That was quick," I said.

"Threw it in the dryer," she replied. "Ten minutes."

"The miracles of modern age," I said. "At home the day workers washed our clothes in concrete tubs, boiled them in a black iron vat and hung them on a line to dry." Every single day laundry flapped in the wind.

The kitchen and the laundry room behind it throbbed with activity, the engine that kept the household running. They were the hottest rooms in the house with boiling pots and baking ovens, steam rising from vats and tubs. A thin veneer of sweat covered the black arms and faces of the cooks and laundry workers. Lye and scorched starch smells mixed with soap, bleach, and pungent kitchen odors.

Conveniently behind the laundry room where she kept an eye on the inner workings of her smooth running empire, Mama had her sewing room. She sat at her throne, a Singer treadle machine with a wrought iron base. In one corner stood a pink, naked form, my first lesson in anatomy. A half-twist increased her bust. One crank lengthened the arms. Mama spread old newspaper on the cutting table and like an architect, drew lines from here to there and then across, creating a skeleton her unerring scissors cut and turned into a garment. The sewing tools and necessities were piled in baskets – buttons, spools, ribbons, tracing wheels, white chalk, measuring tapes. It was here that Mama felt truly at home. This room was hers. The rest of the house belonged to the company.

The laundry and sewing room opened onto a small foyer with a bench where people came and sat, waiting to tell Mama their problems trusting her to solve their troubles.

"And the dance?" asked Olaf. "Did you go to the dance?"

What was he talking about? I hadn't danced in years. Dance? Dance! If I focused on the word, the meaning would resurface, float back into my mind like snagged driftwood unexpectedly cut loose and carried downstream by the current. I concentrated mightily, but the more I thought *dance*, the less I recalled. *Dance* could've been a foreign word. It held no meaning.

A sudden music blast filled the room and without warning, the word slipping past stopped and righted itself, a sensation not unlike swimming to the ocean bottom, running out of breath, struggling to resurface and suddenly breaking through the water with a splash of recognition. "Is that Perez Prado?"

"Yes," replied Connie. "The CD I brought you."

"Perez Prado played at the dance," I said. All the blocks tumbled into place.

"You were there," Olaf reminded me.

Of course I was there! Mama made me a new dress. It had a dark green satin bodice with spaghetti straps, a lighter green tulle skirt, and a grosgrain ribbon sash. My first high heels! Mama and I had crossed the bridge to the shoe shop where the cobbler traced my foot on old newspaper while Mama felt the thin leather strips hanging from pegs on the wall, selecting the ones to be dyed green. Then they argued about the heels, the cobbler wanting them higher than Mama did. They stood like two gladiators in the dark stall smelling of leather, shoe polish and alcohol, flies buzzing over a half-eaten mango, a mangy dog curled in a corner. Mama and the cobbler waved their arms and gestured, throwing their whole bodies into the disagreement. The shoemaker won. My sandals had high, hour-glass shaped heels. Afraid I'd teeter and fall, one night Mama showed me how to hold my head up and glide across the room as gracefully as a gazelle while Daddy watched and moaned, 'She can't grow up! I won't let her grow up!' Mama lent me her pearl necklace. Never had I looked so beautiful and elegant. I was fourteen going on twenty-one.

I wanted Olaf to see me in all my grown-up finery. I yearned to

Cuba on My Mind

eclipse Señorita Evita the way a small moon can once every thousand years darken the sun.

At the dance, I spotted Olaf first, leaning jauntily on the bar across the room, holding a drink he wasn't supposed to have. Circumventing dancing couples, I walked in his direction, not sure what I'd say, just wanting to be near him, start an argument, new or the same old, so that we could spar with words.

He looked up and smiled his crooked smile and my heart jumped. He walked through the swaying crowd toward me, dodging waiters carrying trays, men mopping their brows and women in dazzling jewelry. He avoided his father's elbow moving up and down like a pump handle while his mother jerked her fat hips right and left, an embarrassing moment. He bypassed Mama undulating like a silver snake while Daddy stood immobile as though his feet had ankle weights and it took too much effort to lift them.

We walked toward each other like lovers in a movie scene, or so I thought in my teenage euphoria. Soon we'd meet; he'd touch my shoulder, say something outrageous and the others would be making room for us on the dance floor.

The great expectations took my breath away and right then, right there, my daddy ruined my life. He moved away from Mama and said, 'Excuse me, but I must have the first dance with this beautiful girl.' My heart touched my new high heel slippers.

Mama smiled approval and someone else encircled her waist and she moved aside.

Daddy was a terrible dancer. He had absolutely no rhythm. He held my hand high and I twirled beneath his raised arm. We weren't doing a rumba, or a mambo, or a son. We simply shuffled in place, me looking over Daddy's shoulder for Olaf. As we stepped and turned, new dancing couples whirled around us. Through the moving blur I saw Mr. Van Nuys grab Olaf's elbow and pull him aside. He was giving Olaf a lecture, shaking his finger in Olaf's defiant face, fussing about something, maybe the drinking, who knew. Olaf's mother and father were always in a rage about one thing or another.

We turned again and I lost Olaf and we bumped into Art Cleveland and Margo. We were so jammed in the ballroom that his elbow poked my side.

He raised his voice over the music. 'Pardon me.' He smiled his disfigured, lopsided smile and continued talking to Margo, so naturally I overheard. He was telling her he was a rich man.

'I've managed to sock away a few dollars from my ventures,' he said. 'I have no family. I was married once when I was young.' I supposed he confessed his history in order to erase the past and start over on a clean slate.

Margo raised her head, pretending interest. She looked pale, sick almost. 'What happened?'

'We lived in New York —'

'I can't imagine you living in a metropolis like that.'

'Neither can I, but when you're young and in love you do things you never thought you'd be capable of.'

So! He had been young once; and in love.

Margo looked at him with a new curiosity. 'She died?'

'Oh, no! — She was a ballerina. The situation simply didn't work for either of us. We divorced.'

'Where is she now?' Margo asked, not from curiosity, since she really didn't care, but because she thought he'd expect her to show some interest.

'She teaches dancing — so I was told — in Paris.'

'Do you ever see her?'

'You know what happened to Lot's wife when she looked back? I look ahead to the future. A future with you,' and then, I couldn't believe my ears (if nothing else the man was persistent) he asked her one more time, 'Will you marry me?'

Margo said nothing. I believed she was afraid she'd burst into tears if she opened her mouth.

'Did you hear me?' Art Cleveland was holding her so tightly she looked like a rag doll plastered against him. 'Margo? Dearest?' He gave her waist another squeeze. 'Did you hear —?'

She looked up at his scarred face, his pale, watery eyes and bristly mustache. She hid her face in his lapel and said in a muffled voice, 'I heard you.'

Both Daddy and I thought the *merengue* would never end. For a moment I hoped he'd call it quits and we'd walk away, but I hesitated, wanting to hear Margo's answer.

'You're a great dancer, Daddy.'

'Lying never gets you anywhere, Kitty Kat,' he whispered. 'What do you think?' He'd been listening, too.

'She turned him down once in the library. I heard her.'

'She might change her mind.'

'Because? — '

'Because she's nearing thirty; because the captain is here with Evita; Because Art is rich. There are worse things than marrying a rich man.'

'But she doesn't love him!'

'Ah, love. Love comes and goes. He likes books, music, art, travel. Margo doesn't realize it, but she and Art have a lot in common. She'd be happy.'

'But happy isn't — '

'A fever? — But it's a warm blanket you can wrap around you your whole life.'

Mr. Corman and his wife made a wide, wild turn that sent us crashing into Margo and Mr. Cleveland. The old man laughed and swayed and bent Margo backwards and leaned over her forever. Margo inhaled deeply, opened her eyes wide, looked into the scarred face and uttered one word. 'Yes.'

Art Cleveland released Margo. He put both hands down on the dance floor, kicked his heels over his head and turned a cartwheel. Coins fell out of his pockets and clinked on the polished floor. His glasses flew in one direction and his red tie swung in another.

Olaf, hurrying across the ballroom avoided Mr. Cleveland sprawled on the floor and the people bending over him, including Daddy — an utter commotion. Olaf looked through me as though I were a pane of glass, not even saying 'hello.'

My disappointment was like an anchor dropped into the sea. The weight stopped all movement. I felt a new and rare pain, a sensation so acute I held back tears. I knew where he was headed without turning my head. Through the music, laughter and tinkling glasses, Señorita Evita's distinctive laughter floated over the terrace. Like a fish caught on a hook, the sound reeled in Olaf. At that moment I hated the Spanish teacher with a will and a depth I didn't know existed.

Unable to stop myself, not knowing what I planned to do, I followed Olaf. He made his way across the ballroom, but for whatever reason, didn't step outside. He bounded up the curving staircase to the second floor. Too eager, too anxious to walk, he ran down the musty mildewed hallway and burst into the balcony overlooking the terrace.

Señorita Evita was dancing with Jack King, dancing in the moonlit night, in the warm, sultry, gardenia-scented night. They twirled round and round, King's hand possessively on the Spanish teacher's hip, her head tilted back, the long lashes curling up, coal black eyes sparkling, moonbeams sliding through the inky black hair like a live, electric current.

From the balcony, Olaf looked down on Evita Aluso. Her moves in the red, strapless dress were quick, graceful; her multiple turns a maddening whirl. The way she swayed her hips, rotated her shoulders, the erotic tremor that passed through her body as she lost herself in the drum beats, mesmerized Olaf.

He wasn't aware I stood a few feet behind him. He didn't see the pink geranium boxes attached to the balcony railing or the green ferns hanging from the eaves or the colorful Chinese lanterns decorating the coconut trees. He didn't hear the shrieks and laughter or the tinkling glasses or the music. He didn't notice the gigantic orange moon, so low in the sky it looked easy to touch. Nothing was real to him but the red blur below. He heard only the steady tap...tap...tap of Miss Evita's stiletto heels striking the flagstone terrace. Thin sandal straps encircled her slim ankles. Her toenails were painted red.

He rubbed a hand across his chest and drew a sharp breath. He moaned as if something inside him had given way, been crushed. He lost all restraint. Unable to resist the lure of the swirling skirt and the scarlet toenails, he leaned far, far over the balcony railing.

As the Ruizes climbed the steps to the front door, the guards had deserted their entry posts. The band had stopped playing and someone spoke into the microphone, the agitated voice carrying over the room. 'Doctor Ruiz! Is Doctor Ruiz in the house? We have an emergency.'

Hidden in the balcony's shadow, I stared at the catastrophe below, knowing I should make myself scarce, yet I stayed, glued to the spot. Below, the dancing couples had stopped mid-step and were bending over Olaf or crouching next to him. When they saw Doctor Ruiz coming, they parted like the Red Sea and let him through. He was our healer, the good doctor who cured our illnesses and bound our wounds. At times like these, there was no question. He was one of us.

Olaf had landed face down, his shoulders and head on the green lawn; the lower half of his body on the flagstones, legs splayed. Doctor Ruiz's first order was to Erik Van Nuys. 'Don't touch him,' he said to the agitated father who was about to lift his son's inert body. 'Send for a stretcher. What happened?'

'I don't know.'

Jack King stood with his arm around Señorita Evita's waist. 'The crazy kid jumped from the balcony.'

'Showing off again for Miss Evita.' The remark came from Olaf's younger sister, Gretchie, an obnoxious little pest who always wanted to tag along with Olaf and me. We'd swat her away as if she were a bothersome fly.

Mr. Van Nuys looked up from his son and the attending doctor. He turned to face Señorita Evita. 'What's this all about?' he asked in a stern voice.

Olaf had not spoken to his father since the afternoon Mr. Van Nuys came to the school. Olaf told me that himself. He said he hated the bastard.

'I can assure you I have no idea,' replied the Spanish teacher coldly.

How could Señorita Evita not be aware that Olaf was in love with her? The way he mooned around her, she had to know. Her name scribbled on every book and paper he owned! Deliriously happy to stay an extra year in the eighth grade!

'Showing off,' Gretchie said.

I restrained the urge to jump off the balcony and shake that stupid girl, but Mrs. Van Nuys beat me to it. She grabbed her daughter and rattled her bones. 'Stop it! Stop it right this minute! My little boy! My son! What's happened to my son?'

Everybody's attention was centered on Olaf. The dancers pressed close to get a first-hand look at the crazy Van Nuys boy who should've been sent off to school a year ago and wasn't.

The doctor squatted next to the unconscious Olaf. He moved experienced hands over Olaf's back, felt his arms, legs, fingered his neck. 'He's lucky his head hit the soft ground and not the flagstones. He most likely has a concussion — doesn't look like anything is broken except that left leg. We'll take some X-rays. Everybody relax. He's not going to die.'

The diagnosis whipped through the ballroom as if propelled by a high wind.

'Please, all of you,' Doctor Ruiz said with authority. On medical grounds he had no trepidations. He was in full charge. 'Go back to dancing. Olaf will be fine. He's now discovered diving from a balcony isn't such a good idea.'

The stretcher arrived. The doctor supervised the transfer. 'Careful. Slip it under him. Don't jar him. Move back, all of you. Give him some air. Evita,' he said, 'Do me a great favor.'

'Anything, Alejandro — '

'Paquito is here.'

Her eyebrows shot up to her hairline.

Doctor Ruiz shrugged. 'I can't explain now. Find him. Stay with him.'

'At once — ' She kissed the captain full on the lips. 'I'll be back, love,' and left the captain stranded on the terrace.

From my perch on the balcony, I watched the men carry Olaf away, his mother sobbing and wailing in hysterical drunkenness, his father on the other side and the doctor following.

Suddenly I was overcome with a terror that someone would find me on the balcony and think I pushed Olaf over the railing. In nervous agitation, I flew down the stairs and into the grand ball room. I slid into the sparkling, sequined crowd clutching rum drinks and dissolving into laughter and gaiety now that the crisis was under control.

Perez Prado and his band never quit playing. A doleful "*Guantanamera*" accompanied the procession walking through the ballroom to the street and into a waiting ambulance.

Doctor Ruiz had said Olaf wasn't going to die. I kept repeating to myself — *he's not going to die, not going to die.* What would I do if he died?

Señorita Evita didn't look long or far for Paquito. He sat by himself at the doctor's table, unsure whether he should stay put or join the crowd drawn to the accident scene. He looked like the Egyptian Sphinx, parallel arms extended on the table, ramrod spine and face blank, speechless; motionless except for the feet beneath the table. The hem of the white tablecloth skimming the floor twitched in time to the drum beat and the rhythm.

The Spanish teacher spotted me scurrying through the whirling, twirling couples. I wasn't sure where I was going, but I had to escape, flee the club, go outside, lose myself and forget this terrible night.

'Hey! Cata! Over here!' Señorita Evita waved in my direction, motioned me toward the table where a black boy dressed in a white linen suit looked completely out of place. An alien would've appeared more at home. 'This is Paquito,' she said, 'And he wants to dance.'

'Yes,' the boy replied, 'on the street.'

Doctor Ruiz's wife, returning from the commotion on the terrace, overheard the remark. 'Absolutely not,' she said. 'You will dance right there.' She pointed to the gyrating couples bumping against each other on the dance floor.

Paquito looked pained. The hurt in his eyes matched mine. We were both rejected and confused. We were trapped. We had no idea what to do. A few minutes ago I was dreaming of dancing with Olaf and now it appeared that I'd be dancing with a black boy — impossible! Yet there he was, standing before me, every move, every look tentative, his concern and fear even greater than mine.

I extended my hand at the same time he offered his. Our fingertips touched.

The excitement caused by Olaf's fall quickly receded, overcome by a new aberration. The administrator's daughter dancing with Doctor Ruiz's illegitimate son! What was this world coming to?

Chapter 17

I loved my daughter, but she had inherited an unfortunate disposition: her grandfather Erik's temper and Olaf's bullheadedness. The McAuley's tolerance and good humor, so evident in Daddy, and the Spanish grace and serenity, Mama's hallmark, were missing from Katherine's makeup. She disrupted any room she entered. Type "A" personality, psychiatrists labeled this compulsion to be constantly in control.

She swept into the bedroom and saw Olaf, Connie and me huddled over the recorder and interrupted my narrative. "What are you up to?" she asked, neither expecting nor receiving an answer from anyone. Her decision as to our state and condition was already made. "Wayne Olaf, you have to pack your things. Your room looks like a tornado struck it."

"I've got plenty of time. I'll do that tomorrow."

"We're going to the club for Saturday brunch tomorrow."

"That's fine."

"James and Monroe are teeing off early. Your father has invited Betsy and Barbara to join us for lunch."

"I'm not going."

"You most certainly are. We have to settle this thing."

"It's settled."

"Don't give me that."

Connie said, "Excuse me. I'll go get some orange juice for Gramma."

"Mrs. Van Nuys," Katherine corrected.

"Yes ma'am — for Mrs. Van Nuys."

"She can call me Gramma."

"We can't have the help getting familiar."

Before I retorted to that absurdity, Olaf said, "Stay, Connie. My mother and I have nothing to discuss."

That put Connie on the spot. If she stayed Katherine would be upset and if she left Olaf would resent it. She needed her job. She'd told me so a hundred times.

"I'll be back."

Olaf gave his mother an angry look and stood, ready to go after Connie.

"Sit down. I'm not finished with you," snapped Katherine.

"Yes, you are, Mom," sullen, rebellious. "Do yourself a favor, save yourself some grief."

He was twenty-one for heaven's sake — old enough to decide what he wanted in life and cut his own swath, yet Katherine refused to let him be. When he was gone from the house permanently, what would happen to my daughter? Would the frantic activity that filled her days replace the loss? She had mapped her son's future, made his plans. Barbara would be a beautiful bride, a perfect wife, bear plump, happy children. Katherine's plans were dashed against the rock of Olaf's stubbornness, his reality.

I shared information to smooth the mother-son rift. "Olaf was always crosswise of his father."

"For Pete's sake!" cried Katherine. "What does that have to do with anything? And that easel! What's it doing there again? And the window open! Didn't I tell that girl — ? What in the world? — "

"That's Sunny. I painted the yellow canary for you. I hate yellow. I started to make him green."

"How did you — ?"

"Connie brought the cage to my room."

The bird's little head was cocked at a defiant angle reminiscent of my own. Connie had pointed to the vertical lines and said my paintings had a common thread running through them. Maybe I did feel trapped by my failing body, well-meaning children and society's rules.

"Connie! Connie! Connie! That's all I hear. Connie is taking over this house — "

"Katherine, take a breath," I said.

Connie returned with the orange juice and the room fell silent.

Without asking, she knew the discussion had been about her. "Is something wrong?" she asked.

"Nothing — my mother hasn't gotten it through her head that I'm not marrying Barbara."

Such open defiance sent Katherine into a tailspin. She pivoted on one heel and as she left the room, she sent a volley over her shoulder, "I'll talk to you later — in private."

Olaf had the last word before the door slammed. "It won't do you any good."

A deep silence followed Katherine's departure. Which one of us was responsible for the tirade? Was I the culprit for taking up so much of her time? Olaf for not marrying Barbara? Connie for doing her job? Or was Katherine fed up with life in general and venting her frustrations on us?

Connie held a tumbler next to my chin and placed the bent straw in my mouth. "Take a sip — orange juice — it's good for you. Don't get excited. Remember your blood pressure."

I was more confused than ever. All this disruption took its toll and I closed my eyes and escaped into the consoling darkness where I often took refuge. Sometimes when the others thought I was asleep, I was awake but absent, consciously withdrawing from silly quarrels that made little difference so near the end.

When I rejoined the living, Olaf was still at my bedside holding his head in his hands, elbows propped on the mattress.

"What is it?" I asked.

He hesitated, reluctant to pass his burden onto my weak shoulders.

"You can tell me."

His question startled me. "Gramma, are you afraid to die?"

Whatever brought that on? "Of course not — it's the ultimate trip and you don't have to bother packing. I know where I'm going."

"Where to? — Mars? Around the universe and back to earth in somebody else's body? To a kingdom inhabited by angels and paved with gold?"

"I don't know the exact location, but I do know with certainty that I'm going home to Olaf and Mama and Daddy. Wherever they are, they are waiting for me."

"How can you be so sure?"

"Because I believe in an Almighty God who through his son, Jesus Christ gave us the blueprint for a good life, then gifted us with the free will to follow it or not. In His house are many mansions and He went ahead to prepare them for us. That's my belief. The Jews have theirs; the Hindus theirs. By whatever conveyance, whatever sacred Entity, all people aspire to reach a higher plateau where there is peace and love and joy and heavenly perfection. Earth is merely a transition. We pass through on the way somewhere else."

It came to me then — was it days, maybe weeks later? — why I wanted Handel's *Messiah*. The CD was for Olaf, so he could hear the glorious music and understand the greatness, the mysteries of Christ. I waved my hand toward the bedside table. "It's there somewhere. Connie brought it."

He was silent, paid no attention. Something mighty was bothering my grandson. "Have you ever thought about suicide?" he asked.

His question was so dire and unexpected that in my mind I bolted upright, though in actuality only my head left the pillow. He got my full and instant attention. "No! Absolutely not! That's the cowardly way out, selfish and self-indulgent. Someone who commits suicide leaves those who loved him saddled with a load of guilt that affects their lives forever. Why are you asking?"

After another long silence, came the choked confession, "I don't want to be a lawyer."

I had to suppress a cackle. That was it? — All of it? How young people turned mole hills into mountains!

"I've made such a mess of things. I don't want to be lawyer. I'm not marrying Barbara — after she left for Pensacola and Dad towed my car away, I began looking for a way out of this mess I've made and I'm stuck — "

"The only mess you've made is to be a dutiful son."

"Babs and I are under so much pressure to marry each other! It's like our parents were engineering a merger not a wedding. We're trapped. I hate it! I hate my life!" He choked on the words. "I don't want to be a lawyer! I hate the law! I hate school!" He wiped his nose on his shirt sleeve, hid his face in his arms and said in a muffled voice, "I'm sorry. I have no business weighing you down — it's just that they have my life all mapped out for me. They've put me in this niche, got me into this rut, and I'm trapped. I can't get out."

I placed my hand on his bowed head — hair thick, red and luxurious like his grandfather's when he was young.

"Let me tell you about these two sisters. The good sister obeyed her parents, did everything they asked. The other went off on her own, told Mom and Dad to fuck it — "

"Gramma! — "

"Jane's exact words — sometimes, you know, you just have to get it off your chest. Jane wandered around the world and ended up in Hawaii. That's where I met her. She was the best surfer on the North Shore. She loved the ocean, lived on the beach in a tent and took up with a dark skinned Polynesian. She managed to scrape together enough money to enroll in the University of Hawaii and earned a degree in oceanography. For years she stumbled here and there — you have to live close to the ocean to get a job under water. Nobody hired a woman for such dangerous work. Oh, yes, she had to battle that bias, too. She finally found work with Shell Oil, Scotland's North Sea, weather rough; waves twenty-feet high. She followed her muse, left the lover behind. She discovered something — a reef, or a deposit of some sort. I can't recall, but it was major, major. She became the most respected person in her field. Her consulting fees ran into thousands. She sent for the Polynesian and brought him to meet Mom and Dad. She'd been alienated from her parents for years. She and the dark-skinned man weren't married and had no intentions of marrying, a real scandal in those days. And you know what?"

"What?"

"Her lovers, live-ins, hippie lifestyle and her lack of interest in anything material didn't matter. Her visit home was like the return of the prodigal son — daughter, in her case. Her parents were so proud of her. They had all her newspaper clippings; recorded every television interview she ever gave; bought the documentaries she made; the books she'd written. What do you think she would've accomplished if she'd stayed home and been a good daughter like her sister?"

"But I'm their only son!" His voice caught in his throat, the anguished cry of an obedient, dutiful son.

"So? I was the only daughter and I eloped with Olaf. Mama and Daddy learned to live with their disappointment. People get over disappointments, but if you eclipse your life to make somebody else happy, that has such a negative effect on you, the chain of discontent travels through from one generation to another."

"Mom says it's natural to have doubts. All of this — " he waved his hands at the house in general, the utter wealth that composed their life — "doesn't make my parents happy."

"No argument there."

He held his head between his hands and pressed his temples, a tormented gesture that touched my heart.

"If you had no one to consider, if you had only you to please, what would you do?"

"Easy! I love tinkering with cars. I went to Giovingo's garage — he's Connie's father, y'know — and the old man and I worked on my Studebaker. He's ancient, but he knows so much! When I looked up, it was dark. Time had no meaning."

The son of the lawyer and the society leader a grease monkey! The idea was so far to the left, such a 90-degree turn in the road that my mind couldn't bend around it.

"I want to design cars — but not just the ordinary kind. In order to do that, you have to know all there is to know about motors and suspensions, transmissions. You can learn it out of a book, but nothing beats hands on. I've designed a prototype of a sleek machine that uses solar power and has retractable wheels and can ascend to a height of sixteen feet. Picture it, Gramma! No traffic jams. Get stuck in a lane, pull back a throttle and your car is in the air!" His eyes sparkled with the genuine light that comes when one truly believes.

I had seen many impossible innovations during my lifetime — TV, cell phones, laser surgery and space travel — and minute inventions like Velcro and Post-Its that made life easier, but a car that lifted into the air and flew? "Then do it," I murmured "It's your life, your decision."

Inner turmoil gritted his teeth. "I might not make it — might spend my entire life doing something that could fail. I won't be rich and respected."

"You can never tell. Van Gogh never sold the first painting and was he successful? I'd say so. Life isn't about money, Olaf. Life is about doing something with your God-given talent, about developing a sense of worth. Your father is a good lawyer because he values what he does. You have to trust your instincts."

"Yeah, sure — how am I going to face Mom and tell her I want to drop out of Tulane and be a mechanic?"

The thought was so ridiculous, we both burst out laughing.

"It'll be difficult," I said, "but she has her reasonable moments." I found the Bible by my bed. Waiting to go, the blueprint became all important. I flipped through the well worn pages. "Read her this." I handed Olaf the Bible opened to Corinthians.

He gingerly held the Sacred Book as if it was an egg and the shell easily broken. He scanned the passage where the Apostle Paul wrote to the congregation that every part of a body was of equal importance, the feet as necessary as the eye, the hand as significant as the ear. Olaf looked at me, his lopsided grin back in place. "You think she'll buy a mechanic being as important as a lawyer?"

"The lawyer does have to get in his car and drive to work, doesn't he?"

"They've spent so much money sending me to Tulane. Dad's whole family graduated from Tulane."

"And you're so near the end — why not finish then do whatever you want?"

"I've thought about that. But I'm afraid a diploma will eliminate any choice I might have."

"Could very well be — " The decisions my inexperienced grandson made at this stage of his life would forever affect him. Would that old people had young people's energy and that young people had the wisdom acquired with age!

My Mama and Nanny Carmen cried for days when they heard that Olaf and I had eloped. My last summer at home, after Olaf came down from the hills, he asked me to come with him to Hawaii. I said no — my father would forbid such a trip; my mother would be heartbroken. I dutifully returned for my last year at Newcomb College, unpacked my suitcase and strolled around the campus, talked to my returning friends, sat through a few classes, the familiar enveloping me like a warm security blanket. Newcomb was a good school and I loved the challenge, the academic atmosphere, the intense concentration to reach the end and graduation. I was a good obedient daughter and following my parent's plans for me wasn't a hardship until Olaf offered an alternative. I remembered Zoila's words when Margo let Captain Jack walk out of her life — 'If Margo wanted that man enough, she would give into her passion and chase after him.'

I repacked my suitcase and bought a ticket to Maui. I called Olaf from the airport. He was so excited! We ran toward each other and he lifted me off my feet, twirled me around and showered me with kisses. His arms were home. I was safe there, happy, comfortable, warm. Nothing else in the whole entire world, in the vast universe mattered. We were together again, now and forever. We were meant to be.

Nanny Carmen said Mama who coped with every tragedy, solved every problem, took care of everyone's needs, the pillar of strength, collapsed and took to her bed. Daddy couldn't believe his sweet young daughter had turned into a disobedient rebel. He sent a telegram: "*Come home immediately.*" I replied with one word: "*NO.*"

Life was a series of crossroads and everyone arrived at the crucial point carrying their baggage. My grandson was no different. He was filled with angst.

"I don't know what to do! What should I do?"

"Only you can decide that. Find that CD on the table, go over there and slip it in the machine, listen to the glory of God, the wonder of God, unfetter your mind, loosen the ties that bind, and do what your heart tells you."

The glorious music of Handel's Messiah filled the room.

***

When Connie brought the lunch tray, she was strangely subdued.

Olaf asked roughly, "and what's wrong with you?"

"Nothing — " she wasn't a natural born liar. She set down the tray. "Wayne, can you help her? I'll be in the kitchen."

"In the kitchen!" we both exclaimed at once.

"Mrs. Kennedy thinks that as long as Olaf is sitting by Mrs. Van Nuy's bedside, there's no point in two of us being here, and she's probably right. I can help in the kitchen."

Katherine must be losing her mind. The three of us huddled like football players in a losing game. We needed a supreme strategy to conquer this latest challenge. When did this situation turn into us against her?

"I know — I know — I know," I said.

Olaf asked, "What do you know, Gramma?"

"Connie must quit. Katsy has left her no choice. There are other jobs, other old people who need her special care. You, Olaf, have to get a grip and start living your own life."

The young people turned to each other, a deep, penetrating look in their eyes. "And you?" asked Connie, gently rubbing my arm. "What about you?"

***

After Connie left, hopefully not for the kitchen, Olaf said, "Mom has to control everything and everybody. Somebody told Mom I took Connie to the movies. You know how it is here — a person can't do anything without it being broadcast all over town."

"You took Connie to the movies — when?" The girl worked days, studied nights. "She didn't mention having a date with you."

"Last Saturday after Barbara threw her fit and Daddy towed my car, I was mad as hell at everybody. Connie and I got to talking — she saved my wheels, y'know. She went to the movies with me to cheer me up. She has that kindness about her, y'know, always wanting to fix things, make everybody happy. Unfortunately, Jimmy Monroe, Barbara's brother was there. That didn't help matters much. He must've told his Mom who told my Mom. So — " after a prolonged silence, he asked, "You really ran off with my grandfather?"

"Sure did."

"After the dance — when he fell off the balcony?"

"Oh, no, — Years later. After the episode at the club, he hobbled around on crutches for six weeks."

"Last night I listened to your *Messiah*, over and over again," he said, "and I brought you something. Remember I said I would?" He dug in his pocket. "You said you wanted to try a joint." He withdrew a lighter, lit one end of the funny looking cigarette, took a puff and placed the slim cylinder between my lips, instructing me to draw easily so I wouldn't choke.

With trembling fingers I held the joint and inhaled deeply, held the smoke in my mouth, then let it out and giggled, my voice cracking and tinkling like glass shattering. A sweet aroma permeated the room. I felt young and mischievous, doing the forbidden once again, breaking the rules, swinging over the cliff, one-upping Katherine.

"You like it?" Olaf asked.

"Don't tell your mother."

"I guess not! Finish telling me about the dance."

"Aren't you tired of all that ancient history?"

"No. I want to hear more. What happened after the dance?"

I didn't answer right then and there. Olaf patiently waited until the joint burnt down to a stub, then he took it, left the room and flushed it down the toilet.

Somehow or other, I was floating above the bed, a light-headed sensation, and the colors were very bright, strong, deep colors that I liked, that I used in my paintings, my paintings that Katherine didn't like and never hung up in her decorator perfect mansion.

"After Olaf got off crutches, his father exiled him to Trinity Lutheran High School in Boston. I finished the eighth grade and came to Sacred Heart Academy in New Orleans. Olaf and I sailed on the S. S. Preston with Captain Jack. We left Cuba behind, but carried the island in our hearts. We made a pact to stay in touch, a youthful oath, pricked our fingers and blended our blood. I never heard from him again. I came home in the summer and vacationed on Puerto Bello beach. Mr. Van Nuys wouldn't let Olaf come home. I didn't see him for four years. Olaf spent every summer at his grandparent's tulip farm near Amsterdam where he hoed and weeded the long flower rows and got reacquainted with his sister, Birgette, and her toddler, Ilsa. He became very attached to Ilsa. Ilsita, he called the child, but he grew to hate flowers, any flower, but particularly tulips. I'd plant a rose bush or caladiums and he'd run right over them with the lawn mower. We had constant fights over my garden. His mother became a total drunk. Mr. Van Nuys crossed the bridge and found himself a woman." My throat felt dry and scratchy. "Water? — A little water, please, Olaf."

He shook the pitcher. "I'll go get some more."

He left the room and I sank into the past, into the warm sunny world where palms waved in the breeze, hibiscuses bloomed big as dinner plates, the air carried a strong cigar smell and bongo drums beat a steady rhythm.

***

Olaf was nineteen years old the summer he graduated from Trinity Lutheran High School in Boston and came home for the summer. He announced to his father, 'If you make me go to college, I'll flunk out.'

The elder Van Nuys had spent good money sending Olaf to Trinity and this was the thanks he got. Four years in a hard-line school advocating strong discipline, and his son returned with a high school diploma and no change in attitude.

'You'll do as I say,' the father said.

'Don't ruin my summer, Pops.'

'Pops? — '

'Daddy-O — '

Gretchen raised her gin and tonic and favored her son with a lopsided smile, 'Cheeri-O — , Daddy-O.'

The Van Nuys sat on their veranda. The June afternoon heat warmed the still air. The humidity was stifling. Not a good day for an argument.

'If you don't go to college, what do you propose to do?' Olaf's father asked, tight lipped.

'Join the Marines.'

'You're Dutch, not American.'

'They'll let Dutch enlist.'

'If they do, it won't be you.'

Cuba on My Mind

A sullen silence enveloped the veranda, father and son in deep thought, donning their battle armor.

Olaf's mother fanned herself with a straw mat and broke the stillness. 'There's no telling where you'd end up with that outfit. I do like their uniforms, though — very smart.' She swallowed gin tonic and made a gurgling sound. 'Here's a better idea. Why don't you join Fidel Castro's revolution? He's stumbling around up in the Sierras vowing to overthrow Dictator Batista. He's gathered a little band together. They make a lot of noise.'

His father lost patience, 'For heaven's sake, Gretchen.'

'It's a lot closer,' replied Gretchen. 'And you know the rebels and Batista soldiers only skirmish five days a week. Saturday and Sunday everybody hikes up the trails and picnics with the troops. You could come home on weekends, Olaf. I'd like that. I've missed you. It's been lonesome here — Birgette gone, you gone and soon Gretchie will leave us, too.' The thought was more than she could bear. She wailed for another drink, whining like high wind.

Her husband drummed the rocker arm, willing patience. 'You don't know what you're saying. You're drunk.'

'Don't be silly. I know perfectly well what I'm saying. It's a noble, hopeless revolution. Those wretched people have no guns and no bullets. Olaf would be perfectly safe with them.' The conversation tired her out. She closed her eyes.

Mr. Van Nuys removed the glass from her hand. 'I don't know what to do with her.'

'Grandmother Van Nuys thinks you're cruel to keep Mom here. She thinks you should bring her back to Amsterdam.'

'In three years I retire. I can't just chuck it all and leave.'

'In three years the peasants will have taken over the country and you won't have a choice but to leave.'

'I doubt that. This will all blow over, the same as the other uprisings have.'

'Is it true they have no weapons?'

'Pretty much — they operate by disruption, tearing up train tracks, digging trenches across the roads, stealing gas. It's an aggravation, but hardly a menace.'

'I think before I join up, I'll go for a long swim. Is that okay?'

His mother opened her eyes a slit. 'You can't swim up the mountain,' she said.

***

How I missed the ocean! The warm sand beach! The drifting seaweed! The wind carrying the salty smell! The sun! The palm trees! The coconuts, mangoes, yellow banana spread like hands and sea grapes that dyed the tongue purple! The mountains! The jungles! Everything! The musical lilt of Spanish!

A first language came naturally. The second one, super-imposed over the first, required even unconscious concentration, an alert mind. The South's drawl was nowhere near the British English Miss Kelly taught us or Daddy's Scottish burr. Adjusting to the new sounds took months. I had trouble recognizing words buried in dialect. Southerners called everyone 'hawney' and 'shugah' common endearments, referring to sweetness; 'y'all' meant everybody; and 'fixin' dinner' was a meal being prepared not repaired. Then there was a catch-all, impossible word — 'mess' — your face is a mess; he caught a mess of fish; don't mess with me.

Daddy had assured me New Orleans had a tropical climate. Then why were the winters so harsh? I'd wake up in January, look out the dorm window and see white frost coating the roofs across the street, the drainage ditches covered with thin ice, and in the air, a piercing, humid chill that hurt the bones. The first year I bought sweaters and warm socks and a wool coat, heavy, uncomfortable clothing.

Between school terms, I returned from exile. Not having to think to understand was like a mental vacation. I spent three glorious, lazy months at our cottage by the sea, tanning my body and absorbing my surroundings. To humor me, Daddy and Mama left the West Indies Banes house and moved eight miles across the mountain and to the beach, though they seldom stayed for long. They were too busy, Daddy running the company and Mama not so secretly helping the revolutionary movement. They came and went. Instead of Manco, the big Haitian, Ugo, stayed with Carmen and me. My parents couldn't spare Manco. He had become their trusted, right-armed man.

When I graduated from Sacred Heart High School and returned home for the summer, I was so anxious to see the beach!

'I'll drive,' I told José, jumping behind the Jeep's steering wheel.

He got in the passenger seat. Carmen sat in the back, every spare inch round us packed with supplies — food, linens, silverware. Nothing was ever left at the beach house that the humidity didn't cover with green mold.

Eight miles was a short distance in the States, but not so in the tropics. The road hacked through the mountain jungle was a dirt lane, passable in dry weather, but last night's rain turned the narrow lane to mud. A truck had slipped and slid and lay overturned in a gully, stuck in red mud. Two men leaned against the front fender and smoked cigarettes.

I was home! — home with people who knew not road rage or time clocks, who weren't impatient to get anywhere, who intrinsically understood that every problem would eventually be solved and there was no point in fretting about it; who knew the first vehicle to appear would not pass them by.

I stopped the Jeep and José called out, '*Que pasa, amigo?*'

The mustached man laughed. 'Here we are.'

José jumped from the Jeep and walked to the rear. Groaning her objections, Carmen climbed down from the back seat. José moved aside the boxes looking for the hook and chain.

While the three men dragged the chain and decided where to place the hook, the clouds like a flock wooly white sheep moved west and the sun came out with magnificent force. The heat bathed the men in sweat and they took a cigarette break. One shimmied up a coconut trunk, took out his machete and cut green coconuts. They fell to the ground like unexploded bombs. With one quick motion, the second man sliced off the top and brought Carmen and me two coconuts filled with cool, delicious water.

'*Gracias,*' Carmen said.

After another smoke and more coconut water, José said, 'Here, let me,' and I jumped from behind the wheel.

The sun was straight in the sky when with much yelling and shouting, wheels spinning and splattering mud, the overturned truck was back on the road again.

What a glory to see the horizon! How I missed that defining arc, that curving line that delineated the end of the world as far as the eye could see and the heart could comprehend. This wonderful parameter was lost when living inland.

I raced through the beach house, wriggled into a bathing suit and was on the strand, running toward our ocean swimming pool before Carmen and José had removed the first box from the Jeep. I scampered down the seaweed strewn beach, arms opened wide, taking in my world — blue sea, green mountains, golden sand, the endless sky. I ran down the familiar planks of the boardwalk enclosing our swimming area and plunged head first into a cresting wave. Surfacing, I became one with the universal movement, born to the rhythm and the flow. I swam to the floating platform anchored midway and climbed the ladder.

The tide was at its peak, the ocean one huge roll and swell, inhaling, exhaling, a gigantic watery lung gasping in measured sequence, trapped between the horizon and the shore.

Sitting on the floating platform, cleansing, healing salt water washing over me, I regretted that my first dip into the sea hadn't been at low tide, when the water was calm as glass and swimming was like jumping into an aquarium filled with tropical fish-orange, yellow, black, violet, iridescent green, blue, the sardine schools a moving silver slash. Stinging lavender globs hung suspended, tentacles drifting. Through the clear aquamarine water the sandy bottom was visible and the sea denizens flittered, darted and shimmered, a living, moving biota, my first painting.

Now, at high tide, I was grateful for the concrete piling driven at intervals into the ocean bottom. The grid let water in and kept big fish out. A boardwalk ran all the way around the enclosure. The big rollers washed over the diving boards placed at the two furthest corners and over the benches on the beach side.

The water was warm; the sun glowing. The moon would be out tonight, golden and full. Beach bums worshipped the sun and respected the moon. The sun was bigger, stronger more powerful, but the sweet, romantic moon controlled the tides.

Someone hollered.

I shaded my eyes with a hand and looked blindly into the glare. Olaf? It was Olaf! Olaf was home!

He stood on the boardwalk clad in white trunks, his normally golden skin milky white from Boston winters and Amsterdam's tropical deprivation. He waved his arms over his head, pointing to something.

A huge wave swept two dolphins over the boardwalk, trapped them inside the swimming pool enclosure. They swam circles, rising out of the water, arching their backs, sliding under.

Olaf dove in. His lung capacity far exceeded mine. Once, we had timed each other and he stayed under for an amazing two minutes, while I managed to hold my breath a little over one. 'Hi,' he said, emerging near the ladder, gagging and choking on brine, shaking water from his eyes and ears. 'Let's ride!'

Four years apart melted like ice cream in hot weather. Our separation hadn't abolished his daring taunts, nor quenched the spark that made me rise to the challenge. With outstanding ease and comfort, the years dissolved and we resumed our lives exactly where we'd left off.

The first dolphin passed very close to me. I grabbed for the slippery dorsal fin. Missed!

The second dolphin shot past and when it dipped, Olaf rolled upon its back.

If he could do it, so could I!

Water streamed off the dolphin's sleek back as it broke the surface and lunged in a great upward arc. I seized a tail fluke. As the fish headed downward, I clung tightly, light-headed, holding my breath. My eardrums rang from the pressure. The dolphin's squeaks and whistles, their life song, vibrated through my body like electric tremors. My lungs were about to burst.

I twisted my body this way, that way, maneuvering the fish out of its blind circling toward the open sea.

The timing had to be precise. The force of the incoming wave had to be withstood; the outgoing one caught exactly when it crested, when the swell reached its peak and the spewing white foam swept over the boardwalk.

On the third try, the dolphin and I washed over the man-made barrier into the open ocean. The fish traveled swiftly, slipping through the waves, rising and dipping, going under and breaking the surface.

We hung onto the tough, slippery backs. For a distance the fish swam together. Dolphins were playful. They liked company. Seldom did one see a lone dolphin. Olaf and I rode side by side, clinging to fins and flukes, dipping, rising, submerging and exploding to the surface, water cascading from our heads and shoulders.

'The dolphins came to greet us!' I yelled against the wind. 'You think they missed us?'

The fish, saddled with the unfamiliar weight, headed for the outer reef. The waves crashing against the rocks were like steeds with foaming white manes and muscled legs drawn to jump a barrier. Beyond the coral, the sea floor plunged abruptly and the water went from blue to deep purple.

The sun disappeared behind a cloud bank, taking with it the diamond sparkles dancing on the water. A late afternoon thunderstorm, a quick, unexpected tropical burst, turned the sky a molten gray, the sea a leaden gray, the wind and rain a misty gray. The raindrops stung like needles.

Olaf and I slid off the dolphins. My foot hit the sharp coral. We turned our faces toward the thin white shoreline a good distance away, swimming Australian crawl, breast stroke, side stroke, free style; other times floating on our backs, rain like a whip lash, terns curiously watching as they bravely danced in the wind, curtsying to the waves.

The rain didn't stop and we'd made little progress, our strokes powerless against the wind and waves that pushed and pulled us back and forth. Without the warming sun, the water quickly turned cold. Too tired to swim, we treaded water.

A huge waved dragged us under. We emerged coughing and wheezing. 'Keep moving,' Olaf cried. 'It'll pass.'

Salt stung my foot. I felt the gash. Bleeding? Sharks smelled blood. 'Olaf! Olaf!'

The current had pushed us apart. I lost sight of him, and barely heard his cry, 'Here! Over here!'

Darkness came quickly, a black curtain abruptly descending. On the shore far away one dim yellow glow was visible. That would be the *cofradia*, the fisherman's clubhouse. That beacon was lit every night for fishermen returning after dark.

Something touched my leg and I cried out.

'It's ... me,' Olaf wheezed between breaths. 'Stay ... together.'

Born by the sea, we loved it and had a natural fear of it, for we knew what it did in anger. We bobbed up and down interminably.

'It's passing,' gasped Olaf.

Abruptly, the same way the storm arrived, it departed. The rain stopped and the thunder melted. The wind dwindled. Only the ocean stayed angry.

Above the roaring waves and the whining wind, we both heard a strange, creaking sound. Again, it came — a long creak, a silence, another creak. A long, dark shadow glided over the opening in the reef, one piercing yellow eye.

My teeth chattered beyond control. Olaf shucked his white bathing trunks and waved them in the air. 'Here! Here!' The yellow eye moved closer. The creaking grew louder. 'It's a boat! Yell! Yell!'

A dark shadow rowed standing, the skiff steady in the water, riding the heavy waves. A lantern mounted on a pole cast the eerie light. The fisherman extended an oar, yelled, 'Grab it! Grab it!'

After several tries, we both flopped into the boat, nearly swamping it.

'*Cuidado*,' the fisherman spoke in Spanish. 'You don't want to be shark bait.' He hit the water with his flat oar. 'Get away from here, you heathen.'

The fisherman's trained eye followed the fin we couldn't see as it cut a line through the dark water.

The boat was filled with fish not quite dead, strong smelling, flipping and flopping in the skiff's bottom. I slipped and slid through the slimy pile, looking for a place to sit and found a coiled net near the prow.

'I'll put the sail up,' the fisherman said. 'The wind is normal.'

'I'll help,' volunteered Olaf as he unsteadily wriggled back into his bathing trunks.

'Just stay where you are.'

The fisherman struggled with the mast, raised the sail and adjusted its angle. The steady wind caught the canvas and it billowed out and we sailed easily toward the single light in the little harbor.

When I jumped out of the boat, a wave caught me behind the knees and I toppled. Olaf helped the fisherman pull the skiff as far up on the sand then waded over to where I floated face-down in the water. He grabbed me around the waist and pulled me ashore. I flopped like a half-dead fish upon the beach.

'The great swimmer drowned?'

I didn't answer.

'Catica — ' he used the familiar, endearing form of Catalina.

I rolled over gasping and shuddering, sticking a finger in my ear, blowing salt spray out my nose and laughed, 'Never! — I can out swim you any day of the week.'

'But never on Sunday.'

His eyes met mine and we touched upon a perfect understanding, a knowledge deep and true that bypassed reason and logic and came straight from just knowing, the way one knew hunger, or breathing, or approaching death and we both looked quickly away, as if we'd unintentionally plucked a hidden string that sent forth, like the dolphin's song, secret vibrations.

The fisherman took down the mast, rolled up the sail, and tied it securely.

'What about the fish?' Olaf asked the fisherman. 'Can we help you?'

'Leave it alone,' the man replied. 'My boy will take care of it. Let's go into the *cofradia* for hot coffee.'

'Thank you very much.' I wrapped my arms around myself to keep warm as I limped to the clubhouse. 'You saved us.'

'You are fools,' said the fisherman.

Olaf said, 'And you are Rojas. I know that white beard. Remember me? I helped you mend your nets one rainy afternoon many summers ago.'

'The boy with the head of fire? — '

'Yep, that was me.'

'Where have you been?'

'Away at school — you have a great catch today. What kind?'

'Red snappers, mostly, — magnificent catch — three days' work. I was close to Haitian waters. Juan and I will sell them at the market tomorrow.'

'Lucky for us you were late,' Olaf said. 'We could still be treading water out there.'

'Probably not — sharks eat you by now.'

Beneath the thatched roof of the clubhouse portico several men huddled. As we approached, someone lit another carbide lamp.

In the dim glow cast by the hanging lanterns Rojas was the first to see the uniforms blocking the way. 'Here they come.' he said. 'You'd best get your story straight and stick to it. Find a good reason for being out at sea in the night. These Batista people twist things to suit themselves. They are very nervous.'

Two guards followed a flashlight's yellow beam. They shone the light in our faces and we halted. They had pistols strapped to their belts.

Rojas greeted the one walking slightly ahead. 'Hola, Bebo.'

Bebo! The mean, hateful guard who'd thrown Reverend Juarez in jail, who'd kicked the sailor, harassed the street woman; the brutish pig that was happiest when terrifying someone.

'Hola, amigo, are these the missing ones?' He pointed to Olaf and to me shivering in wet bathing suits.

'These are the only two I saw about to drown out there.'

Olaf introduced himself. 'I'm Olaf Van Nuys and this is Catalin — '

'Spare me the formalities. I know who you are,' the guard, Bebo, said. 'Señor Van Nuys called the Coast Guard. They are looking for you. He also called us. The mountains are our jurisdiction. He had a premonition that you had gone to the Sierras to join the rebels. Now, that's not true, is it?' Soft, smooth voice with steel edge; an iron fist in a velvet glove.

Olaf and I lived in the American Colony. This insolent guard had no authority in our compound. Chief Heinz was in charge there. I laughed in his face. 'Why in the world would Olaf want to do that?'

Bebo's sinister smile lifted his handlebar mustache and sank his weasel eyes into his fat cheeks. 'A little adventure, maybe?'

Olaf bristled. 'And what if I do go? What business is it of yours?'

Wrong question! I knew that right away.

'That, my man, is not advisable.' And as if turning a new page, knowing our chapter was closed, he couldn't touch us, he turned his attention to Rojas, 'What's in the boat, amigo?'

'Three days' work."

'You return at this late hour? —'

'The fish were biting.'

'And what else?'

'Nothing else — '

Bebo turned to his partner, who'd been silent so far. They looked at each other solemnly, then suddenly, without warning, as if they'd agreed on a plan through telepathic communication, they took three big steps forward. I jumped to one side, Olaf to the other. Rojas stood his ground. Bebo pushed him roughly aside. The fisherman watched helplessly as the two guards grabbed the wooden skiff and rocked it from side to side. They overturned the boat.

'You can't do that!' Olaf cried.

'Yes, they can,' said Rojas, 'sons of bitches.'

The silver, red-bellied fish slid into the water. The nets, harpoon, fish lines and hooks bobbed a few minutes, then disappeared. The plastic water jug danced on the waves.

Chapter 18

When Olaf and I returned to my beach house, Carmen was un-raveling like a ball of yarn, agitated beyond reason — 'By God! By God! And you in my charge!' She threw her arms around me and showered my face with kisses 'My little girl! My little girl! What was I to do?' She grabbed my shoulders and shook me. 'Don't you ever dare do that again, you hear me? I must've walked a hundred kilometers looking for you! Your mother has sent for us! We are to go home to-morrow! Where have you been?'

'We were at the *cofradia*. They dumped Roja's fish — '

'I don't care about that. I can't find you! I'm looking every-where!'

'Don't have a heart attack.'

'And you — you!' She poked Olaf in the chest with a closed fist. 'You're nothing but trouble. No good! Trouble! Get out of here!'

'Okay! Okay!' Olaf yelled at her. 'I'm going to my house!'

The Van Nuys had their own house. Every USSCo employee was assigned a beach house.

'Be careful,' I said.

He smiled his lopsided grin. 'Careful takes the joy out of life.'

'Come inside,' Carmen snapped, her patience worn thin.

'I need to go to the bathroom.'

She wasn't about to let me disappear again. 'I'll go with you.'

She held the kerosene lamp high as we made our way to the out-house. Daddy had designed an innovation soon copied by others. He'd built a raised platform and installed a toilet seat with a lid over the hole in the ground. The place was a smelly closet.

'You're coming in with me?'

'You're not funny. Here's the lamp and I'll be right outside.'

I entered the closet, shoved the door shut, and latched it closed with the leather loop that hooked to a nail. A kerosene glow lit the cubicle. Through the cracks in the plank door, I saw Nanny Carmen's bulky shadow guarding the entrance – 'How about a cup of tea?'

'We don't have the Lipton you like. It's all gone.'

'Coffee, then – '

'A little flan? – you must be hungry.'

We were back on sure footing again. My business finished, Nanny and I followed the path to the house. The night was black as pitch. The lamp cast a small circular glow. We placed our surroundings by sound: the ocean's measured roar, the mountain wind's whining complaint, the windmill's creaking blades.

The beach house was built on pilings, the height necessary to be above high tide; split palm trunks for wall; thatched fronds for a roof.

'I'm sleeping down here,' I said, pointing to the black void beneath the house. The hammock strung between two posts next to a storage room that held the beach paraphernalia, life vests, floats, towels, sand buckets, plastic shovels, was my favorite bed.

'Don't even think it. Only one sleeping down here is Big Ugo. Nothing is safe anymore. It's dangerous. Besides, we haven't straightened down here yet. The chairs and tables are still half-buried in sand.'

She pushed me ahead, up the stairs to the open porch above. Behind it were an enclosed sleeping area and a crude kitchen. The billowing wind turned the windmill paddles that provided electricity. The bare yellow bulbs hanging from the rafters blinked uncertainly and cast an opaque glow.

'Take a hot bath,' Carmen said. 'I will heat the water.'

Rain had filled the cistern and wind powered the windmill. All systems were on go, otherwise it was kerosene lamps and water stored in jugs.

As I sat eating flan and sipping coffee, I heard Nanny and Big Ugo talking in the kitchen. He was stoking the wood stove to heat the water and by his tone he was flirting with Carmen, though there was no understanding what he said, his deep gruff voice an impossible mixture of French patois and Spanish. After a while he carried two big buckets into the bathroom cubicle and filled the tin tub with steaming water.

Carmen poured in bubble bath I had brought from the States and I sank deep into the soapy froth, relaxing in the tub. How wonderful to be home!

Next morning Carmen was in a fever to return to Banes. She came from the mountains and hated the beach. Sending her to Puerto Bello for three months was as bad for her as nine months in Louisiana were for me.

The three of us piled into the jeep, Ugo taking up the whole back seat, and I drove up the mountain trail to the crest. I looked over my shoulder and saw the ocean five miles away, the spot where the worshippers brought the sainted virgin to pray for rain. We descended on the other side into Banes, past the railroad yard, the hospital, the USSCo office buildings, and up steep Calle Iglesia, the white clapboard Adventist Church on the corner, the rambling yellow boarding house for single employees, the egg-yolk colored stucco dwellings with red tile roofs, paradise hemmed by scarlet bougainvillea. We reached our hilltop house and I stopped the Jeep abruptly, stunned by what I saw.

People gathered on our driveway blocked our way. It appeared as if an entire civil guard platoon milled about. Men holding large cameras with flash attachments pushed close to the padlocked main gate. Our gate was never closed, much less chained shut. A soldier with an M-16 slung over his shoulder blocked the entrance.

What was this armed guard doing here? Had the militia come to arrest Mama for her political activities? — her open criticism of the president? — her activism for the poor and the disenfranchised? How often had I heard Daddy warn Mama that what she was doing was extremely dangerous? She not only jeopardized her own safety, but she was compromising the safety of the company and all its employees. 'And what about the Cuban people? — ' Mama always replied, fire in her eyes. 'What about their future? Does that matter to U. S. Sugar?'

I looked nervously at the guards, the photographers, the town people who seldom crossed into the American Colony, milling around our gate. A respectful distance away, the beggars gathered, hands extended more from habit than expectancy.

'What is it?' I asked Carmen.

'Who knows? Those bastards probably took over the house — USSCo, too. Things aren't the same.'

A guard approached us and said, 'You must leave.'

The crowd turned, watching.

'*Qué pasa?* – ' Carmen asked the armed soldier.

'Nobody enters,' he replied. 'The General is coming.'

Carmen found that hard to believe, 'Batista?'

'What other General is there?'

'Well, let us through. We live here.'

'Nobody passes.'

In the back seat, Ugo was struck mute. Sweat dampened his forehead and glistened on his black cheeks. Fear's rancid odor enveloped him. He slapped his chest and moaned, 'I have no papers, no papers.' He swung his heavy legs over the side and with a crouching run disappeared into the crowd.

A defiant Carmen got out of the Jeep. 'Come on,' she said to me. 'This goose can't keep us from entering our own house.'

She took a step to circumvent the soldier. With one swift, practiced motion, the M-16 was off his shoulder and poking her in the stomach.

'Oh, for heaven's sakes!' Carmen swatted the barrel aside with the same force and determination with which she'd chopped the snake's head. 'Put that thing up before you kill somebody. This is Catalina McAuley, the Administrator's daughter.' She grasped my elbow and pulled me forward and ordered the soldier, 'Go inside. Ask somebody. We'll wait here. Look, there comes José.' She raised her arms above her head and waved, 'José! José! Go find Caridad, or Mister Hoo. Tell them this man won't let us in.'

Eventually, the soldier let Carmen and me through without further incident. Mama met us at the door. She kissed me lightly on the cheek. 'Get dressed right away. President Batista is on his way. Hurry! – hurry!'

The tension in the house made the floor boards creak. The apprehension exuded enough pressure to buckle the walls. The usually ebullient servants glided from room to room like shadows. Earlier, the militia had entered the house, gone through every room, opened every drawer and looked into every closet. One soldier had gone so far as to lift the heavy black iron pot lid and taste the stew cooking on the stove, causing Margarita to cower in her own kitchen. The cook lacked Carmen's mettle.

Carmen said, 'Take a quick shower.'

I was in and out in no time. I entered the bedroom wrapped in a towel.

'Put this on,' Carmen held a green sheath with pink roses, 'Hurry!'

'Carmen, remember the day we rode in the Sierras? When we went to see your family? I talked to the peasants.'

'Hush. Let me comb your hair.'

'They were all for Fidel. They're supplying him with food and shelter. They say they're Fidel's own private CIA. Nobody gets past them to the top of the mountain.'

'Shhh, girl — don't say such things. Anybody can hear. Quick, put these on.' She held the green dance slippers in her hands. 'Come. Come. Let's do something with your hair,' and running a comb through the unruly auburn curls, she admonished, 'Catica, go in there and be nice. Be careful what you say. Don't stir up The Man.'

'The pretty mulatto? — '

'Oh, my God — there you go. If he hears that, he'll send you to the dungeon. Be polite for your mother's sake. Come! Come! Let's go. He's coming! He's coming!'

Mama and Daddy sat on the veranda rockers waiting for the honored guest. Mama's rocker creaked as it moved back and forth. Daddy's clasped hands rested on his knees. Both had their eyes trained on the flower-lined walk leading from the street to the front door. The president stood under the gate's scarlet bougainvillea arbor, posing for photographers. Flashbulbs went off. The general wasn't clad in his usual uniform adorned with ribbons and medals. He wore a white linen suit. He'd discarded the visor military cap for a smart Panama straw.

My bedroom window opened onto the veranda. I heard Mama

and Daddy talking, their voices low and reserved.

'Today,' Daddy said, 'our man is not the army dictator who rules by force. He is a business man, a civilian, like me.'

'That is not so,' Mama replied through clenched teeth, a smile of greeting tight on her lips. 'You don't walk around with six armed guards.'

'But I do have the big Haitian. Ugo could toss those six without much effort.' Daddy snickered. 'President Truman must be mad as hell.'

'The very idea of sending American troops to monitor our voting! Who does he think he is? That American muscle of theirs! So obvious! So insulting! We would've stopped Batista and held democratic elections ourselves if Truman had only left us alone. I know it!'

'So much for democratic Cuba, the example for all Latin America to follow,' Daddy couldn't resist gouging Mama a bit. 'You know the Americans consider Cuba their territory, another Puerto Rico. I bet it never entered Truman's head that Batista would board a yacht in broad daylight, sail from Miami, rally his old army buddies and cancel the election. Batista left Truman with egg on his face,' Daddy mused. 'There must be consequences.'

'We've had consequences! — Eddie Chibás dead!' Mama's agitation added a timbre to her voice. She had actively supported Eddie Chibás for president, incurring both Daddy's wrath and the U. S. Sugar Company's. Her actions negated the neutrality of the foreign powers.

'Democracy is a wonderful thing in theory,' Daddy said. 'In practice it is war and bloodshed. Chibás was destined for death, one way or another. He set himself up. Either Batista or the Americans or a disgruntled follower was bound to bring him down. He knew that.'

'He was a great man. He wept over our future.'

Mama sat down the entire household and made us listen to CMQ 'Hour of the People,' Chibás's program following the Albertíco Limón soap opera. He spoke at length over the glorious future awaiting Cuba once the populace roused and went to the polls and elected a leader of their very own choice. He exhorted the people, urging them to rally and take control. Their destiny was in their hands — a simple "X" on a ballot. Listeners glued to radios heard his plea: 'Fight forever! Never give up!' After a long, static-filled pause, he quoted the well-known line from the national anthem, *Himno de Bayamo,* 'To die for the country is to live!'

The shot was heard from one end of the island to the other. The country reeled from the consequences. Chibás's death made it so easy for Batista.

'Freeze that smile,' Daddy said. 'Here he comes.'

Dictator Batista passed through the crimson arbor and came down the flower-bordered lane. He walked in the sun's spotlight, in noon's silver heat, flanked by six men in khaki uniforms and dark glasses. He swaggered toward the veranda, a definite strut to his stride, a man who had conquered all and knew it.

The house servants peeked from behind the curtains. Carmen, agog with excitement said, 'There he is! *El Hombre!*'

'*El Sargentico!*' I said with great sarcasm. We'd studied in school how the Little Sergeant had back in the '30s rallied the army and deposed the then dictator, the cruel and ruthless Machado. The lowly foot soldier was Cuba's new savior.

'*El Guajirito de Banes,*' Nanny Carmen said — the little peasant from Banes.

And then, to end it together on a high note, we both cried, '*El Tigre!*' the Tiger.

My parents rose and greeted the President with formality. Daddy extended his hand. 'Welcome.'

Mama didn't trust her tongue to form flattering words. Batista removed the Panama hat. His jet black hair, pomaded and slick, grew straight from his forehead without part or widow's peak, thick and shaped like a helmet. He brought Mama's outstretched hand to his lips and kissed the fingertips.

She mustered a bland compliment. 'The people are very happy about the new park in La Guira.'

The dark, miserable slum across the Banes River was Batista's birth place. In the shanty town lived the down-and-out, mixed breeds, displaced Indians, Negroes without work, beggars, and derelicts — lesser people. This uncertain background showed in Batista's dark, round face, an unusual face because he was clean shaven, without mustache or beard, uncommon for a Cuban man. He had flat nostrils, thick arched brows, and quick sharp eyes with a slight oblique tilt, features attributed to a mixed Asian-European-African ancestry.

'This afternoon when you unveil your mother's bust, we will be at the ceremony,' Mama said. 'A beautiful gesture.'

Behind the curtains, I whispered to Nanny Carmen, 'I thought she hated him.'

'She does,' replied Carmen.

'She's not acting like it. Remember she said it was a crime and a sin to make his mother's bust bigger than José Martí's, and worse yet to have the nerve to place it higher. Nobody, she said, was above José Martí.'

'By God, girl, El Hombre is the president. She has to be courteous.'

Daddy ushered President Batista and his two bodyguards into the living room. The four armed soldiers remained on the veranda.

'Please have a seat, General.' Daddy motioned to the bodyguards, 'Please. Have a seat.'

Two cushioned couches faced each other on either side of a glass-topped coffee table with ivory tusk legs. The president ignored their comfort and sat in a straight-armed, cane-bottomed mahogany chair. His back to the wall, he faced the entrance. Mama sat on the edge of her chair, her slim ankles crossed. 'It's our pleasure to introduce you to our daughter.'

That was my cue. I stepped into the room in my high heeled green shoes, holding my head high like Mama had taught me.

President Fulgencio Batista rose. So did the bodyguards. So did Daddy. Only Mama was left seated.

'My pleasure,' I murmured, extending my hand. I was head and shoulders taller than he was.

The president clasped my hands. His palms were warm and moist. 'The pleasure is mine.' He turned to his hosts. 'You have a beautiful daughter. Where have you been hiding her?'

Mama forced a smile, 'In New Orleans. She graduated this term.'

'What next?' the president asked.

I sat on the couch next to Daddy. He dropped an arm around my shoulders. I hadn't told anybody, but now I dropped the bomb. 'I'm hoping to go to the University of Havana and major in art.'

Daddy's hand tightened on my shoulder, a sudden unexpected grip. Mama looked at Daddy and when their gazes met, I saw displeasure in her eyes.

A sneer disfigured The Man's face, but he quickly rearranged his features into a more pleasant look. 'Unfortunately, the University is temporarily closed. Such disruption by students! We hope to reorganize and reopen by the next term. When you come to Havana, you must visit the presidential palace.'

Margarita, the cook, dressed for the occasion in a gray uniform with a white embroidered apron and a starched white cap, brought coffee, the cups rattling on the tray. Her black shoes were new, tight on her feet. She walked pigeon-toed. She set the silver tray on the coffee table and with self-conscious little bows awkwardly backed away.

'Let's drink the coffee while it's hot.' Mama's eyes were blazing, but her hand was steady as she poured. 'We are very honored by this unexpected visit,' she said. 'Is there something in particular that brought you here?'

'Your reputation, madam, that's what brought me here. Stories of your legendary, charitable works are known as far as Havana. I understand the poor call you *Santa Caridad*, or *La Bendita*.'

Mama waved a depreciatory hand. 'That is very much exaggerated.'

If he knew about Mama's good works, he was certainly aware of her political activism.

'This time I want to change things,' the President said. 'Make a difference.'

Though sincerity vibrated in his voice, Mama was dubious. 'Our people perish because they can't pay a doctor, much less a hospital. We find babies dead on the streets. We need health care.'

'A priority,' replied the President, looking into the naked, direct eyes that so openly beseeched.

'Education,' she said. 'If we teach our people to read and write, they can find employment.' The intensity made her pupils shine with a radiant luminescence.

Daddy couldn't resist a little biting sarcasm. 'And they could read a ballot.'

'Naturally,' the dictator agreed.

'Employment,' Mama's voice didn't waver, but the tone went low, as if it took all her strength to make these huge demands, 'wages decent enough for survival.'

'That is good, Caridad. We believe in the same things, but you have to talk to Mr. McAuley about wages.' Batista favored Daddy with an oily smile. 'U. S. Sugar employs most of your people here.'

Daddy laughed ruefully. 'The Company loves you, General. These years have been the most prosperous we've ever experienced. Sugar prices are booming and you keep the political atmosphere stable and under control. We are very encouraged.'

'Yes. The Americans are building hotels and factories. They are growing sugarcane, tobacco, pineapples and bananas. We do all in our power to accommodate our foreign investors.'

Daddy said, 'Don't forget the casinos and nightclubs in Havana.' The Mafia had converted the capital into a second Las Vegas. Money hungry, power mad men who smoked big cigars and wore trench coats came from Chicago, New York, Los Angeles, Miami. They had bought a president and owned the house.

Mama gave Daddy a – stop that! – look. 'U. S. Sugar would never voluntarily raise the workers' pay,' she said. 'The government must pass laws for a minimum wage.'

'I understand. We will do what we can. In any case, you have a strong influence in Oriente Province, and I need someone who can talk to the *guajiros*, someone who understands them and can help me solve their problems. We don't want little problems to become big problems, do we? Will you help me?' The President's eyes were small and shrewd like an elephant's. Daddy left the couch and stood behind Mama's chair. He placed a cautious hand on her shoulder.

Flattered to be among the chosen, Mama responded with emotion. 'If you will do the right thing, if you will be fair, I will help in any way I can.'

Cuba on My Mind

A sidelong smile parted the President's thick lips. 'Good!' he said, slapping his knee. 'That is news very, very welcome.' He took Mama's arm and raised it as if he were a judge administering an oath. 'You are hereby appointed Minister of Music.'

Mama looked up quickly, her eyes suddenly blank like an empty blackboard before a single word was written on its slate surface. 'What are you talking about? I don't know a thing about music.' She lowered her arm. 'I don't play a piano. I don't know one note from another. I can't even carry a tune.'

'You don't have to know music,' the president replied smoothly. 'I need you on my team. You will be handsomely paid.'

'And what will my duties be?'

'Visit a public school every once in a while, something like that.'

In the silence that followed, a breeze swept across the veranda, rattling the canvas awning rolled half way down against the burning sun. The unexpected gust, warm and tropical, brought a chill into the living room as though the wind had come directly from the Arctic.

Daddy had remained silent during the exchange. Mama touched the big hand resting lightly on her shoulder. 'No, thank you. I appreciate the thought, but the answer is no.' Before Batista opened his mouth to reply, she continued. 'I won't be that easily eliminated. You can't quiet my voice with such an ignoble gesture, Fulgencio. I thought you were a better man than that.'

The bodyguards were on their feet.

'It's all right.' The president motioned them back. 'It's all right.' Immediately, he rose and jammed his Panama straw on his head. 'Are you sure of this? Won't you reconsider?'

'No —'

Such courage! Such poise! I had never been prouder of my mother.

'*Entonces, muy buenas tardes, amiga —* '

The president abruptly turned on his heel, a military movement. His entourage followed in tangent, veering with him like spokes on a wheel. As he hastened down the steps, he miscalculated and put his left foot down too soon. His knee buckled and he lost his balance. A bodyguard reached out and steadied him.

Daddy had followed the honored guest to the door. 'General, were you about to fall?'

The president brushed off his trousers and quickly regained his composure. 'Not at all,' he replied. 'That was merely a slip.'

'Well, be very careful,' Daddy said, 'very careful.'

Cuba on My Mind

Chapter 19

At this stage in life, the most aggravating aspect was losing track of time. Was today Tuesday or Thursday — morning or afternoon? Had I gone to the bathroom once already? Was this pressure on my bladder a second emptying? Had I eaten dinner or was that a lunch tray Connie brought? Connie — had I seen Connie today? Had I just talked to Batista? Was he sitting across from Mama in the living room? Floating between two worlds was like clinging to slippery rocks on a cliff. Without warning the hold gave way and the mind plummeted through time and space.

"Where's Connie?" I asked Olaf, suddenly and unexpectedly swinging into the now, into the present, cognizant of what was going on around me, filled with energy like an incoming tide, a vigorous wave rolling upon the sands of today — a good feeling.

"It's Sunday. She didn't come today."

"She quit?"

"I don't think so. She's taking a day off to settle things in her mind."

"And you?"

"I'm not going back to school." The decision weighed heavy on his shoulders. "I found an apartment. I'm taking a semester to think things over."

"Where is the apartment?"

"It's on Prytania Street near Mr. Giovingo's garage. He said it was okay to leave the Stu there and he'd help me work on it. Gramma, I showed him my design and he was carried away. I blew his mind! He says it's *plausible*!"

"That's great. You told your mother yet?"

"No. I'm delaying the slaughter. She's gonna kill me."

"You're not becoming a lawyer and you're not marrying Barbara?"

"That's right."

"Thank goodness. Don't you feel a great sense of freedom?"

"No. I'm confused and depressed."

"Too bad there's not an *iyalocha* available to divine your future."

"*Iyalocha?* – "

"A religious witch – "

"She told you your future?"

"Exactly – "

"Were you ever as confused as I am?"

"I suppose so, though I knew from a young age I was an artist. Whether I was successful or not, whether the paintings sold or not didn't matter. And I wanted to be with Olaf always. I never went with anybody else. In one of her fits, Carmen dragged me to her *iyalocha*. The woman could see into the future."

"You went to see a witch?"

"A priestess – "

***

I didn't want to be there, wasn't happy about it. I stood in the doorway, under a big silver cross nailed to the transom and refused to enter.

Carmen had brought me to this tumbled down shack in La Guira where the Santeria priestess, disciple of the ocean goddess, Yemaya, lived. The old woman sat cross-legged like a Buddha on a straw mat and smoked a Partagas. A blue velvet cloak stained and faded by age covered her wizened body, the folds draped about her. White feathers circled the hemline like a foaming barrier reef. Navy panels hung from the shoulders, each side decorated with three appliqué fish: tails yellow, red, green; fins bright gold; eyes black sequins glinting evil. The smell of cigar, garlic, stale peanut oil and Flit insect repellant enveloped the cloak and clung to the room. Gray strands of hair escaped from under a blue beaded scarf.

A sagging sofa and two chairs with holes in the cane seats were pushed against the blue wall to create greater space for the session. On a makeshift altar for the Christians' benefit sat a Virgin Mary statue. The ocean goddess, Yemaya, painted an electric blue, reigned atop the television set.

In the overpowering blue room, I noticed two very white pigeons, heads tucked under wings, a conscious effort to erase themselves. An unfettered red rooster cackled and picked cracker bits from a pan on the wood floor; on the window sill, a green lizard, sunbathing.

I said to Nanny Carmen, 'This isn't a good idea,' and refused to budge from the doorway.

'Don't you be a turkey,' she replied. 'We're here now. She can see into the future. What is bad about that?'

'You go ahead and believe it.'

The old woman was seriously drawing on the cigar and chanting between breaths. '*Omi tutu laro ero pesi laba koko lado per leri wi be mo iga be riga boya i –* ' She withdrew cowrie shells from a straw basket and threw them into the air. They clattered to the floor. '*Omi tutu laro ero pesi labe –* ' she motioned for me to come and sit.

I didn't budge.

Nanny Carmen nudged me between the shoulder blades and pushed me into the room. 'Sit there.' She pointed to a low, three-legged stool.

With each chant the priestess in the velvet cape underwent a transformation. She drew all energy to her, absorbed the force and synthesized the power. Her body expanded. Her dark eyes were spark plugs of light. Sweat glistened on her forehead.

She pulled me into the séance, blurred my consciousness. The past fell away; the future never was. Present only. The room melted, the blue ceiling dripping onto the blue wall, the blue floor, the blue virgin, blue swirling like the sea, like ocean waves.

'*Omi tutu laro ero pesi labe ... pesi labe fi ro fi ro fi ro!*' The iyalocha chanted very fast, her tongue darting like a bell clapper. She reached for a stone covered with hieroglyphs and kissed it. '*Omi tutu laro ero pesi labe –* what's your name?'

'Catalina.'

'*Fi ro. Fi ro.* There is more. *Pesi pesi labe labe.* More! More!'

'Catalina McAuley.'

'*Bale abo! Bale abo! Bale abo!* What's your number? I need a number!'

'I don't know.'

The iyalocha wanted a number. 'Everybody has a number.'

'Not me.'

Carmen confirmed the deficiency. 'This girl has no number.'

'No good number? No bad number?'

Carmen's bad luck number was six. On the sixth day of the month, she never budged from her room. The other servants understood the bad number's significance and consequences. On that day, they pitched in and did Carmen's work.

Lacking a number was a drawback. The iyalocha did her best to compensate. 'Fidel has a number,' she said 'twenty-six. He was born in 1926, led the Moncada revolt in '52 which is double 26. You see the importance? How old are you?'

'Sixteen.'

'Then your number must be eight.'

'Her mother has a number eight,' Carmen said.

Mama didn't believe in numerology, yet every week she bought lottery tickets numbered eight or multiples of eight. She picked December 8 for her wedding day. I was born on the 24th, a multiple of eight.

'Then there is no other choice.' The iyalocha drew two more stones from the basket and cast them into the air. *'Pesi pesi labe labe.* Pick a stone. *Fi ro! Fi ro!* Touch! Touch the stone! Eight! Eight! Touch the stone!'

This shrunken old woman puffing on a cigar, playing with stones could no more foretell the future than the fabled man on the moon. She chanted for three or four minutes, maybe hours. The monotonous, repetitive syllables danced in the smoke-filled room. The sounds bounced from the floor, slid up the walls, made their way through the gray cloud to the ceiling. The intonations filled all the space, left room for nothing else. Vibrations with nowhere to go seeped into my body, absorbed through the pores.

The iyalocha stared at me with a penetrating and powerful glare, the same frightening, crazed look I'd seen on those who had lost their senses and abandoned their minds, empty bottles drained of living liquid.

'Touch the stone! Quickly! Quickly! — ' the authority in her voice drew forth my hand.

Without warning the chanting stopped. The abrupt silence charged the room with expectation. With a forceful movement, the iyalocha flung an arm and threw a cowrie shell onto the mat, muttering, muttering. She scooped up the shell, spat on it, tossed it again ... again. She looked up with great conviction and said, 'You will not die.'

The pronouncement caught me off balance. Life, I was attuned to. Death hadn't entered my mind. Young people owned immortality. I grasped the stone tightly in my hand and turned to Carmen. 'What is she talking about?'

Another puff on the cigar and the iyalocha threw down the cowrie shells once more. Each shell had one side painted blue and the other left the natural pearly color. Eight shells were at the iyalocha's feet, four with the blue side up, four with the natural color. She raked them all back into her lap and wrote down numbers on a little pad. 'Good,' she said. 'Good,' she said. 'You will be rescued. Rescued by someone from your past, someone you know ... you know ... well.'

'Rescued from what?'

The woman sent the cowrie shells crashing to the floor again. All eight landed blue side up. Was that good or bad? The hair on my arms bristled. The stone I clutched radiated a heat so intense my palms sweated. The iyalocha held my life's span in the cowrie shells and in the numbers she wrote down on the pad; from birth to death and all the years between.

I leaned forward, Carmen crowding near.

'Omi tutu laro ero pesi labe ... pesi labe fi ro fi ro fi ro! ... Peril,' muttered the iyalocha, shaking all over. 'Great peril. I feel a shadow ... heavy, heavy.'

As if on cue, a young boy entered the room. He gave the cage in the corner a kick. 'You need a dove?'

Eyes closed in a deep squint, face frowning, the iyalocha replied through painful breaths that made her grimace. 'This one calls for the strong blood of a rooster.'

I shot Carmen a fearful look. 'She's not going to — '

The boy chased the rooster around the room, cornered and grabbed it. With both hands he clutched the squawking fowl, wings trapped and hard marble eyes about to pop out of its head. He carefully placed the bird, crowing shrilly, eyes roaming wild into the priestess's extended hands. One wing wriggled loose from the iyalocha's grip. The feathered warrior fought fate, flapping furiously, yellow legs with splayed toes and nail-sharp talons extended, the hard, pointed beak piercing the executioner's hand.

With one swift motion, the iyalocha clasped the rooster's neck and flung it around once, twice.

The sudden movement caused her cloak to fly open, exposing a soft silk lining painted in blue, aqua and yellow swirls, random squiggles, cubes, circles outlined in gold, lines that flowed and ebbed soft and cool, pink and pale green like a calm sea reflecting the heavens. She clutched the robe shut, but again the folds opened to reveal the cloak's underside, comforting, smooth, peaceful, the very opposite of the heavy, sodden velvet.

The stone I clutched grew unbearably hot. The burning sensation in my palms spread to my wrists. Heat radiated from my finger tips.

The iyalocha placed the rooster's neck under her canvas espadrille and separated the head from the body with one tough yank. Blood gushed out, staining the comb and wattle. Walking slowly, holding the headless rooster upside down, the priestess circled the stool where I sat petrified, a blood ring staining the wooden floor, the disgust in my stomach rising to my throat.

The iyalocha plucked a tail feather, dipped it in blood and before I leaned away, she touched my forehead with the feather, anointed me. The remaining blood she poured into a cracked china cup and offered to Yemaha, sea goddess. As she did this, a strong convulsion engulfed her. She toppled and fell face-down upon the floor.

***

"What in the world?" I heard Katherine ask. "What's that smell?"

"Smell?" Olaf narrowed his eyes in warning. "I don't smell any-

Cuba on My Mind

thing."

My daughter drifted into my vision, my consciousness, yellow jaundiced color, melancholy gold like withered autumn leaves.

"Look at her eyes!" Katherine said. "The pupils are dilated."

"She's agitated," Olaf said. "She's chanting some mumbo-jum-bo."

"I'm calling Doctor Jonathan."

"There's no need."

Fingers encircled my wrist. "Her pulse is erratic."

Olaf said. "Let her be, Mom."

"Are you yellow?" I asked. "I don't like yellow."

"I"m wearing a yellow suit, if that's what you're talking about — "

"It was so crazy, Katherine. You can't begin to believe how crazy it was."

"What was, Mama?"

"*Firolo firolo bale fi ro lo ba le abo fi ro lo fi ro lo bale abo fi ro fi ro lo bale.*"

"Wayne! Her legs are drawing up."

"*Fi ro lo fi ro lo bale abo fi ro fi ro ...* "

"She's delirious, Wayne."

"She's remembering things, Mom."

"Her mind is going, can't you see that?"

"We need to call Connie."

"Connie? Why in the world would I call Connie? I'm calling Doctor Jonathan."

"Connie has a knack for calming her down."

"I'm sending for the doctor." Katherine's voice rose in alarm. "Stay with her, okay?" She left the room.

Heat generated from my body as if a sudden fever had entered my bones. The cold, damp perspiration sapped what little energy I had and left me limp. I pushed off the covers. "My name is Catalina McAuley Van Nuys."

Olaf urgently grasped my hand. "That's you, Gramma. C'mon — don't stare at me that way. It's scary." I couldn't let go the stones. He pried my fingers open.

Someone was restraining me. Heavy hands pressed my shoulders.

"Mom's gone to call Doctor Jonathan."

"You know what she told me?"

"Who told you? What?"

Quick running steps on the hallway and Katherine was back in the room. "Help me, quick, Wayne. Doctor Jonathan said call and ambulance and take her to the emergency room. He'll meet us there."

"Mom, she doesn't need to go to the emergency room. She doesn't like to ride in an ambulance. Listen to me. Connie can calm her down."

"Do as I say!"

My feet touched bottom. The current pulled the sand through my toes. All was dark except for one light shaft cutting through the inky water. I reached for it and soared upwards to a cliff higher, taller than any I'd seen before bathed in silver light that came directly from the sun and dazzled the vision. I stood on the rim and wrapped my legs around a liana. I raised both arms, lifted my hips, and with one violent thrust forward reached for the heights.

"Gramma! – Gramma! – Oh my God!"

Connie burst through the door. "I'm here. Let me help."

Thudding feet and heavy breaths, lots of confusion and Olaf's strong arms lifted me onto the bed.

"How'd she fall?" Connie asked.

"I don't know," Olaf replied. "She bolted upright without warning and toppled."

A pain, new and acute, pierced my midsection.

Katherine struggled with the wadded sheets. Connie straightened my nightgown, pulled it down below my waist. The excruciating pain took my breath away.

"I think she's broken a rib," Connie said. Her cool hand pushed matted hair away from my forehead.

"She doesn't weigh a hundred pounds." Katherine had a real sadness in her voice. "The ambulance is on its way."

I didn't want an ambulance or procedures or well-meaning people poking and punching on me. The time had come to cast away the empty shell. Why didn't my loving daughter understand that?

Cuba on My Mind

Chapter 20

Connie moved silently about the room, straightening the clutter on the night table, adjusting the arm chair doilies, opening and closing drawers.

"What day is it?" I asked in a voice so weak I had trouble hearing myself.

"Thursday — "

"I didn't die."

"Nope — you came close, though."

"Well. The good news about death is it happens only once."

"Unless you're resurrected — then you might die twice."

I liked her sense of humor. "I hope not."

The exit no longer worried me. The slowness was disturbing and upsetting. Why not wham-bam as Olaf did? Why this prolonged departure? Why did death circle around me, teasing, tantalizing and closing in ever so slowly? Was there a purpose to it?

"That Doctor Jonathan should've just let me go — sent me on my way."

"Wayne wouldn't let him. He wants the end of the story and he said his mother pushed away the papers. She loves you very much. "

"Loves me to death — "

We both laughed. Connie had an infectious giggle. My cackle crinkled like dry paper. Staying in the now took too much concentration, too great an effort. I drifted away and smelled the sea, the salt in the air; heard the waves swishing in and out, the whining wind; saw the palm trees dip and sway. My breath took on the rhythm, floating on the gentle waves, my body light and weightless. How long was I gone — a minute or perhaps a day? Time no longer had relevance.

When a big swell washed me back into the present, my mouth was gritty, filled with sand. "Water," I murmured.

I felt Connie's sweet breath when she bent down to place the straw between my lips, heard her voice tinkling like bells, "Pull hard." She placed a cold, damp washcloth on my forehead. The coolness soothed my brow.

A movement drew my eye. "Who's that?"

"Wayne," Connie answered.

"Who's Wayne?"

The person who leaned over my bed said, "I'm your grandson, Gramma, Wayne Olaf."

I recognized his smell, gasoline and oil absorbed through the pores. "Oh, yes," my gnarled fingers made a crooked victory sign.

The young people didn't laugh. The humor escaped them. Olaf and Connie whispered across the hospital bed, looking so stricken that I felt it necessary to ask, "Am I dead?" How did dead feel? Would I recognize the event? Had I disappeared from their visual range like a blip on a radar screen? Was I in a new zone where I heard and saw them but they had lost me forever? Their youthful faces should've been bright with smiles, not draped in sadness. "What's wrong?"

"Nothing," they replied together.

"Well, then. Let me tell you about El Cojo."

"No, Gramma. We're done. We're not doing this anymore."

My mind slipped from level to level like a tern in high wind. "I want to."

"No. You just rest."

Rest! Rest! I was going into a forever rest! "Did I tell you Nanny Carmen took me to see the *iyalocha*?"

"Yes, you did.'

"We left there and headed for home."

The thought of Carmen brought a pain to my heart that hurt more than the broken rib. How I fussed at her! Took her for granted! Always there for me when I needed her and when I didn't. Whenever I raised a finger or lifted an eyelid, she moved at my command. She was, in the true Biblical sense of the word, my handmaid.

***

The *iyalocha* business had shaken me badly and I wasn't happy that Carmen subjected me to such gross stupidity. 'You were crazy to take me there,' I said.

'The problem is you don't have a number. I've told your mother that,' replied Carmen in a quarrelsome voice. 'You need a number. That's why the iyalocah was so confused. No number.'

Leaving the *iyalocha's* place Carmen and I walked through the civil town, down the one lane streets with carts and horses and manure piles; past the material shop with its brightly colored cotton lengths flapping in the breeze; the butcher shop, flies covering beef shanks and limp, yellow-skinned chickens hung from iron hooks; the shoe shop; the *almacén* where wooden crates and burlap sacks filled with beans, rice and oranges blocked the sidewalk; past the bloody bucket outside the dentist's door; past the letter-writing scribe slumped in a chair waiting for business. Three Civil Guards emerged from an old, moldy stucco building, their *cuartel*; headquarters. Two leaned against the building and lit up — on break, probably. Bebo, the fat one who dumped Rojas's fish, dropped down into a wooden chair and tilted it on its back legs. He removed a cigar from his shirt pocket. His roving eye surveyed the street and stopped on Nanny Carmen.

'Quick!' she said. 'Cross the street.' She greeted the skinny black woman hanging onto the lamppost. 'Be careful, Consuelo.'

A strong aromatic coffee smell stopped us and we entered the Chinaman's café through the big, open doors so Carmen could have a cup. I had one, too, black, strong, two spoonfuls of brown sugar. The coffee burned like rum when it hit my stomach.

The Chinaman approached and asked Carmen, 'Howsa wife?'

'Same as always — and you? — '

'No change. Day in, day out' — wok, wok, wok — '

'Well, then.' She placed two *pesetas* on the table. 'We're on our way.'

Around the corner, across the bridge, Calle Iglesia, up the hill, home. Perhaps because the iyalocha had predicted that I wouldn't die, that I would be saved, I had an apprehension, an eagerness to depart the civil town and get to the American Colony and the safety of my house — not that I believed her.

An accident had occurred on the bridge. A rattletrap truck had careened into the railing and hung precariously over the edge. With much shouting and arm-waving, two men were wrapping a chain around a railroad tie dragged by two oxen. The chain was hooked to the truck axle. Vendors, beggars, street boys, cooks and maids on their way to market stopped to observe the distraction. Drawn by the noise, the homeless climbed from the bank below, everybody offering unsolicited advice on the best way to shove or pull.

'Ya! Ya! Vamos! Vamos!' A man prodded the oxen with a sharp stick. The animals didn't budge.

A street boy suggested. 'Beat their rumps!'

The confusion stopped us. Carmen, drawing on her infinite Latin patience, said, 'Wait. They'll clear this soon enough. We should've waited. Manco was coming to pick us up in the car.'

'He couldn't get across the bridge, either.'

'It's not safe walking the streets these days.'

'Be quiet, old woman. You give me a headache. You've been saying that since I got here. We're almost home.'

We leaned against the bridge railing, waiting for the oxen to do their job. The bridge had wide planks with cracks between them and as the oxen humped their huge backs and strained forward the planks bowed.

A man clad in a burlap tunic and using a crutch approached. He was followed by pale, sick-looking, snotty-nosed children, little hands clinging to the rope belt around his waist. He observed the accident and veered aside. In his arms he cradled a babe.

Leaning over the railing, Carmen and I watched as he wrestled his way down the muddy bank, forcibly pulling his crutch in and out of the mire then springing forward on his good limb, the children tagging behind him. He disappeared into the misty darkness.

A man's voice came from under the bridge, 'Hand me that baby.'

I recognized the raspy, phlegmatic voice and asked Carmen, 'She's still there?'

'Mayor of the underworld,' replied Carmen.

'Come here,' the crone said. 'Come with me.' She enticed the children, who hung back. 'I have bread and rice and beans for you.'

The children too weak to assimilate the invitation to eat, too shy, too scared, didn't move. 'You'll be all right' the crone said. 'Come! Come!'

Leaning further over the railing, I saw her silhouette emerge from the shadows. Like a shepherdess leading her flock she guided the children between the barnacled pillars and the dying campfire embers to a safe, dry spot. They followed docile and quiet as sheep.

The crone asked the man, 'How is it going?'

'The same — no guns — no ammunition — no petrol, yet Fidel is certain we will overcome. Will she come?'

'Yes — in the morning — every Tuesday.'

'Will she take them?'

'Of course she will take them. She wants to take them. She wants all children, all people, to be well-fed and healthy. She is a true angel.'

'Does she know?'

'What difference does that make? They are children and they are sick and they need help. That is all she cares about. It doesn't matter where they come from,' and after a pause, 'she knows.'

I asked Nanny Carmen, 'They're talking about Mama?'

'Yes. Santa Caridad.'

From below rose the man's question, 'How about the orphanage and the American hospital?'

The crone explained. 'What do the nuns care? Sister Maria is not political, and it is Doctor Ruiz who runs the hospital. You know that. He saved your life.'

'A difficult enough life it has been.'

'Better life with one leg, than death with two.'

'That's *El Cojo*!' Carmen said admiration in her voice. "He's legendary!'

'Saved my life for what?' asked *El Cojo* — 'to steal gas and burn cane fields and lead children down the mountain? I want action! I can fight! Victor knows I can fight!'

The crone appeased him. 'What you do is more important. Any man can fight! But you! You are their Acquisition Man. You can find whatever they need.'

He was fixed on fighting, obsessed by the thought. 'Victor knows

I can fight better than the best soldier.'

'Victor is still there?'

'Yes. Now he's a field commander. Fidel should send him back to the post office. He has a head so big it wouldn't fit in a railroad box-car. Why do you think he doesn't let me participate in the skirmishes, because I'm lame? No! Because he's afraid I'll out-fight him, out-shine him and become greater than him. He couldn't survive that.'

'He does have a great ego, but then, don't they all, César?'

A great hue and cry rose from the people on the bridge as the oxen jerked forward and the truck teetered on the brink about to go over the side. A woman screamed. Carmen watched in stoic silence. The truck settled back down and a hush came over the crowd.

'One day soon I will show Victor. I will do something of such great value to the cause that he and Ché and Paco and Fidel himself will have to take notice.'

I leaned far over the side of the bridge and saw the old crone and the lame man sitting on the boulders below.

'Don't do something stupid,' the crone replied. 'Remember your limitations.'

El Cojo was filled with rage. 'I have no limitations!'

'Of course you don't,' agreed the crone in a conciliatory voice. 'Thanks for bringing the children. The task may not seem important to you, but you're rescuing the future of our nation.'

El Cojo held the tin cup to his lips and drank coffee. 'Doctor Ruiz could expose us,' he said fretfully. 'These children leave a wide trail.'

'Doctor Ruiz has no reason to. You don't sneak the children into the American Hospital. I don't take them there. Caridad does that every Tuesday — as many as the truck will hold. Think about it. Who at the American Hospital or the Flower of Charity or the Salvation Army would dare tell Caridad no?'

'I don't trust Doctor Ruiz.' El Cojo carped like a worry wart.

'The good doctor is not blind, dumb or stupid. He knows these children are not sons and daughters of company employees. You are in much more danger when you walk past the Civil Guard headquarters.'

'The guards are with us.'

'Until they are not,' said the old crone.

'What happens if Mister *Hoo* finds out?'

'Never will he know as long as nobody talks. Down here we say nothing. Caridad and Doctor Ruiz keep their mouths shut. We are Cubans, for God's sake. These are our people. Here, have more coffee,' and after a slight pause, 'he knows. Are you going back today?'

'Without delay — '

A little voice wailed, 'Please! Please! Don't leave me here. Take me home!'

'Don't worry,' the crone said. 'The child will get over it. Take a little bread.'

'No. Give it to the children.'

'Sit for a small minute, then. Catch your breath.'

'A van will pick me up in a few minutes. It will honk twice. Listen for it.'

On the bridge the oxen took a step forward and with a great rattle the truck came off the railing along with a few rotten boards. The people cheered and moved away. The chain around the railroad tie clanged as it hit the iron nails on the span's uneven planks. The truck owner sat behind the steering wheel, grinning happily. He waved his straw hat to the crowd.

A van with horn blaring careened onto the bridge. The lame man stood up, saw me leaning over the bridge rail and asked, 'Who is that?'

'Caridad's daughter,' the crone replied. 'She and Carmen crossed into the civil town.'

The old woman knew who came and went and what happened. She tracked better than the CIA.

'The company administrator's daughter!' The man's voice had a sinister edge, an excited timbre.

'He knows me?' I asked Carmen.

'Everybody knows you, love,' my nanny replied.

The crowd dispersed; the span cleared. Everyone went about their business. The beggars returned to their usual corners, by the Chinaman's Café, by the shops. They drew their knobby knees to their chins and extended arms holding tin cups. The vendors went back to their abandoned carts and kiosks. The pedestrians walked on to finish their business.

The oxen pulling the truck lumbered across the bridge, the driver poking the beasts, forcing them to one side, chains clattering and clanging, making room for the brown van blowing its horn.

Carmen and I started across as the lame man hobbled up the bank, the crutch under his armpit, jerking one hip, swinging his good leg with effort, reaching the bridge.

As he neared I saw him clearly, scraggly black beard, dark aviator glasses and tattered straw hat low on his forehead. He hobbled forward, the burlap tunic swinging open revealing an artificial limb secured in place right below the knee by a rope tied around a cushioned pad. He thrust forth a peg-leg made of dark wood that tapered to a point.

The pedestrian lane was one person wide. I walked in front, sulking. At my heels Carmen grumbled and fussed. The lame man walked toward us with a hop and a swing. We stopped face to face. I moved to one side and so did he, then I went the other way and he did also. We were doing a chicken dance when suddenly he grabbed the railing for support, whipped the crutch from under his arm and struck a blow to my head. My arms flew up to protect myself. The second strike caught me across the temple and my legs gave way.

It all happened so quickly, I didn't understand how Carmen had time to spring to my defense. She shot past me like a bull charging a red cape and kicked the one-legged man, kicked wood under the homespun tunic and the artificial leg came loose, toppled to one side. A knowing look sprang wild into Carmen's eyes and she cried in a fierce voice like a yelping animal caught in a trap. 'It's you! It's you! El Cojo! That's you!'

I knew him then, too, the leg and the blood and the boot pointing up, the outrage that he had the nerve to attack me twice, that Carmen had to save me twice.

Carmen retreated two steps, bowed her head and humped her shoulders like the oxen and charged. Clinging to the railing, the lame man shifted his great torso. Carmen rammed into his midsection and

Cuba on My Mind

he swung his crutch like a wood axe. The blow hit Carmen across her lowered neck. Her head flopped to one side. Her hands flew up; she gave a snort, gasped, fell.

The van honked.

'Stop! — ' I cried, hand flying to the lump on my forehead swelling like a grapefruit, positioning my feet, finding my knees, bracing my arms on the rough planks, blood streaming down my face as I half crawled, half walked to reach Carmen. 'Stop!'

The next blow struck my shoulder and I went down.

The one-legged man shoved his bloody crutch under his armpit. 'You, my beautiful one, will bring a fortune. Your father will give the company away to get his little girl back.' Grabbing me by the hair and dragging me as if I were a sack of sugar, he hobbled toward the waiting van. 'Before I send you back I will deliver to him a little gift, your leg, wrapped in newspaper, my demands attached. You think he will like that?'

In a dizzying swirl, consciousness slipped away. I mustered my little remaining energy and kicked with all my might.

A vehicle sped onto the bridge, swerved to avoid hitting the stopped van and almost ran over us. One look and Olaf sprang from the Land Rover and leapt onto the lame man's back, jumped on him as if he were vaulting onto a saddle. He kicked the crutch from under the man's armpit, grabbed his hair and yanked back his head. El Cojo lost his grip on me and I fell on the rough planks.

El Cojo toppled, Olaf on him, striking with rock-hard fists, punching the man's stomach, his kidneys, his miserable life. Without leg or crutch, El Cojo put up a terrific fight. He was strong, spry as a mountain goat. They grappled like fighting bears, rolling over and over. Olaf grabbed the burlap tunic and jerked the man upright.

El Cojo yelled at the van driver. 'Help me! Help me, you fool!'

The fleeing van almost hit three Civil Guards summoned by those looking from afar. Two hurried to the altercation, billy clubs in hand. Fat Bebo followed, taking his time, puffing his cigar.

The homeless ones who had scurried like rats up the river bank and stood in a silent huddle watching scrambled away when they saw the guards. The beggars stared and kept a distance. A straggling pedestrian quickly scampered across, not wanting to be a witness, to become entangled in the Guardia Civil justice system. A few street boys remained glued to the violence, too captivated to care about the consequences.

With one murderous jerk, Olaf tore off El Cojo's rope-belt and bound his wrists. He dragged the thwarted abductor still kicking his one leg in a hopeless fight, toward the first guard to reach the bridge.

El Cojo spit contempt. The bloody gob dribbled from the side of his mouth and smeared his black beard. Olaf didn't release his grasp on El Cojo until the Civil Guards trapped the one-legged man securely between them. His crutch gone, El Cojo was forced to lean for support on one man and then the other.

Fat Bebo lumbered onto the bridge, his sharp eyes noting every detail.

Olaf said, 'Take this man and hold him for the Company. Mr. McAuley will want to deal with him.'

Bebo replied, his voice mean and silky. 'The company administrator has no jurisdiction on our side of the bridge. What happened here?'

El Cojo threw back rebellious shoulders, 'These sons of whores — '

'Arrest this man!' cried Olaf.

Olaf put an arm around my waist and helped me to my feet. The whole world swam in a whirling mist. The van, beggars, bridge railing, river bank, went round and round, topsy-turvy. Bells rang in my head and distant voices shouted in my ear. I heard the *iyalocha's* dismal chanting.

Bebo narrowed his weasel eyes, deliberately took one long drag on his cigar, removed it from between his fat lips, and examined the ashes gathering on the glowing tip. 'Are you telling me how to do my job?'

'I'm asking you to hold this man until Chief Heinz gets here.'

'Chief Heinz, eh? — is that what you said? Did I hear right? You want USSCo's Nazi man to come into my town, my side of the bridge to deal with this — ' he looked contemptuously at El Cojo — 'this traitor to his country, this scum, this cockroach?'

Cuba on My Mind

'Yes!'

'This varmint that I can step on and crush beneath my heel?' His fat greasy face was an inch away from El Cojo's nose. The lame man struggled to free himself from the clutches of the two civil guards, no fear in his eyes only smoldering and disdain.

'Yes!' said Olaf. 'That's your job! Do it!'

Bebo stepped around Carmen where she lay on the bridge, legs splayed, head at a crazy angle, looking up. Blood matted her wiry black hair. Her eyes were open, a blank look in them. He leaned over her and retrieved the bloody crutch and the cracked wooden leg from where they'd fallen by my nanny's side.

'Carmen, please, Olaf. Carmen — '

El Cojo twisted his torso and rammed a powerful shoulder against the guard to his left. The man bent double, uttering a stream of profanity, and grabbed his gut. El Cojo raised a defiant chin, drew his lips into an angry bow and cried, 'Do you know who I am?'

An oily smile crossed Bebo's face, 'No, tell me — let me think — are you the El Cojo known as the Acquisition Man? The one who steals guns and medicine and food for the revolution — '

'If you touch one hair on my head, the *barbudos* will stream down that mountain and — '

Bebo's mean noisy laugh cut off El Cojo's threat. He said to the guards, his voice heavy with simulated boredom. 'One tells me how to do my job; the other threatens me.' He asked his cohorts, 'What is a man to do?' He placed the crutch under his armpit, leaned heavily on it and balanced the wooden leg in the crook of his arm.

The guards stared blankly ahead, tussling and holding the lame man who didn't cease his struggles.

'Let me see — let me review this — tell you what I know — you — ' he flat-handed El Cojo's face. The slap stung and El Cojo's head jerk-ed to one side. 'You bring the children from the hills, Santa Caridad takes them from under the bridge to the American Hospital; Doctor Ruiz takes care of them. We know that and look the other way. They are children. The only thing we don't know is why — ' he pointed to me — 'this *gringa* crosses the bridge to have her fortune told.'

'Carmen,' I sobbed uncontrollably, incoherent, not registering anything the guard said. 'Carmen, please, Olaf. Carmen, please.'

Bebo said to the guards. 'Let that worm go.'

The guards snapped to attention, not sure they'd heard correctly and held on tighter.

El Cojo yelled, the screaming words tearing from his throat like a madman's shrieking. 'You dare call me a worm! Batista scum! When we overcome we will hang you by your thumbs from the nearest tree!'

'Don't push your luck, my friend,' warned Bebo, and to the guards, 'Did you hear me? Let him go!'

The men released their prey. He teetered momentarily then balanced himself like a crane standing on one leg.

Bebo extended the crutch and the wooden leg to the lame man. 'You will need these.'

El Cojo lunged for the crutch just out of his grasp, lost his balance and toppled. With the bloody crutch Bebo poked the downed man in the chest, the stomach, and then a violent shove to the groin that made El Cojo draw his one leg in pain. Bebo dangled the crutch near El Cojo's face. The lame man lurched for it. Bebo jerked the crutch away and hurled it like a javelin over the bridge railing, 'and how about this?' He waved the wooden leg before its owner. 'You'll need this, too.' He sent the wooden leg sailing after the crutch.

El Cojo raised an angry fist. 'Your mother is a whore!'

Bebo turned to his fellow guards. 'You saw me. You heard me. I let this man go and what is my reward — insults to my mother!' Bebo kicked El Cojo. 'Send him after his crutch and his leg.'

Fighting and screaming, arms flaying, his one good leg trapped, El Cojo resisted the guards. One put his arms under the lame man's shoulders and the other grabbed his one leg; together they hoisted him over the railing and swung him into space.

A great 'oooh' escaped the stunned crowd standing on the river bank, watching. As they backed further away, they invoked God, Christ and the Holy Spirit, seeking help, seeking mercy. A woman shrieked.

Not a sound or a murmur came from those living under the bridge.

The whimpering I heard was my own. The mewing fell like strange sounds on my ears. My leg wrapped in newspaper; Carmen not moving; El Cojo flung to his death. What next? What next? I edged away from the Land Rover and shuffled toward Carmen, every step overwhelming pain, knotted stomach wrenching and heaving vomit.

I leaned on the railing for support. 'Olaf! Please! Please! Carmen!'

Olaf squatted next to Carmen and placed two fingers on my nanny's neck. Almost immediately he looked up and said, 'Get in the Rover.' When I didn't move he stood and scooped me in his arms, the pain so unbearably excruciating, the world slipped away, but an adrenaline surge brought me back.

'I'm not leaving her!'

He said very quietly. 'Yes, you are. There's nothing we can do. I'll get one of ours to come get her.'

Chapter 21

They crowded into my bedroom, the ones here and the ones gone away, shadows and colored bursts moving through a veil, a gray fog separating us. Katherine was standing far, far away a frightened look on her pale face, her hand firmly grasping my foot under the white sheet, holding on. James wearing a suit and tie sat in dark cobwebs holding a book, aimlessly rifling the pages as if to discover something lost. The red streak was Olaf's hair, his fire head; his hand rested on my cold arm. His fingers once felt warm, but no more. Connie — why were tears running down that sweet girl's cheeks?

No one sat in the wicker rocker across the room — my daddy's rocker, my husband's rocker, a vacant throne. The green and pink flowered cushions made it look like a woman's chair, a place to nurse a baby or croon a child to sleep, curl up and read a book. Yet men had always sat in it, looking misplaced amid the delicate weave of the pencil-thin reeds, their big field boots and rough khaki pants an anachronism. I must tell my grandson that the chair was his.

Without looking, I knew it was raining. I felt the atmospheric ache in every bone. The water dripping from the roof eaves had a rhythm and so did death relentlessly scraping a windowpane, rapping for entry. The only element not in sync with the universe was my breath. It came at odd moments, erratically, from all directions. My lungs wheezed and rasped as I struggled to reach and trap the air, an eerie Banshee wail escaping my lips.

The ocean waves sighed in, sighed out. A soft breeze whispered a lilting tune, died down. The coconut fronds bowed and waved. A rainbow arched across the sky.

Olaf and Connie whispered across the bed. I couldn't hear or understand. Next time I looked, he was standing next to Connie, his arm around her shoulder, her head resting against his heart. Her hand clutched his shirt collar.

Olaf had to know the whole story — how circumstances ended my life in Cuba, my youth. It was important that he understood that when one phase ended another began. There was no beginning and no end only the everlasting horizon arc stretching forever, unchanging, unaffected by time, eternal.

The words in my mind came out a gurgling, spitting sound.

***

Newcomb College offered studies abroad. I spent one summer roaming Europe visiting the great museums, another in Paris attending the École de Arte, learning the craft, living in a garret with two schoolmates, having the time of my life, the days so crammed full that if I was homesick for my island or lovesick for my Olaf, I had no time to think or dwell upon it.

June, 1959, I returned to Cuba. My last summer at home! The crocodile had opened its big jaws and swallowed our life. I lay on my stomach on the warm sand one last time. Olaf on his side, head propped on one hand, dribbled sand on my bare back. 'Tell me what happened,' I said.

'Where do you want to start?'

'With you — whatever possessed you?'

'I guess I caught the fever. You would've, too, if you'd been here. Fidel sparked everyone's imagination. He built hope in people's hearts, stick by stick, the way wood is stacked up for a big bonfire.'

'But you are one of us!'

'C'mon, Catica! — we knew what we were doing was wrong — taking their land and working their people for ten cents an hour. We made them our slaves and built thatched huts for them while we lived like kings and queens in our yellow palaces.'

'So you went up into the Sierras for two years — two whole years?'

'Eighteen months, actually — I came home and told the old man I was joining the Marines. He went through the roof and Mama suggested in her drunken stupor, that I go up into the mountains and fight with the *barbudos* — remember, Dad sent that pig, Bebo, to look for me and he dumped Rojas's fish, his whole three-day catch — '

'Of course I remember.'

'It made sense to fight right here in my own country, close to home — '

'This isn't our country.'

'It's more our home to us than any other place.'

'But why join a doomed revolution?'

'The revolution should've been doomed. By all accounts you're right. But there was this wonderful spirit about it — I can't exactly explain. I joined partly for the adventure, the thrill of it — the rush. Partly because all the others in the company were too old, too set in their ways, their thinking too rigid to be of any help, except your mother. She is a magnificent woman.'

'Fidel's new government took over our company.'

'A big mistake, but it's a fact. Those peasants don't know a thing about running a sugar operation. They just want their land back, Cuban soil for Cuban people. Right after the takeover, the *guajiros* stood in long lines at government land offices waiting for land deeds, any little plot, something permanent, something their own.'

'Those plantations are ours. We bought and paid for them.'

'Mostly we stole them from the rightful owners.'

'You sound brainwashed.'

'More tired than brainwashed — why should one country come into another country and like a parasite suck the life out of the host?'

'Because U. S. Sugar has money, resources, know-how and they don't.'

'You sound like your father. Your mother thinks differently. She'd say what made the Americans rich was the cheap Cuban labor, slave labor, really. Fidel is right. The wealth needs to be redistributed more evenly.'

'You're talking socialism.'

'Call it what you wish.'

I raised both eyebrows and shook my head. A political discussion was a dead end. We'd never convince each other. I changed the subject. 'Tell me about Manco and the Rolls.'

'That was bad. There was no reason for it. On the day of triumph, the rebels streamed down the mountain. What a sight they were! Dirty, foul-smelling, wild-haired, their unkempt black beards down to their chests — '

'Did you have a beard?'

'I did — I did! Only mine was red. The men were half-dressed, most without boots, and the ones with boots had them tied with rope and string. The *barbudos* lacked bare necessities. They had nothing except a blind faith in Fidel's dream. When Batista fled to Miami, the army and the civil guard went into complete disarray, no commander and no discipline. Initially, the rebels pouring into the towns were orderly and restrained, not really sure they'd won the war, since no major combat ever occurred, no bodies strewn on a battlefield, only this long, extended quiet. Around our necks we wore the red bandanas, the revolution's symbol. There were many women, too. The people in Banes lined the streets and waved red scarves and Cuban flags. They threw kisses. The priests on the sidewalks hoisted chalices and crosses, blessing the liberators. Father Juan Antonio stood before the Cathedral, handing bottles of communion wine to the weary soldiers. The grateful nuns kissed the crosses hanging around their necks and they held them forth in blessing. Barefoot kids ran alongside. We were proud. This revolution would change lives, provide opportunity. The whole thing was better than carnival, a great sight to see.'

'And on our side? — '

'A deathly pall — no movement. The green shutters drawn on all the houses. Your father and mine and everybody else with a gun or rifle cocked and ready. Chief Heinz had taken the weapons away from the company guards. He didn't trust anyone.'

'Is it true about Chief Heinz?'

'Yes. He was a Nazi, after all. A few months after the new regime took over Fidel sent the military after Chief Heinz. They were to execute him for his war crimes. Chief Heinz went to your father's office seeking help. He and your dad always got along. It was daybreak and Mr. McAuley wasn't there. He was out in the fields, surveying the damage. Boston was raising hell, demanding an accounting. What happened to the sugar? Where was the freighter? Confusion reigned.

Those Boston people had no clue. Chief Heinz sat behind the desk in your dad's chair, waiting for your him to arrive. He heard the sharp rap on the door, a military knock he recognized right away. He panicked. Instead of opening the door, he unsheathed that big Luger he wore strapped to his waist and put the gun to his head. The cleanup crew said it was awful, brains all over the place.'

'Oh, my God! — and Frau Heinz?'

'Going back to Germany wasn't an option. For some time she was under house arrest, but then USSCo headquarters sent down word she had to leave the company house since her husband was no longer an employee — the Boston brass was still under the delusion they owned the company — so she'd have to be confined somewhere else. Ironic, isn't it, their jealous care of the yellow houses? The militia took over the house and released Frau Heinz. She disappeared into the civil town, melted into the populace. She's living in La Guira.'

'The shanty town! — '

'Yes. The others have forgotten her but your mother visits her every week. She's not afraid of La Guira.'

'What happened to the Doberman pinschers?'

'Victor killed the dogs, one bullet to the head each.'

I'd heard this news from Mama, from friends, but I wanted to hear the facts from Olaf, so that his familiar voice would convince me and I would finally grasp once and for all, the whole tapestry of our world before it totally unraveled.

'And Gretchen?'

'I'm so proud of Gretchen. That little twerp had more gumption than all the rest of us. She and Dad are back in Holland. Dad's growing tulips. Can you believe that? Tulips! They took Mumsie's ashes with them.'

'Did it affect her — the kidnapping? Leave lasting scars?'

'No, she weathered the whole business like a real trouper — never talks about it. In the end, though she went through awful ordeals, she understood — she really understood. She got caught up in it, like I did.' Olaf reached over and took my hand in his. 'People need heroes and there was no one more heroic than Fidel.'

'What a triumph it must've been when the men came down from

Cuba on My Mind

the mountains! What a tragedy for the company!'

'Joy and sadness; elation and fear; a great noise on the civil town side — as the day wore on the louder the people got, a New Year's day fiesta like no one had ever seen before — beer, wine and rum — a good celebration for a long-earned victory. The people, caught up in the moment, danced in the streets — at long last — Cuba for the Cubans. They were so happy — frenzied — singing and drinking. Sometime in the afternoon, Victor sent a soldier across the bridge to get the Rolls Royce and drive it to Dominguez Plaza, run it up the steps and place it right in the middle of the park, next to the kiosk where the firemen's band plays.

'Manco sat himself in the driver's seat. 'Nobody is taking my car,' he said.

The *barbudos* laughed. 'This car belongs to the gringos.'

Manco said, 'This is the people's car, and if the people want this Rolls, I will drive it across the bridge.'

'The rebel objected, but your mother came out and convinced the man it was all right to let Manco drive.'

'What was Daddy doing all this time?'

'He and Dad and all the others were trying to salvage what was left. All the tractors and heavy equipment on the outlying plantations had been stolen; the cane fields set on fire; the sugar mill up in smoke. Nothing smells worse than sugar burning. It makes you puke, it's such a stink. They knew it was only a matter of time before the rebels crossed the bridge and destroyed the colony.'

'Did they burn the golf course?'

'First thing — Y'know how all that watering and pampering of grass galled the Cubans, particularly during the dry season.'

'They didn't torch the houses. Why?'

'Because of your mother maybe or maybe because Mirta had moved back into her parents' house and she had Fidelito with her. Maybe because they planned to put up dividers and turn our houses into apartments. Victor said six families could live in your house.'

'Olaf, don't you feel awful that you helped bring down the company? You sabotaged us! You're worse than a turncoat!'

The color rose in his neck and stained his cheeks red. 'It was the right thing.'

'Come now!'

'Divided loyalties are a torment.'

'By definition, loyalty can't be divided! Never mind! What happened to Manco? Finish telling me.'

'Manco went into that little room behind the garage where your cook hung banana bunches to ripen, the room where he polished shoes in his spare time. He found his uniform, the blue one with the gold stripe down the trousers, and changed from his soiled clothes into it and sat behind the steering wheel, tall and straight, as dignified as a presidential driver, a bearded rebel on the passenger side.'

'I bet he wasn't pleased to have that filth sitting inside his automobile.'

'Manco drove through town slowly, the people cheering the car. You know how they loved that Rolls. It was the people's car. Your father always let them have it for weddings and funerals and processions and parades and any other occasion they wanted. Everybody waved and yelled 'Manco! Manco!' He looked straight ahead, ignoring the commotion. Across the bridge, right there by the Chinaman's Café, the crowd thronged into the street and stopped the car. Li Wong darted out, waving his fat hands in the air, saying 'no ploblem, no ploblem,' his usual admonition.

'The men hadn't had a drink in months — no rum, no *agua ardiente*, no *cervesas* — Fidel's rule, no liquor in the hills, and they guzzled rum by the gallon when they hit town. They were crazy drunk. One man reached out and touched the Rolls and Manco said 'Get your dirty hands off this car.' The soldier yanked Manco by the collar, jerked him from the driver's seat, flung him up against the fender and beat him with his fists. Manco slid to the ground, his one arm extended, trying to protect the Rolls, more worried about the car than his bloody face. The drunken mob engulfed the Rolls and rocked it from side to side. A man opened the hood and ripped out wires. Another opened the trunk and took out the spare. Manco was half-blinded by the blows and the blood pouring down his face, trying to scramble to his feet, and they were all laughing and drinking.'

'You stood by and let all this happen? You let that rabble kill

Cuba on My Mind

Manco?'

'I did my best to stop it, but it was no use. The people struck like a hurricane. They were blinded by hate — y'know how they hated the company because they had no choice — they had to work there or starve. They were deaf to reason, as if poor Manco embodied every curse that ever came upon them. They forgot Manco had helped them again and again — all the time, your *chofer* only had one stipulation. 'Don't touch the Rolls.'

'The more he protected the car, the more determined they became. They'd show him! They set about destroying the Rolls with a vengeance, laughing and carrying on, beating it with rocks and sticks. What a solid car! They had a hard time denting it.' Olaf swallowed hard. 'I couldn't stop them. I swear to God I couldn't stop them — not single-handedly — though Lord knows I tried. There were too many of them. I had nowhere to turn for help. Victor stood there, a satisfied look in his eye and a smile on his face. If this was triumph, it didn't taste like victory to me. Evita ran out of the Chinaman's place and tore into Victor. He laughed and pushed her away. She sprung back, furious, and he slapped her face and knocked her down.'

'Señorita Evita! — what was she doing there?'

'She came down from the mountain with the others. She is a liberator. She fell truly in love with a poet named Abel who was part of the revolution. Batista's soldiers captured and tortured him. They sent Evita his eyeballs wrapped in her own lace handkerchief. She quit teaching and went up into the mountains determined to avenge his death. People said she kept those eyeballs in a glass jar beside her bed wherever she slept so she would never forget.' Olaf continued with a wry chuckle. 'Evita had a lot of men — my father and I included — but she was really in love with this poet. He was very poor, from the mountains. He wrote poems for the revolution and inspiring songs.'

'Remember when Captain Jack was going to marry her because she was pregnant?'

'Yes. She told that tale as a favor to old man Cleveland. He wanted Margo to marry him. He gave Evita this huge diamond to remove Jack King, his big obstacle. Cleveland had money coming out his ears, a rich old man. Evita sold that diamond and bought arms and ammunition and she herself brought them up to the mountain, leading a mule loaded with guns and bullets. She was welcomed as if she were Christmas. Evita did everybody a good turn. She had a big heart. She knew Margo was much better off married to Mr. Cleveland, one of her own sort, than to Captain Jack.'

'Finish what happened to Manco.'

'That's it. They killed him and set the Rolls on fire. The gasoline tank caught and exploded like a bomb. Next day your father sent a flatbed truck into the civil town, and the workmen lifted the Rolls' warped, black chassis on board, Manco's charred remains behind the wheel. His face was beyond recognition. Your father found the chauffeur's cap and set it on his head, the same jaunty angle as when he was alive. He had workers dig a huge pit behind the garage at your house, back near the river. Manco's remains and the remains of the Rolls Royce now rest in peace.'

'Where was Mama during all this? She won't talk about it to me or anybody else.'

'She was there, tears running down her cheeks, greatly disturbed by the events — first thing the rebels did when they came down the mountain was kill an innocent man — her innocent man. We stood by the gravesite and the priest read the Bible, words nobody heard over the wailing of Manco's wife. Your mother's face was set, her lips pinched. She had her arm around the widow trying to console her. Your father was purple all the way to the top of his bald head, he was so mad. He was ready to go after the culprits. Your mother looked Mr. McAuley straight in the eye, with that keen look that can pin you to a wall, and said, 'We will not avenge one death with another. That is the cycle we must break if we are to be truly free.'

'Manco is dead and Carmen is dead, and the company is going to close down,' a wistful note entered my voice.

'Yes,' replied Olaf. 'Nothing in Cuba will ever be the same again.'

We lay side by side for a long time. The sun dried our wet bathing suits. The warm rays warmed our skin, a delicious touch. The sea spilled upon the golden sand. I lay with half-shut eyes, Olaf on one elbow, watching my face, gazing at my lips as if he were waiting to kiss me and then he leaned over and did, again and again, tremendous soft breathless stabs that stirred a drowning passion. I wrapped my tanned arms around him to keep from going under.

'Are we all leaving?' I murmured, holding back my tears.

'I'd say within a year U. S. Sugar as we know it will be gone. The Colony will be absorbed into the civil town.'

'I don't believe that. They can't undo in one year what it took a lifetime to build.'

'If you hate enough or love enough or want enough, certain tenacity takes over.'

'Cuba is our home!'

'Not five minutes ago you told me it wasn't our country, and you are right. We are, in effect, wanderers — nomads. When there's no profit in staying in a place, we leave, move on to the next.'

I was silent for a long time, my nose nestled under his chin, my cheek warm against his neck. 'Will I ever see you again?'

He rolled away from me and looked deep into my eyes. 'Sure,' he said. 'Think Hawaii, Dole pineapples. We'll go together.'

'What do you mean?'

'We've grown sugar cane in Cuba. We'll grow pineapples in Hawaii. There's no difference. Climate's the same.'

'No, I mean about going together.'

'We are bound by the dolphin's song. We could never be apart.'

Never apart ... never apart ... never apart — I was looking — looking everywhere—

So many faces in the room — sad faces; serious faces; tearful eyes; hushed voices coming through the misty gloom. I looked for my Olaf in the rising, falling tide; the blowing, waning breeze; the dipping rustling sugar cane stalks; the silky white mariposa clumps.

Oh, there! Khaki sleeves rolled to the elbow — Olaf's outstretched arm! His hand reached for mine and holding tightly onto each other, our fingers intertwined, we ascended to the top of the cliff, wrapped our legs around a trailing liana, swung out ... swung back ... soared up and reached a rainbow as our grandson silently, gently dropped into the old brown wicker rocker.

Katie Wainwright   240

The End

photo: Patricia Steib

I was born in Banes, Cuba 1935. My father, William Howard Cameron was Scot; my mother, Angela Martinez, was Cuban. My father worked for United Fruit Company growing sugar cane. I went to high school in Louisiana and married Carl T. Wainwright in 1953. Between five children and work, I managed to get a B.A. in Education from Southeastern Louisiana University. Writing has always been my hobby. In a crazy household, it helped maintain my sanity. Until now I never tried to publish anything because I didn't want a hobby to become a second job, although I did write 'Travelin,' articles from travelers around the world, including some of my own travels, for the *Hammond Daily Star* for 5 years. I also wrote 'A Date with Kate' for the *Hammond Sun* for nearly fifteen years. *Solar Today, Inside Northside, Christian Science Monitor,* and *Chicago Tribune* have also published articles I have written.